Pyotr Tchaikovsky

Titles in the series Critical Lives present the work of leading cultural figures of the modern period. Each book explores the life of the artist, writer, philosopher or architect in question and relates it to their major works.

In the same series

Antonin Artaud *David A. Shafer*
Roland Barthes *Andy Stafford*
Georges Bataille *Stuart Kendall*
Charles Baudelaire *Rosemary Lloyd*
Simone de Beauvoir *Ursula Tidd*
Samuel Beckett *Andrew Gibson*
Walter Benjamin *Esther Leslie*
John Berger *Andy Merrifield*
Jorge Luis Borges *Jason Wilson*
Constantin Brancusi *Sanda Miller*
Bertolt Brecht *Philip Glahn*
Charles Bukowski *David Stephen Calonne*
William S. Burroughs *Phil Baker*
John Cage *Rob Haskins*
Albert Camus *Edward J. Hughes*
Fidel Castro *Nick Caistor*
Paul Cézanne *Jon Kear*
Coco Chanel *Linda Simon*
Noam Chomsky *Wolfgang B. Sperlich*
Jean Cocteau *James S. Williams*
Salvador Dalí *Mary Ann Caws*
Guy Debord *Andy Merrifield*
Claude Debussy *David J. Code*
Fyodor Dostoevsky *Robert Bird*
Marcel Duchamp *Caroline Cros*
Sergei Eisenstein *Mike O'Mahony*
Michel Foucault *David Macey*
Mahatma Gandhi *Douglas Allen*
Jean Genet *Stephen Barber*
Allen Ginsberg *Steve Finbow*
Václav Havel *Kieran Williams*
Ernest Hemingway *Verna Kale*
Derek Jarman *Michael Charlesworth*
Alfred Jarry *Jill Fell*
James Joyce *Andrew Gibson*
Carl Jung *Paul Bishop*

Franz Kafka *Sander L. Gilman*
Frida Kahlo *Gannit Ankori*
Yves Klein *Nuit Banai*
Akira Kurosawa *Peter Wild*
Lenin *Lars T. Lih*
Stéphane Mallarmé *Roger Pearson*
Gabriel García Márquez *Stephen M. Hart*
Karl Marx *Paul Thomas*
Henry Miller *David Stephen Calonne*
Yukio Mishima *Damian Flanagan*
Eadweard Muybridge *Marta Braun*
Vladimir Nabokov *Barbara Wyllie*
Pablo Neruda *Dominic Moran*
Georgia O'Keeffe *Nancy J. Scott*
Octavio Paz *Nick Caistor*
Pablo Picasso *Mary Ann Caws*
Edgar Allan Poe *Kevin J. Hayes*
Ezra Pound *Alec Marsh*
Marcel Proust *Adam Watt*
John Ruskin *Andrew Ballantyne*
Jean-Paul Sartre *Andrew Leak*
Erik Satie *Mary E. Davis*
Arthur Schopenhauer *Peter B. Lewis*
Adam Smith *Jonathan Conlin*
Susan Sontag *Jerome Boyd Maunsell*
Gertrude Stein *Lucy Daniel*
Igor Stravinsky *Jonathan Cross*
Pyotr Tchaikovsky *Philip Ross Bullock*
Leon Trotsky *Paul Le Blanc*
Richard Wagner *Raymond Furness*
Simone Weil *Palle Yourgrau*
Tennessee Williams *Paul Ibell*
Ludwig Wittgenstein *Edward Kanterian*
Virginia Woolf *Ira Nadel*
Frank Lloyd Wright *Robert McCarter*

Pyotr Tchaikovsky

Philip Ross Bullock

REAKTION BOOKS

For Abi, Toby, David and Helen

Published by Reaktion Books Ltd
Unit 32, Waterside
44–48 Wharf Road
London N1 7UX, UK

www.reaktionbooks.co.uk

First published 2016
Copyright © Philip Ross Bullock 2016

Printed and bound in Great Britain by Bell & Bain, Glasgow

A catalogue record for this book is available from the British Library

ISBN 978 1 78023 654 4

Contents

Editorial Note

Until 1918 Russia used the Julian rather than the Gregorian calendar, meaning that in the nineteenth century it was twelve days behind the West. For the sake of simplicity and readability, dates are given solely according to the Julian calendar. Where, in a few instances, dates of events in western Europe and America are given according to the Gregorian calendar, this is noted by use of 'n.s.' (for 'new style'). Most Russian names are transliterated according to a modified version of British Standard 2979: 1958, although familiar versions such as Benois, Cui, Diaghilev and – of course – Pyotr Ilyich Tchaikovsky himself – have been preferred where they exist.

Tchaikovsky aged 52, St Petersburg, 1892.

Introduction: 'The Intimate World of My Feelings and Thoughts'

Writing to his friend and secretary Isaak Glikman on 3 February 1967, Dmitry Shostakovich meditated on the subject of mortality – both his own and that of his precursors:

> I am thinking a lot about life, death and careers. Thus, recalling the life of certain famous . . . people, I am coming to the conclusion that not all of them died at the right time. For instance, Musorgsky died before his time. The same can be said of Pushkin, Lermontov and several others. But Tchaikovsky should have died earlier. He lived a little too long, and for that reason his death, or rather his final days were terrible.[1]

Shostakovich was right; Tchaikovsky did not die at the right time (although surely few would agree that he lived 'a little too long'). His death on 25 October 1893 was tragic not just because it was a painful and ignoble affair, but because it has cast a lamentable pall over his life and how that life is written and read. Coming just nine days after the premiere of his Symphony No. 6, a work interpreted by many at the time as a requiem and by some ever since as a suicide note, Tchaikovsky's death has been extensively and even excessively interpreted as the key to the life that preceded it. Yet there was nothing inevitable about his death, and still less so about the unfolding of his life. Everything that Tchaikovsky did involved a choice, or at least a conscious examination of his motives. He was decidedly not a victim of circumstance or conspiracy, much less a pathological case study in melancholia or sexual guilt. Rather, he was a sophisticated and self-aware agent in the evolving social, economic and artistic culture of Imperial Russia in the second half of the nineteenth century.

So what would be our image of Tchaikovsky had he died under different circumstances? If, in the wake of his disastrous marriage in July 1877, he had succeeded in taking his own life, as his friend Nikolay Kashkin later alleged he had tried to do (although the claim is disputed), he would be remembered as the composer of three operas (*The Voevoda*, *The Oprichnik* and *Vakula the Smith*), a ballet (*Swan Lake*), three symphonies, a piano concerto, the orchestral fantasias *Romeo and Juliet* and *Francesca da Rimini*, and three string quartets, as well as a substantial body of songs and instrumental pieces. Had he lived a little longer, dying at the age of 42 as his near-contemporary Modest Musorgsky did, he would have added such masterpieces as the Symphony No. 4, *Eugene Onegin* and the Violin Concerto to this already impressive oeuvre. Knowledge of his failed marriage would have added scandal to his reputation, and some might have sought to claim the Piano Trio, written to honour the recently deceased Nikolay Rubinstein and dedicated 'à la mémoire d'un grand artiste', as his own memorial.

It is more interesting, though, to speculate as to what might have happened to Tchaikovsky's career had he not died in 1893. If, like Nikolay Rimsky-Korsakov, he had lived to the age of 64, he would doubtless have become the *éminence grise* of Russia's Silver Age, feted by a new generation of artists such as Alexandre Benois and Sergey Diaghilev. He might well have returned to the idea of collaborating with Anton Chekhov on an operatic version of 'Bela', the first story of Mikhail Lermontov's novel *A Hero of Our Time*, which the two men first discussed in late 1889. Other tantalizingly unrealized operatic projects included an adaptation of George Eliot's 'The Sad Fortunes of the Reverend Amos Barton' and 'Mr

Gilfil's Love Story', which Tchaikovsky read in the final years of his life. The Symphony No. 6 would not then be seen as an ending, but as a turning point in the development of musical history, and its composer would surely have continued his role as a sought-after ambassador for Russian music in Europe and America.

Had Tchaikovsky lived to the age of 82 – like Vladimir Stasov or Leo Tolstoy – he would have witnessed Diaghilev's success in western Europe and might even have been enticed into writing for the Ballets Russes. Indeed, given his monarchist sympathies and connections with the Imperial court, Tchaikovsky would probably have found himself in emigration, most likely in his beloved Paris. His attitude to the compositions of Gustav Mahler, Richard Strauss, Claude Debussy, Maurice Ravel, Jean Sibelius, Igor Stravinsky or Sergey Prokofiev is harder to guess; perhaps – like his near-contemporaries Camille Saint-Saëns (1835–1921) and Gabriel Fauré (1845–1924) – he would have seemed like some strange hangover of the nineteenth century and a living link between late Romanticism and early modernism.

Yet the fact remains that Tchaikovsky died when he did, and in tragic circumstances, whose nature is disputed to this day. His life and death have become public property, and have long played a role in the development of Russia's national myths both at home and abroad. In the summer of 2013, for example, Tchaikovsky's name found itself caught up in the international scandal surrounding the Russian parliament's decision to enact a law banning the promotion of 'non-traditional sexual relationships' to minors. The script for a new cinematic biography was allegedly rewritten to remove any reference to his sexuality, and the country's minister of culture even claimed that there was no evidence at all that the composer was gay. Vladimir Putin, the Russian president, tried to downplay the situation, declaring that Russians loved Tchaikovsky despite his sexuality, but this did little to prevent calls in the West for a boycott of a production of *Eugene Onegin* that opened the autumn season at New York's Metropolitan Opera. Starring diva Anna Netrebko and conducted by Valery Gergiev, the opera came to symbolize the complex relationship between art, politics, sexuality and national identity that has long defined Tchaikovsky's posthumous reputation.[2]

So can such myths and controversies be peeled away to reveal something of the man himself? To an extent, they can. Tchaikovsky's life is one of the most thoroughly documented of any musician, not least because he was as fluent a writer as he was a composer. Starting with the three-volume biography that his brother, Modest Tchaikovsky, published at the start of the twentieth century, critics have mined more than five thousand letters, a number of surviving diaries and a substantial body of memoir literature to fashion intimate and detailed portraits of their subject.[3] Galina von Meck, the granddaughter of Tchaikovsky's patron, Nadezhda von Meck, even went so far as to subtitle her translation of a selection of his letters 'an autobiography',[4] and works such as Alexandra Orlova's *Tchaikovsky: A Self-portrait* (1990) and Alexander Poznansky's *Tchaikovsky: The Quest for the Inner Man* (1991), not to mention any number of other biographies, have drawn extensively on such documents to create compelling portraits of the composer and his world, although their emphases can be radically different and even downright contradictory.[5]

The temptation to look to Tchaikovsky's letters as an infallible source of information about his personality and creativity is natural enough. Writing to Nadezhda von Meck in February 1878, Tchaikovsky stated directly that 'the value of a letter lies in the extent to which the person writing it remains himself, and does not pose or pretend.'[6] The previous November, he had even referred to his correspondence with her as 'my diary'.[7] Certainly, much of his correspondence gives an impression of extreme self-revelation, and his letters to von Meck – as well as those to his siblings (especially his younger twin brothers, Anatoly and Modest), his publisher Pyotr Jurgenson and his fellow composer Sergey Taneev – have allowed biographers to establish a detailed and variegated picture of his life. Reading the often substantial number of letters that Tchaikovsky would write in a single day can be a revealing experience; the florid and carefully crafted outpourings of artistic inspiration characteristic of his letters to von Meck, for instance, read rather differently when placed alongside the brisk, funny and often vulgar missives that he would pen to Jurgenson (which were published in complete and unexpurgated form only in 2011 and 2013).[8]

Yet in a diary entry dating from June 1888, Tchaikovsky questioned the notion that letters were necessarily reliable as sources able to shed light on his personality:

> It seems to me that letters are never entirely sincere, at least judging by myself. Regardless of my correspondent or my reason for writing, I am always concerned about the impression that the letter will produce not only on my correspondent, but even on some casual reader. As a result, I pose. Sometimes I *try* to make the tone of the letter simple and sincere, that is, to make it *seem* so. But, apart from letters written in a moment of *emotion*, I am never myself in a letter. However, letters of this latter variety are always a source of regret and sorrow, sometimes even painfully so. Whenever I read the letters of eminent people published after their deaths, I am always troubled by a vague feeling of falseness and deceit.[9]

Tchaikovsky's reference to 'some casual reader' is highly significant, as is that to 'the letters of eminent people published after their deaths'. Tchaikovsky lived at a time when the documentary study of artists' lives was establishing itself as a new and important literary and historical genre, and he enjoyed such works as Otto Jahn's biography of Wolfgang Amadeus Mozart (1856) and the posthumous memoirs of Mikhail Glinka, published in 1870 (he was less taken with the correspondence of Nikolay Gogol, first published in 1847, noting in his diary 'how disagreeable our great figures are, apart from Pushkin').[10]

Yet Tchaikovsky's pleasure in reading the biographies of other artists was tempered by an awareness that his own life would one day become public property, as he noted to von Meck in August 1880:

> The idea that one day I may actually achieve a small dose
> of fame and that interest in my music will stimulate
> interest in me personally is very burdensome. Not because
> I am afraid of society. Hand on heart, I can say that my
> conscience is clear and that I have nothing to be ashamed
> of; but to think that one day people will try to penetrate
> the intimate world of my feelings and thoughts, everything
> that throughout my life I have so carefully hidden from
> contact with the crowd – that is very sad and unpleasant.[11]

Unpleasant this may have been, but Tchaikovsky was under little illusion as to its inevitability; almost everything he wrote – at least from the mid-1870s onwards – was written in full awareness that it might one day be made public and used to illuminate his life and works.

If Tchaikovsky's written words need to be approached with caution, then a similar claim might be made about his musical compositions. As has often been noted, they frequently give a sense of speaking, of somehow communicating a truth inexpressible through mere verbal language. Such was the force of a claim that the composer himself made to von Meck in 1878:

> You ask me, my friend, whether I have ever known *non-platonic love*. *Both yes and no*. If the question is put slightly differently, and you ask whether I have experienced complete happiness in love, then I should answer: *No, no* and *no*!!! In any case, I think

that the answer to this question can be found in my music. If you were to ask me whether I understand all the potency, all the immeasurable force of this feeling, then I should answer: *Yes, yes and yes*, and should say again that I have lovingly made repeated attempts to express through music both the torment and bliss of love. I do not know whether I have succeeded; or rather, I leave it to others to judge. I cannot agree with you at all that music *cannot convey the all-embracing characteristics* of love as an emotion. I am of the complete opposite view, believing that *music alone is capable* of achieving this. You say that *words* are required here. Not at all! It is precisely words that are not required, and where they are powerless, a more eloquent language appears in all its armour, that is, music.[12]

This famous passage is often read for the light it appears to shed on Tchaikovsky's sexuality and what – if anything – von Meck might have known about it. Read more attentively, however, it makes more sense as a statement of Tchaikovsky's artistic conviction that music is eminently capable of expressing human emotion and experience. Yet care must be taken here too. Writing to von Meck that same year, he cautioned against any directly autobiographical interpretation of his works:

Those who believe that the creative artist is capable of using his art to express what he feels at the very moment he *experiences* it are wrong. Both sad and joyful feelings are always expressed *retrospectively*, so to speak. Without having any particular reason for feeling joyful, I can immerse myself in a mood of cheerful creativity, and by contrast, I can produce in happy circumstances a piece which is steeped in the gloomiest and most desolate of feelings. In short, the artist lives a double life: the everyday life of humanity and the artistic one, and it is not always the case that these two lives coincide.[13]

Tchaikovsky's works are profoundly expressive, yet what they say is often unclear, just as the relationship between the circumstances of his life and the 'meaning' of his compositions is rarely unequivocal.

What mattered above all, then, was not whether audiences could interpret Tchaikovsky's works in a literal sense, but what use they could make of the feelings his music engendered in them. Von Meck, for instance, claimed that 'in your music, I hear myself, my condition, I sense in it echoes of my feelings, my thoughts, my melancholy',[14] and she was far from being the only one to treat Tchaikovsky's compositions as a canvas onto which to project her own emotions. And it was not just individuals such as von Meck or Tolstoy – who wept on hearing the slow movement of the String Quartet No. 1 – who made up Tchaikovsky's audience. The wider public on whom he depended for his financial well-being, whether in the form of publication royalties or box office revenue, also subscribed to the 'legibility' of both his works and the artistic personality they intuited within them. In his biography, Modest records the following 'amusing episode' between the composer and one of his many unnamed admirers, which took place during a journey down the river Volga in May 1888:

> Pyotr Ilyich had so artfully arranged his relationship with his fellow travellers that no one knew who he was. And so one day, during an improvised musical soirée arranged by the first-class passengers, Pyotr Ilyich was called upon to accompany some lady amateur, who, as she sang one of his own songs, criticized the inaccuracy of his playing. When he timidly tried to object, she replied that she must know best, 'because Tchaikovsky himself went through these romances with her teacher'.[15]

Behind the assertion of a direct musical lineage lies the fact that cheap and accessible publications (such as those issued by Jurgenson) did much to promote the composer's celebrity outside the salons, opera houses and concert halls of the capitals. Well beyond Moscow and St Petersburg, his works – not just songs and instrumental works, but extracts from his operas, as well as piano arrangements of his orchestral works for four hands – circulated in the towns and cities of the Russian Empire, creating communities of newly cultured Russians who came to know the composer through print culture, amateur performance and their own imaginations.

Tchaikovsky himself was all too aware of the nature of his relationship with the growing public for classical music in Russia in the second half of the nineteenth century. As he wrote to his friend and fellow composer Taneev in August 1880:

> I compose, that is, through the language of music, I pour out my moods and feelings, and of course, like anybody who has, or claims to have, something to say, I need people to listen to me. And the more they listen to me, the more congenial this is to me. In this respect, of course I love *fame* and strive for it with all my soul . . . However, it does not follow from this that I love the manifestations of *fame* that take the form of luncheons, suppers and musical soirées, at which I have suffered, as I always suffer in the company of people who are alien to me. If I did enjoy drawing the attention of the public and of society to myself, to my personality, then it would be all too easy to spend my whole life at all kinds of social gatherings. But surely you must know that I have never aspired to this, and that, on the contrary, I always strive to bury myself somewhere where I can exist outside of society. I *want, desire and love* people to take an interest in my music, to praise it and love it, but I have never sought to encourage them to take an interest in me *personally*, in my appearance or my conversation.[16]

Over the course of his too-short life, Tchaikovsky found a means – in his works, as in his letters – of projecting an image of himself as a creative individual who was intimate and personal enough to seem real and authentic, while simultaneously guarding his own need for privacy, not to mention established social codes of tact and discretion. Tchaikovsky's genius lay in his ability to translate his own vulnerable and sensitive disposition into an artistic method for engaging the emotions of a wide and growing audience through the projection of a seemingly readable self. And this was not just a question of his own artistic method; it was determined by the times in which he lived too. As Russia evolved from a traditional agrarian society into a modern industrial and urban empire over the course of the nineteenth century, many of its former certainties began to falter. With the weakening of autocratic power and the development of new social classes and identities, especially after the great reforms of the 1860s, there was a growing need for new symbols and certainties around which the nation could unite. Two great figures embody this process above all: in literature, Tolstoy, and in music, Tchaikovsky. How Tchaikovsky intuited the possibilities of – and lived with the consequences of – such celebrity forms the keystone of the life as it is presented in the pages that follow.

1

'I Will Make *Something* of Myself'

The first complete performance of Tchaikovsky's Symphony No. 1 in Moscow on 3 February 1868 was a strange sort of premiere. The third movement scherzo had been heard in concert back in December 1866, and had been repeated – along with the work's slow second movement – the following February. Yet a public hearing of the work in its entirety had been held up by criticism from Tchaikovsky's teachers and colleagues, as well as by his own ill health and artistic anxieties. Its immediate afterlife was just as tentative; despite being received with enthusiasm by its first audience, it would not be heard again until November 1883, when it was given in a revised version that the composer had made in 1874.

Viewed with hindsight, the Symphony No. 1 is, of course, a notable work, both in terms of Tchaikovsky's development as a composer and in the history of Russian music more generally. For one thing, it was an audacious choice for a composer who had not long graduated from the St Petersburg Conservatory and who had taken up the formal study of music as recently as 1861. Writing to his sister Sasha (Alexandra) that December, for instance, he gave notice of a sense of determination, ambition and self-confidence that would come to underpin the rest of his professional life:

> I think I already wrote to say that I have started to study the theory of music, and very successfully, too; I think you will agree that with my considerable talent (I hope you won't take this as

boasting), it would not be unreasonable to try my luck in this field. The only thing that worries me is my lack of character; laziness may get the upper hand and I may not be able to resist; but if this is not the case, then I promise you that I will make *something* of myself . . . Fortunately, there is still some time in hand.[1]

Tchaikovsky was right; he did make something of himself, applying himself to the formal study of music for the next few years with great assiduity and more than a little success. For someone whose only publicly performed works before 1868 had been the *Characteristic Dances*, an Overture in F major, the *Festival Overture on the Danish National Anthem* for orchestra, a single movement of a youthful string quartet and a cantata on Friedrich Schiller's 'Ode to Joy' written as a graduation exercise, a substantial 45-minute symphony in four movements represented a major claim to be taken seriously as a professional composer.

The choice of a symphony was an audacious one for other reasons. Few of Russia's composers before Tchaikovsky had tried their hand at the genre. For all his reputation as the founder of Russian music, Mikhail Glinka never completed one. Associated above all with the Austro-German tradition, it was a form that variously repelled and allured Tchaikovsky's nationalist peers too. Neither César Cui nor Modest Musorgsky wrote one. Alexander Borodin and Nikolay Rimsky-Korsakov each wrote three, although with mixed results. Borodin's Symphony No. 3 is unfinished, and Rimsky-Korsakov revised all of his in the 1880s, even reclassifying his Symphony No. 2 as a symphonic suite with the name *Antar*. Mily Balakirev made just two attempts at the genre: the first was begun in 1864 but not premiered until 1898, and a second was completed as late as 1908. By the time Tchaikovsky's Symphony No. 1 was performed, the only other Russian composer to have established himself as a symphonist was Anton Rubinstein, and his efforts were all too easily denigrated as foreign imports.

Tchaikovsky's Symphony No. 1 can thus be read as a defining statement about its composer's vision of the future of Russian music. With its echoes of Mendelssohn, Schumann and even Berlioz, it fuses western European foreign influences with intonations that would later come to be heard as typically Russian, such as an expansive sense of lyricism, a sectional rather than developmental attitude to musical argument; and movements that included a soulful adagio, a filigree scherzo and a finale based on a folk song (although its exact origins are disputed). Of that decade's other symphonic debuts – Rimsky-Korsakov's in 1865 and Borodin's in 1869 – it was above all Tchaikovsky's that inaugurated a tradition that would go on to include Alexander Glazunov, Vasily Kalinnikov, Alexander Scriabin, Sergey Rachmaninoff, and – eventually – Nikolay Myaskovsky, Sergey Prokofiev and Dmitry Shostakovich.

One further element of the Symphony No. 1 requires comment here: the nature of its programme. For all his academic training, Tchaikovsky nonetheless held that music must be more than a mere mechanistic working-out of notes, ideas and techniques. To this end, he gave a number of his works either explicit programmes or programmatic titles, many derived from literary sources. The Symphony No. 1 is subtitled *Winter Daydreams*, and each of its first two movements carries a subtitle too: 'Daydreams on a Winter Journey' and 'Land of Gloom, Land of Mist'. Yet the work's programmatic element does not mean that Tchaikovsky saw it as merely illustrative. While rejecting the notion of music as an abstract phenomenon, he was equally resistant to the view that art was exclusively referential or representational. His world view was closer to a Romantic one than a realist one, and while he asserted the presence of programmes in his works, he was decidedly not encouraging audiences to engage in acts of inference or decoding. No; the programmatic element in Tchaikovsky's music is an invitation for his listeners to involve themselves in a process of imaginative listening, in which their spontaneous and independent responses are as constitutive of musical meaning as Tchaikovsky's own authorial intentions, and it is remarkable to see the potential of such an approach so profoundly intuited in such an early work as the Symphony No. 1.

So how did Tchaikovsky come to find himself as Russia's first professional composer and a potential national celebrity? Writing to his French publisher, Félix Mackar, in January 1886, he offered the following account of his artistic development from his earliest years in the provincial town of Votkinsk in the Urals, where he was born on 25 April 1840, to his teenage studies in the Russian capital:

My predisposition for music manifested itself at the age of four. My mother, having noticed that I experienced the most vivid form of pleasure when listening to music, engaged a piano teacher, *Marie Markowna*, who taught me the rudiments of music. At the age of ten I was taken away to St Petersburg and enrolled in the *Imperial School of Jurisprudence*, where I spent nine years without seriously occupying myself with music, although towards the end of this period my father arranged for me to take lessons with an excellent pianist, *Mr Rodolphe Kündinger*, then resident in Petersburg. It is to this eminent artist that I am indebted for having understood that my true vocation was music; it was he who introduced me to the classics and opened up new artistic horizons for me. Having completed my study of the *Law* I became an employee of the Ministry of Justice, and for three more years I was forced to neglect music. When *Mr Zaremba*, a theoretician of great merit, established some classes in *theory and composition*, I joined these and my progress was such that when, the following year, *Antoine Rubinstein* founded the *Imperial Conservatory of Music*, I gave up my civil service position entirely and devoted myself entirely to my art . . . In 1865 I completed my studies under the supervision of *Mr Zaremba* and *A. Rubinstein* (the latter taught me orchestration), and my first composition was a cantata on a poem by *Schiller*, '*Joy*', which was performed at the palace of *the late Grand Duchess Hélène*, patroness of the Conservatory. Immediately afterwards I was engaged by *Nicolas Rubinstein* as professor of *composition* at the Moscow Conservatory.[2]

In its essential details, Tchaikovsky's account is correct enough, yet it imposes a degree of retrospective coherence and inevitability about his early years that they decidedly lacked at the time. Music may have been an important feature in the Tchaikovsky household, as it was for many gentry families in the early nineteenth century, yet it was never viewed as anything more than a genteel social accomplishment, as Modest's biography suggests:

> Pyotr Ilyich was born and lived in a place where there was no music other than domestic piano-playing by gentlemen and lady amateurs of the most primitive kind. Alexandra Andreevna [Tchaikovsky's mother] sang sweetly, but played nothing more than dances for her children; at least there is no evidence of a more serious repertoire after the time of her marriage. None of the other members of Ilya Petrovich's [Tchaikovsky's father's] family could manage even as much as this.[3]

Tchaikovsky too remembered his mother's singing voice, writing nostalgically of her performances of Alyabyev's 'Nightingale' – a staple of the nineteenth-century salon repertoire – in a letter to his parents in 1852.[4] Later on in life, Tchaikovsky would also recall the influence on him of an orchestrion, a mechanical instrument that reproduced extracts of operas by Mozart and the *bel canto* Italian composers. Given Tchaikovsky's evident facility as a performer by the time the family settled in St Petersburg in 1852, Modest is probably guilty of downplaying the influence of Pyotr's first teacher, Mariya Palchikova, but there is little in the composer's childhood and youth to suggest that a musical career lay before him.

The Tchaikovsky family, St Petersburg, 1848. From left to right: young Pyotr, his mother Alexandra, his sister Alexandra, his half-sister Zinaida, his brothers Nikolay and Ippolit, and his father Ilya.

One reason for the relatively lowly status of music in the Tchaikovsky household was what Richard Taruskin has referred to as 'the tardy growth and tardier professionalization' of music as a career in the first half of the nineteenth century in Russia, where music was either an accomplishment to be pursued by high-born dilettanti or a trade practised by hired foreigners.[5] Glinka, for instance, can barely be considered a professional musician in any conventional sense; for all his subsequent reputation as Russia's first great composer, his musical career was that of a talented amateur gentleman. Likewise, Zinaida Volkonskaya,

Tchaikovsky (second from the right), with his brothers Anatoly, Nikolay, Ippolit and Modest, St Petersburg, 1890.

who took the title role in her own opera, *Giovanna d'Arco*, in Rome in 1821 and staged Giovanni Paisiello's *La bella molinara* during the Congress of Verona the following year, was just the last in a long line of gifted female aristocrats associated with the Russian court from the eighteenth century onwards.[6] Although of gentry origin, Tchaikovsky's father spent his life as a mining engineer and administrator and often found himself in straitened financial circumstances. He may have enjoyed domestic music-making and even played the flute to a tolerable standard, yet he never intended that his artistically inclined son should embark on any career other than that of a lawyer, civil servant or state administrator (which is what Tchaikovsky's younger brother Anatoly eventually became).

Music was not the only form of artistic accomplishment practised by the young Tchaikovsky. As all members of the Russian gentry at the time did, he read, wrote and spoke French fluently, something that would stand him in good stead throughout his life and especially during his later international career (he would read assiduously in other languages too). Yet his command of the French language was as much literary as it was practical. As a boy, he read widely (a habit he would continue throughout his adult life), and among his earliest surviving artistic endeavours are a number of poems that he wrote in both French and Russian. In part, this was the result of the tastes of his French nanny, Fanny Dürbach, who did much to cultivate 'le petit Pouchkine', as she called the young Pyotr.[7] Tchaikovsky had a distinct and seemingly innate literary sensibility, even if it was his younger brother Modest who eventually turned out to be the aspiring writer in the family.

The prominent role played by literature in Tchaikovsky's life continued during his time at the School of Jurisprudence in St Petersburg, which he attended from the age of twelve (having spent two years at its preparatory school). There was some opportunity for the boys to indulge in music-making, to be sure, but the school no longer supported the kind of serious musical training that had nurtured the careers of Vladimir Stasov and Alexander Serov in the 1830s and 1840s. Even outside the school's official curriculum, literature rather than music predominated. A fellow student, Fyodor Maslov, recalled the extent and quality of Tchaikovsky's contributions to the school's literary journal, yet as far as music was concerned, Tchaikovsky's reputation rested on little more than performing tricks such as 'guessing keys and playing the piano with the keyboard covered by a towel'.[8]

Whether Tchaikovsky was more drawn to literature or music at this stage in his life is, though, beside the point. What matters more is his attitude to art as a vocation, and how this attitude was conditioned by social and cultural factors at the time. One of the two editors of the *School Herald* was Tchaikovsky's exact contemporary, the poet Alexey Apukhtin, and it was Apukhtin rather than Tchaikovsky who seemed to possess the more promising artistic talent, as one contemporary recalled: 'Pyotr Ilyich's fame as a musician was eclipsed by the fame of the poet Apukhtin, in whom we saw a future Pushkin.'[9] Tchaikovsky and Apukhtin were to remain lifelong friends, even if their

Tchaikovsky aged 19, dressed in the uniform of the School of Jurisprudence,
St Petersburg, 1859.

friendship was at times an uneasy one; both were homosexual, but
Tchaikovsky was disconcerted – at least in later life – by Apukhtin's
flamboyance and indiscretion. In the 1850s, however, poet and
composer were members of the same dandyish set, and part and
parcel of this milieu was a playful, dilettante attitude to the arts.
Had Tchaikovsky not ultimately enrolled at the St Petersburg

Conservatory, it is entirely possible that he might have carried on his career as Apukhtin did, whether in literature or in music.

Despite his abundant talent, Apukhtin preferred to live the life of a salaried civil servant. He published little in the periodical press until the 1880s, and for many decades his poetry circulated primarily in manuscript form among the cultural elite. Although he eventually put together a volume of his poetry in 1886, Apukhtin's art was shaped above all by an aristocratic conception of literature as either a gentlemanly accomplishment or a timeless vocation, but certainly not a profession carried out in the public sphere; his was decidedly not a career shaped by the concessions to markets, publishers, readers and critics that the professionalization of literature seemed to entail.

Initially at least, Tchaikovsky's life promised to take the same course. He seems to have neglected his musical training after graduating from the School of Jurisprudence in May 1859. Taking up an appointment in the Ministry of Justice that summer, he spent the next two years living the life of a carefree young bachelor in Russia's northern capital. Modest recalled his brother's 'mania for amateur theatricals', as well as his habit of imitating the movements and gestures of various well-known actresses and divas.[10] Modest also claimed that at some point in the early 1860s, Tchaikovsky found himself caught up in a homosexual scandal, as a result of which he modified his behaviour and submitted to a regime of discipline and discretion that would characterize the rest of his adult life.[11] Nonetheless, the composer never entirely abandoned his youthful playfulness, at least when in the company of intimate and trusted friends. During the visit of Camille Saint-Saëns to Moscow in 1875, for instance, the two composers performed an improvised ballet on the theme of *Pygmalion and Galatea*, accompanied by Nikolay Rubinstein on the piano.[12]

With Tchaikovsky's change in attitude to his private life came a change of attitude towards his life as a musician too.

Tchaikovsky aged 20, St Petersburg, 1860.

Writing to his sister, Sasha, in March 1861, he summarized his recent social life ('I spent Shrovetide in very high spirits and not at all sensibly. I have bid farewell to all those theatres and masquerades – and have now calmed down'), before revealing the details of a conversation he had recently had with his father:

> Papa insists that is it not yet too late for me to become an artist. It would be nice if that were true; but the fact is that even if there is any talent in me, it is probably impossible to develop it now. They have turned me into a civil servant – and a bad one at that; I am trying to mend my ways as much as I can, to devote myself to my official position with greater seriousness – and at the same time I'm supposed to be studying figured bass?[13]

Tchaikovsky's father was evidently proud of his son's embryonic talent, but he was willing to support it only to the extent that it would not detract from his future career as a lawyer or administrator. He was still of the view that the arts were a social accomplishment, even a source of personal pleasure, but certainly not a promising career choice.

Such caution was understandable, not least because it was shared by Tchaikovsky's piano teacher at the time, the German-born Rudolph Kündinger:

> Ilya Tchaikovsky engaged me to give lessons to his son Pyotr, a student at the School of Jurisprudence. From 1855 to 1858 our lessons were interrupted only during the summer months, and my pupil made good progress, though not such as to spark in me any particular hopes for him. When Ilya Petrovich asked me whether it would be worthwhile for his son to dedicate himself wholly to a musical career, I replied in the negative, first of all because I did not see in Pyotr Ilyich the talent that subsequently came to light and, second, because I knew from

my own experience how difficult the position of a 'musician' was at that time in Russia. We were looked down upon in society and treated with condescension, nor was there any serious appreciation or understanding of music as a profession.[14]

Soon, however, the situation was to change profoundly. In 1859 the Russian Musical Society was established by the pianist and composer Anton Rubinstein with support from his influential Imperial patroness, Grand Duchess Elena Pavlovna. From now on, music would enjoy greater social prestige and institutional security than it had previously in Russia. Initially the Society arranged classes in St Petersburg, including lessons in harmony that were taught by Nikolay Zaremba. Tchaikovsky attended these from September 1861, while nominally continuing his official career in the Ministry of Justice. Then, in the autumn of 1862, he became one of the first students to enrol at the city's newly established Conservatory. He officially renounced his post in the civil service the following April, graduating from the Conservatory with a silver medal in December 1865 (the gold medal was not awarded that year).

Tchaikovsky seized this opportunity to make up for his previously piecemeal musical education with uncommon zeal. Putting to good use the work ethic instilled in him first at the Schmelling School in St Petersburg in 1848–9, and then as a boarder at the School of Jurisprudence, he submitted himself to the rigours of the Western-style academic training that the Conservatory offered. He also proved himself able to deal with disappointment and unhappiness. As he began to master the techniques of composition, Tchaikovsky discovered a facility for turning his private emotions into a vivid and expressive musical language that could reach out to audiences who knew nothing of his inner feelings. In particular, Modest claimed that the key to his brother's creativity was his

Tchaikovsky aged 20, dressed in the uniform of the Ministry of Justice,
St Petersburg, 1860.

youthful relationship with Sergey Kireev – 'the strongest, most durable and purest amorous infatuation of his entire life':

> It comprised all the charms, all the sufferings, all the depth and force of a love both luminous and sublime. This was the courtly 'service to the Lady,' without the slightest sensual design or intention. Anyone who doubts the beauty and high poetry of this cult should be pointed to the finest passages of Tchaikovsky's musical oeuvre: the middle portion of *Romeo and Juliet*, *The Tempest*, *Francesca*, Tatyana's letter, which could never have been 'invented' without having first been experienced, and he would never experience in later life so powerful, lasting and torturous an emotion . . .[15]

It was not just failed relationships and erotic longings that formed the basis for the development of his musical voice. His mother died of cholera in 1854, and this single traumatic event haunted him more than any other for the rest of his life. The first of a number of painful losses of friends and family members, it is but one clue to the tragic and fatalistic elements in his character.

The paradox was, however, that Tchaikovsky was able to compose a whole series of intensely emotional, seemingly self-revelatory and often unruly works precisely by a process of methodical self-control. Like Gustave Flaubert or Henrik Ibsen, he was one of those nineteenth-century artists who could challenge bourgeois values in his compositions by espousing a distinctly bourgeois attitude in his professional life. As Flaubert famously put it in a letter to Gertrude Tennant in 1876: 'Be ordered in your life and as ordinary as a bourgeois so that you may be violent and original in your works.'[16] In the case of Tchaikovsky, something of this duality can be traced to the teaching he received at the St Petersburg Conservatory, and to the differing attitudes taken to composition by his two teachers, Zaremba and Rubinstein.

Zaremba's teaching was generally felt to be formal and conservative, focusing on a respect for the classical traditions of the past and a strict adherence to the rules of harmony and counterpoint. Rubinstein, by contrast, was seen to be more imaginative and creative, preferring to judge his students on their ability to find a distinct creative voice of their own. The influence of both men can be discerned throughout Tchaikovsky's oeuvre, combining as it does elements of 'Teutonic' discipline and a looser, more inventive, 'Slavic' flair. Indeed, much of the critical reaction to his works would struggle to disentangle these two elements of his artistic make-up. On the one hand, the nationalist composers would berate him for his rigid, European-style conservatory training. On the other hand, his earliest Western critics would dismiss his music as the very embodiment of the chaotic, primitive and untutored 'Russian soul'. In truth, it was both – and neither. Tchaikovsky's language may have been the product of both Zaremba's and Rubinstein's teaching, but what he had to say was entirely his own. It was this voice that audiences heard in February 1868, when the Symphony No. 1 was heard complete for the first time.

2

'The Only Hope for Our Musical Future'

Work on the Symphony No. 1 coincided with Tchaikovsky's arrival, in January 1866, in Moscow, where he had been engaged to teach classes in harmony for the local branch of the Russian Musical Society. As had previously been the case in St Petersburg, these classes formed the foundation for the subsequent establishment of a fully fledged conservatory, which opened that September. The premiere of the Symphony No. 1 was therefore not simply a crucial event in its composer's professional career; it demonstrated the ambitious role that the conservatories had set themselves in shaping the nation's musical life more generally. As a graduate of one of these institutions, Tchaikovsky was now responsible for passing on at one what he had learned at the other, and in 1871 he published a number of his lectures as *A Guide to the Practical Study of Harmony*, followed by *A Short Manual of Harmony, Adapted for the Study of Church Music in Russia* in 1875 (the success of the former volume in particular can be seen from the fact that it was reprinted in 1876, 1881, 1885 and 1891).

Tchaikovsky's colleague and friend from the St Petersburg Conservatory, Herman Laroche, congratulated him on his appointment as a professor of theory and harmony in Moscow, confidently predicting the future that lay ahead of him:

you are *modern Russia's greatest musical talent*. More powerful and original than Balakirev, more elevated and creative than Serov, immeasurably more educated than Rimsky-Korsakov, *I see in you the greatest, or rather, the only hope for our musical future . . . It is possible that your works will begin only in five years; but these mature, classic works will surpass everything that we have had since Glinka*.[1]

Others were more circumspect. Despite the new status accorded to professional musicians in Imperial Russia, it seemed that Tchaikovsky's father's prejudices were not so easily overcome:

> So now, thank heavens, you have finished your musical education as you wished – and what good has it done you? You say you've been offered a post as a teacher, but that just means you'll be called a professor of music theory with a pitiful salary! . . . Your passion for music is laudable, but, my dear friend, it is a slippery path: the reward for a genius's work always comes much, much later. Just look at Serov, that poor genius of a musician: for all the passion he has put into his work, the only thing he has managed to earn are silver hairs, not silver itself . . . After all, here only Italians like Verdi can command fees of 30,000 roubles for their works. Glinka died a poor man, and none of our other talents are much valued either. Anybody who knows your playing and your other musical gifts will appreciate you even without Rubinstein's approval. So just spit on them and go back to state service again.[2]

Such fears were not entirely without foundation. Tchaikovsky's initial salary was just 50 roubles a month[3] and, at least initially, the financial situation of the Moscow Conservatory itself was distinctly precarious, surviving as an institution largely on the basis of the forceful personality of its director, Nikolay Rubinstein, the brother of Tchaikovsky's former teacher in St Petersburg.

Tchaikovsky, it must be said, was not a natural teacher, although he certainly was a conscientious one. Most of his students were young women, primarily destined for careers as music teachers; though the task of teaching them was as crucial to the musical education of the Russian Empire as was the cultivation of composers and virtuosi, it held little appeal for him.[4] Even before his classes had begun, he wrote to his stepmother, Elizaveta: 'yesterday I had to examine the new students. I must admit that I was terribly afraid at the sight of such a large number of crinolines and chignons.'[5] Neither did his new colleagues inspire him greatly, as he confessed to his brothers Anatoly and Modest: 'In general, the staff of the conservatory here will not be as good as it was in St Petersburg. But there are two or three solid types.'[6] In fact, Tchaikovsky's social circle in Moscow soon became a wide and supportive one. With the move from St Petersburg, he was no longer a promising student, a society dilettante, a loving family member or a former – if unenthusiastic – civil servant; now, he enjoyed the status of a respected professional musician and a leading member of a thriving artistic and bohemian elite, and many of the friends he made at this time remained loyal and supportive throughout his life. It was here, for instance, that Tchaikovsky met Pyotr Jurgenson, the one publisher who would do more than anybody else to promote his works. Two colleagues from the conservatory, Nikolay Kashkin and Karl Albrecht, also became close and trusted friends (Kashkin wrote some of the earliest and most vivid recollections of the composer after his death). Throughout his life, Tchaikovsky would draw much-needed moral and practical support from the extended network of friends and associates that he first established in Moscow in the mid-1860s; their conviction, both collective and individual, that he would prove to be a composer of genius formed the precondition for much of his later success.

The dominant figure in Tchaikovsky's life at this time was, however, Nikolay Rubinstein, who – as director of the Moscow Conservatory – had direct involvement in just about every aspect of his professional career. Moreover, Tchaikovsky's financial

Tchaikovsky's friend and publisher, Pyotr Jurgenson.

circumstances obliged him to lodge with Rubinstein for five or so years (he would not move into an apartment of his own until autumn 1871), and he often chafed at the lack of personal freedom that this arrangement entailed. To be sure, Rubinstein could be high-handed and arrogant, but what bothered Tchaikovsky most was his mentor's extravagant socializing. Barely had he arrived in the city when he wrote to his brothers about the contrast between his own behaviour and that of his mentor: 'Rubinstein, who leads quite a dissipated life, cannot get over his astonishment at my industry.'[7] Clearly the work ethic and discretion that had been the hallmarks of Tchaikovsky's musical training in St Petersburg would be carried over into his life in Moscow too. Although his social life during his first years in Moscow can in no way be described as hermit-like, he was clearly aware of society gossip. Indeed, a scandal that broke out in March 1870, when Rubinstein was required to defend himself in court against allegations that he had mistreated a female student, demonstrated just how easily affairs at the Conservatory could become public knowledge, and Tchaikovsky would have been struck by the implications of the case for both his personal and professional reputation.

Given his musical background, one might expect Tchaikovsky to have continued the traditions advocated by his conservatory teachers, yet it was precisely at this time that Tchaikovsky began a fruitful association with their very adversaries, the so-called 'Mighty Handful' (*Moguchaya Kuchka*). Also known as 'the Balakirev Circle' or 'the New Russian School', the Kuchka was a group of St Petersburg composers who spurned both academic training and the influence of the German classical tradition, while remaining open to the influence of other Western composers such as Hector Berlioz, Franz Liszt and Robert Schumann. Later, Tchaikovsky was to express a number of reservations about their works and aesthetics. Writing to Nadezhda von Meck in late 1877, for instance, he singled out Nikolay Rimsky-Korsakov as the only member of the group to have grasped the necessity of a formal musical education (Rimsky-Korsakov had, somewhat unexpectedly, been appointed professor at the St Petersburg Conservatory in 1870, whereupon he subjected himself to the kind of conventional learning that the Kuchka otherwise eschewed). Alexander Borodin and César Cui had talent, Tchaikovsky admitted, but their dilettantism meant that they were unable to develop it fully, while Mily Balakirev was 'the inventor of all the theories of this strange little group which unites in itself so many untapped, wrongly directed, or prematurely destroyed forces'. Modest Musorgsky was the most ignorant of all, 'an ignoble character, with a fondness for vulgarity, crudeness and roughness'.[8]

In the late 1860s and early 1870s, however, Tchaikovsky and the members of the Kuchka found themselves occupying common artistic ground. Tchaikovsky would use his influence with Nikolay Rubinstein to get their works performed in Moscow, and when Balakirev was deposed as conductor of the Russian Musical Society in St Petersburg in 1869, Tchaikovsky denounced the decision in the press. So close was their association at this time that the de facto spokesperson of the Kuchka, the art historian and critic Vladimir Stasov, even dubbed Tchaikovsky the sixth member of the group.[9] The main appeal of the Kuchka for Tchaikovsky lay in the ways in which their music, for all its technical shortcomings, offered a form of liberation from the limitations of his own academic training. In fact, in the wake of the Symphony No. 1, he was already experimenting with new ways of treating musical form. Between September and December 1868 he completed *Fatum*, an orchestral fantasy with no obvious musical structure other than that dictated by his own imagination. The problem with such forms was, however, that they did not readily show listeners how to follow and make sense of them. This much was intuited by Tchaikovsky's friend Ivan Klimenko, who – according to one version of the story – encouraged the composer to attach a programme to the work:

You must give the listener at least some clue for understanding such a vague title, and if, for some reason or other, you find it impossible to bare your soul to the listener and give a more or less detailed explanation of what you wanted to say in the work, then why not give him at least some hint in the form of an epigraph?

Tchaikovsky agreed to a suggestion, apparently made by Sergey Rachinsky, that a fragment of a longer poem by Konstantin Batyushkov be given by way of programme:

Knowest thou what the grey-haired Melchizedek
Said as he bid farewell to life?: 'Man is born a slave,
A slave he goes to his grave,
And even death will scarce reveal to him
Why he walked this sorrowful vale of tears,
Why he suffered, wept, endured, then vanished!'[10]

The ruse failed. Critics rounded on the disparity between the verses and the music, as well as on a number of perceived weaknesses in the musical construction of the work itself. Tchaikovsky, already dissatisfied with his composition, destroyed the manuscript (it was reconstructed and published after his death on the basis of the surviving orchestral parts).

One of the harshest critics of *Fatum* had been Balakirev, who listed his objections in a series of letters written in March 1869.[11] This was, however, the prelude to a more fruitful collaboration between the two composers, the first and most famous product of which was the fantasy overture *Romeo and Juliet*. In the summer of 1869, Balakirev proposed Shakespeare's play as a theme for a new orchestral work, sketching out not just a detailed literary narrative but a possible musical structure too. Inspiration came slowly at first, and in October 1869 Tchaikovsky was anxious that his underlying conservatory training was getting

Tchaikovsky aged 29, Moscow, 1869.

in the way of poetic inspiration: 'I'm beginning to fear that my muse has flown off to some far-off place (perhaps she's paying Zaremba a visit), and that I may have to wait a long time for her to return.'[12] Such academicism was soon behind him, however, and by the middle of November the overture was complete.

Tchaikovsky's relationship with the Kuchka at this time was so intense that it unleashed a striking tone of intimacy in their letters. Writing to Balakirev, he compared his initial lack of inspiration to a state of castration ('I have become a muse-less musician, or what amounts to the same thing, a testicle-less one'),[13] and later on, Balakirev wrote ecstatically about the work's love theme:

> the second theme in D flat is simply *delightful*. I play it often, and I would really like to give you a kiss for it. Here is all the voluptuousness and sweetness of love . . . When I play it, I imagine you lying naked in your bath . . . with your little tummy being washed with the hot lather of scented soap.[14]

For all this, *Romeo and Juliet* is also a striking assertion of Tchaikovsky's own voice as a composer. Once he had completed the first version of the overture, he refused to let Balakirev see it until after its premiere in Moscow in March 1870. He made further changes that summer, and once the score had been published by the Berlin publisher Bote & Bock in 1871, he rejected Balakirev's promptings to undertake a further revision. (He did, however, return to the score on his own initiative in 1880, and it is in this form that the work is generally heard today.)

Tchaikovsky's growing confidence can be seen by looking beyond his surface treatment of situations and characters derived from Shakespeare's play. As well as its almost pictorial evocations of Friar Laurence, the young lovers and the warring families, the overture has a compelling formal structure that is based on the classical sonata-form principle. Consisting of an introduction, an exposition made up of two contrasting themes, a development section in which the motivic material of these themes is elaborated and explored in greater detail, and a recapitulation in which the material of the exposition is repeated in modified form, *Romeo and Juliet* has a musical coherence that a literary narrative alone could barely have achieved. The lessons of *Fatum* – which had eschewed just such a formal structure – had been learned. Throughout his career, Tchaikovsky remained convinced of the primacy of music as the ultimate form of emotional expression, just as he was happy to use a programme, or at least the suggestion of a programme, inasmuch as it constituted a powerful way of engaging an audience's imagination. The challenge was to come up with a narrative that was credible enough to be sustained by attentive listening, but which did not bind his invention to such a degree that the music became merely illustrative, representational or secondary to external, non-musical stimuli. It was Tchaikovsky's encounter with the Kuchka that helped him to refine a technique that brought elements of programme music to the symphonic tradition, while simultaneously insisting on the rigorous search for form within the more flexible structure of the tone poem.

Romeo and Juliet was a breakthrough work in many ways. It allowed Tchaikovsky to assimilate the two great influences available to him at the time: the academic training offered by the conservatory on the one hand, and the more informal eloquence of the Kuchka on the other. This artistic achievement was matched by commercial success, too, both in Russia and abroad. Published in Berlin, *Romeo and Juliet* was rapidly taken up by orchestras throughout western Europe and laid the early foundations for its composer's eventual international renown. Tchaikovsky would return to the Shakespearean tone poem on later occasions – *The Tempest* (1873), based on a programme suggested by Stasov, and *Hamlet* (1888) – as well as exploring the narrative and emotional potential of other literary sources, such as in *Francesca da Rimini* (1876), derived from a canto in Dante's *Divina Commedia,* and *The Voevoda* (1891), inspired by Pushkin's translation of a poem by Mickiewicz.

Whatever their professional rivalries and disagreements, Tchaikovsky and the Kuchka were linked by a sense of mutual respect as creative artists, as well as by a conviction that Russian music could increasingly hold its own against western European traditions. Writing to his brother Anatoly in early January 1875, Tchaikovsky aptly summed up the situation:

> What an extraordinary thing! These various Cuis, Stasovs and co., although they sometimes play mean tricks on me, can also make me feel that they are much more interested in me than my so-called friends.[15]

Less well known than *Romeo and Juliet* perhaps, yet equally indicative of Tchaikovsky's closeness to the so-called nationalist composers at this time, is the Symphony No. 2 (1872). The Symphony No. 1 had cost him much effort and exhaustion, both physical and psychological, and represents a desire to write within the framework of an inherited canonical form (while simultaneously imbuing it with elements of his own). By contrast, its successor came easily and fluently, the product of an idyllic summer spent on the Ukrainian estate of his sister and brother-in-law at Kamenka, as well as on those of his friends Nikolay Kondratyev and Vladimir Shilovsky at Nizy and Usovo. In his previous orchestral works, Tchaikovsky had employed themes of his own invention. Now, however, he drew on a number of folk songs, which he took from both published sources and directly from the field; he was particularly proud of the version of 'The Crane' that he included in the finale and which, as he wrote to Modest, was sung to him by the steward at Kamenka.[16]

The nationalists were delighted by the work, and not just on account of its obvious local colour (its nickname, 'The Little

Russian', refers to the nineteenth-century Russian name for Ukraine). Unlike melodic and motivic material in the classical Western symphony, which can be developed infinitely according to the composer's inventive capacity, the use of folk songs demanded a somewhat different approach to form. Ever since Glinka's *Kamarinskaya* of 1848 (referred to by Tchaikovsky as 'the acorn' out of which all Russian music subsequently grew),[17] Russian composers had often repeated a folk song melody against a changing background, and Tchaikovsky's use of this technique marked an important contribution to the development of a self-consciously native symphonic tradition. Whether the Symphony No. 2 achieves its ambitions is debatable, and this may have something to do with the borrowed nature of its nationalist rhetoric. The handling of the often wistful folk song sources can at times be overemphatic and even bombastic, especially in the outer two movements, and the repetitive sequences and imitations can outstay their welcome. Tchaikovsky himself clearly had reservations about the work, and in 1880 he substantially revised the first movement, and made a number of other changes elsewhere too.

Tchaikovsky's revisions to the Symphony No. 2 were evidence of his own strict attitude to his works and give some sense of how much, in his own estimation, he still had to learn as a composer. Yet if the successful fusion of influences that was such a feature of *Romeo and Juliet* had still to be fully applied to his output as a symphonist, then his work in the field of opera at this time was yet more uncertain. For a young and ambitious Russian composer, opera presented an obvious, if daunting, challenge. Notwithstanding the crucial role played by Glinka's *A Life for the Tsar* (1836) and *Ruslan and Lyudmila* (1842) as foundational documents in Russia's national tradition, there was a perception that native works still did not enjoy the same prestige as foreign repertoires did, as Tchaikovsky himself argued:

I am prepared to agree that it is unfitting for any *self-respecting* capital to do without an Italian opera. But, listening to Mme Patti's trills, can I, as a Russian musician, forget even for a moment the humiliating situation of our native art in Moscow, where there is neither time nor place for it to find a refuge? Can I forget the pitiful way in which Russian opera vegetates, even while we have in our repertoire several works which any other *self-respecting* capital would regard with pride as its most precious treasures?[18]

Moscow's Bolshoi Theatre and St Petersburg's Mariinsky Theatre were both administered by the Imperial Theatre Directorate. Although it could be a long and trying process to get works staged at these institutions, they offered the possibility of major critical and financial rewards, and success promised to fulfil Tchaikovsky's high-minded patriotic ideals, as well as his pragmatic financial needs.

Tchaikovsky first began to think of writing an opera in late 1866, as he completed work on the Symphony No. 1; the score itself was written between March 1867 and the following summer. For his libretto, Tchaikovsky turned to an existing play, *A Dream on the Volga* by Alexander Ostrovsky, whom he had met soon after arriving in Moscow. In many ways, Ostrovsky was an obvious choice. Tchaikovsky had already written a tone poem based on his most famous play, *The Storm*, while still a student (although the work was not published or performed until after his death). He also provided some instrumental music for a production of his *Dmitry the Pretender and Vasily Shuisky* in 1867 (the story deals with the same historical period as Musorgsky's *Boris Godunov*). As Russia's leading mid-nineteenth-century dramatist, Ostrovsky promised to lend something of his own artistic kudos to the project, as well as producing a scenario that was scenically viable. From the outset, however, the opera was beset with problems. First, Tchaikovsky managed to lose Ostrovsky's libretto for the opening act, and once this had been rewritten, the dramatist left the adaptation of his original play of 1865 to the still young and inexperienced composer. Then Tchaikovsky delayed the premiere of the new work from September 1868 to early 1869 in order to allow greater time for rehearsals.

At its premiere at Moscow's Bolshoi Theatre on 30 January 1869, *The Voevoda* (as the opera was now called) took fifteen curtain calls, yet its success was short-lived and it ran for just four more complete performances.[19] Its first night had been a benefit performance for the soprano, Alexandra Menshikova, a practice common enough when it came to new stage works in the nineteenth century (the premiere in 1874 of the revised version of Musorgsky's *Boris Godunov* was given in honour of Yuliya Platonova, and as late as 1896 Anton Chekhov's *The Seagull* was staged as a benefit for the actress Elizaveta Levkeeva). Disappointed by both the poor performance and the critical reaction, Tchaikovsky withdrew the score and – as he had done with *Fatum* – destroyed it. Part of the problem, as Laroche saw it, was Tchaikovsky's inability to fuse Western and Russian influences into a single whole. Despite its libretto on a Russian historical theme, it betrayed too great a debt to the very foreign influences it set out to counter:

> Mr Tchaikovsky's style wavers between German (predominantly) and Italian styles . . . But from time to time in *The Voevoda* there appear Russian folktunes which the composer takes as themes for extensive development, and which he treats with indubitable taste and refinement. It is these songs more than anything that expose the non-Russian character of all the remaining numbers.

More presciently, Laroche also singled out Tchaikovsky's tendency to think symphonically rather than scenically:

> Mr Tchaikovsky shares with the most recent German
> composers a predilection for the orchestra and indifference
> to the human voice . . . Very often the sonorous, beautiful
> scoring completely drowns the performers' voices, and the
> spectator on such occasions can only look in his libretto
> and simply guess what they are singing about.[20]

No one could accuse the mature Tchaikovsky of 'indifference to
the human voice', and as a song composer he found a natural
and spontaneous form of intimate lyricism from the outset.
Yet in his early operas, he struggled to reconcile the competing
demands of melodic expressivity, dramatic structure and musical
form. Tchaikovsky himself would echo Laroche's assessments
in his own commentary on *Vakula the Smith* (1874), which – as
he wrote to von Meck – suffered from 'an agglomeration and
superfluity of detail, tiresome chromatic harmonies, and a sense
of shapelessness and incompleteness in the individual numbers.
C'est un menu surchargé de plats épicés.'[21] Even before the failure
of *The Voevoda*, Tchaikovsky had begun work on a second opera
– a setting of Friedrich de la Motte Fouqué's *Undine*, in a Russian
version by Vladimir Sollogub, and a premonition of the fairytale
theme that would be so central to his later ballets. Rejected by
the Theatre Directorate, *Undine* never even made it to the stage
and was subsequently destroyed by its composer. Plans for an
opera called *Mandragora*, with a libretto by Rachinsky, similarly
came to nothing, apart from a 'Chorus of Flowers and Insects'.

Tchaikovsky's efforts were not wasted, however. Each of the
suppressed scores yielded ideas that could be reused successfully
elsewhere, echoing a practice seen more widely in his music at
this time. Material from his overture *The Storm*, as well as from
a piano sonata written while still a student, found its way into
the Symphony No. 1, for instance, and a duet in *The Voevoda* was
based on an aria first heard in the graduation cantata, *To Joy*.

Despite its dramatic failings, Tchaikovsky obviously knew that the new music for *The Voevoda* was too good to waste, and as late as 1875–6 he was raiding the score – as well as that of *Undine* – for *Swan Lake*. *Undine* also provided the music for the slow movement of the Symphony No. 2, suggesting a potential link between the fairy tale subject-matter of the opera and the folkloric tenor of the symphony. Such a practice was understandable enough from both a pragmatic and a creative point of view; when faced with pressing deadlines, or merely a musical idea too inspired to reject outright, Tchaikovsky was only too likely to recycle existing material. This habit may also shed light on the question of the relationship between Tchaikovsky's music and the ideas it is sometimes held to represent. Whatever the original inspiration behind particular musical ideas, the significance of such ideas inevitably alters when they are translated into new and different contexts. Programmes and programmatic titles may suggest something of a work's original inspiration, as well as functioning as some sort of retrospective commentary on a particular work, yet the actual meaning of individual musical ideas is far from straightforward.

The most extensive instance of reworking at this time was Tchaikovsky's next opera, *The Oprichnik*, the first act of which was based substantially on the first act of *The Voevoda*. Another complex historical melodrama on a Russian theme, it is the first of Tchaikovsky's operas to have survived and shows his continued determination to establish himself as a dramatic, as well as a symphonic, composer. Like the Symphony No. 2, *The Oprichnik* is a work shaped in part by Tchaikovsky's closeness to members of the Kuchka in the early 1870s. The original play on which it was based, Ivan Lazhechnikov's historical tragedy *The Oprichnik*, dated from 1842, when it was immediately banned by the censor on account of its depiction of the *oprichnina*, the personal bodyguards of Ivan IV (known better by his nickname, 'the Terrible'). Published only in 1859 and staged for the first time in 1867, its fate was not unlike that of another historical tragedy that had only recently been adapted as an opera: Alexander Pushkin's *Boris Godunov*, which, although written in 1824–5 and published in 1830, was not cleared for performance until 1866 (when, of course, it attracted the attention of Musorgsky).[22] Clearly, both composers were responding to the more liberal reign of Alexander II and the possibilities it offered for exploring previously taboo topics on the stage. Yet both composers found themselves struggling with the expectations of Russian audiences at the time. Musorgky's revision of his original version of *Boris Godunov* added an entirely new strand to its plot, granting substantial romantic interest to an opera that had been emotionally stark to begin with. Given his more cosmopolitan tastes, it is not surprising that Tchaikovsky's opera should show the influence of the kind of foreign models that were still so popular with contemporary audiences (for Gerald Abraham, it amounted to little more than 'Meyerbeer translated into Russian').[23]

Tchaikovsky worked on *The Oprichnik* between 1870 and 1872, crafting his own libretto, just as he had with *The Voevoda*. Premiered in St Petersburg on 12 April 1874 at a benefit performance for its conductor, Eduard Nápravník, it had run for fourteen performances by 1881 (a creditable number for new Russian operas at this time, as Modest points out, citing comparisons with Rimsky-Korsakov's *The Maid of Pskov*, Dargomyzhsky's *The Stone Guest*, Musorgsky's *Boris Godunov*, and Cui's *William Ratcliff* and *Angelo*).[24] After performances in Kiev and Odessa, it opened at the Bolshoi Theatre on 4 May 1875; yet despite positive reviews from a number of friends, Tchaikovsky could still confess to his brother Anatoly that 'I *hate The Oprichnik* with every force of my soul!'[25] Quite what offended him so much is hard to gauge; certainly, had the vocal score not already been published by Bessel in 1874, it is possible that the opera would have been withdrawn and even destroyed. Perhaps Tchaikovsky realized that the shortcomings of *The Oprichnik* were the very ones that had bedevilled his earlier operas. Already during the rehearsals for the first run in St Petersburg, Nápravník proposed a number of revisions, arguing that the lush orchestration overwhelmed the singers and that the work's symphonic, rather than dramatic, attitude to musical form impeded the unfolding of the stage action.[26] Admittedly, the persistence of such critical judgements may ultimately say more about contemporary tastes than about Tchaikovsky's inherent strengths as an opera composer; yet the fact that *The Oprichnik* has barely flourished even in Russia, with its long tradition of convoluted historical melodrama, suggests that Tchaikovsky was still struggling to find his voice.

By the time of the premiere of *The Oprichnik*, Tchaikovsky – who had just turned 34 – was known as the composer of two operas, one of which had been withdrawn, and two symphonies, neither of which had yet been published. Despite a growing reputation and the support of a group of friends and colleagues in both Moscow and St Petersburg, the only work that could be said to confirm Laroche's claim that Tchaikovsky would become Russia's greatest composer was *Romeo and Juliet*. This state of affairs was reflected in his financial situation too. Although Tchaikovsky's salary at the Moscow Conservatory had risen considerably since his appointment (1,500 roubles by 1871, rising to 2,300 roubles the next year), and he derived a further supplementary income as a critic for the *Contemporary Chronicle* and the *Russian Register*, it would be some time before Tchaikovsky could consider himself financially stable, let alone affluent.[27] At the opening night of *The Oprichnik* in St Petersburg, Ilya Petrovich claimed that he would still have been happier to see his son awarded the Order of St Anna, first class – an honour traditionally bestowed on high-ranking civil servants and distinguished military officers.[28]

However, this picture of Tchaikovsky's slow path to success is true only if one focuses on the supposedly major genres of symphonic music and opera, which were crucial in establishing critical and social success at the time and which have tended to

Tchaikovsky aged 33, St Petersburg, 1874.

dominate the narratives of so many histories and biographies
ever since. If one turns instead to song and chamber music, then
one encounters a composer who found a confident creative voice

much earlier, and it was this voice that allowed Tchaikovsky to establish a durable – as well as profitable – relationship with the broad and educated audience that existed beyond Russia's capital cities and their artistic elites. Given the relatively limited number of performances of his operas and symphonies, it was through song and instrumental music that Tchaikovsky first established his reputation with audiences and performers. Some of these works are undeniably slight, such as the *potpourri* on themes from the discarded *Voevoda* for solo piano published under the pseudonym H. Cramer in 1868. Yet given the enormous task of educating and providing for Russia's musical tastes, such works are as important as opera and symphonic music, both in the composer's biography and in the history of nineteenth-century Russian music, if not indeed more so.

There has been a long tradition of dismissing Tchaikovsky's songs as sentimental hack work; Cui in particular was contemptuous of his handling of words, seeing in his songs only the most generalized form of emotion.[29] Yet this is to misunderstand Tchaikovsky's attitude to the form. When members of the Kuchka fetishized a scrupulous attitude to text as the defining feature of all vocal music, whether opera or song, they ran the risk of seeing music as fundamentally subservient to verbal content. In the Kuchka's most extreme works, such as Musorgsky's almost naturalistic songs of the 1860s, music becomes the faithful reproduction of an external reality. Tchaikovsky had no time for such realism, preferring a looser, more associative relationship between music and its sister arts. In his hands, song becomes a freer form of aesthetic experience, in which the composer's reluctance to determine details of performance and articulation create correspondingly greater space for singers and audiences to inhabit. Through his choice of texts, treatment of words and musical language, Tchaikovsky came up with a form of lyric expression that was maximally suggestive yet minimally referential, a combination that formed the basis for the subsequent commercial and popular success of his songs.[30]

Tchaikovsky's first published songs date from late 1869, and it is clear from his correspondence that he saw the task of writing them as primarily mercenary. Yet it is inconceivable that he would have gone on to write more than one hundred songs, many of them the most characteristic examples of his genius, had he not also derived considerable artistic and personal satisfaction from doing so.[31] Tchaikovsky was a voracious reader with a well-developed literary sensibility, and his songs constitute both a diary of his private reading and an insight into how poetry circulated through musical adaptation at a time when amateur music-making was a defining feature of Russian polite society. The songs from 1869 – published by Jurgenson as Tchaikovsky's Opus 6 – are typical of his approach. The group, which consists of six songs, takes an anthological approach to poetry. There are two songs to texts by Alexey Tolstoy and one with words by Evdokiya Rostopchina (very much the kind of female salon poet often dismissed in or entirely excluded from standard literary histories of Russia). Alongside these Russian originals sit translations by Lev Mey of poems by Heinrich Heine and Johann Wolfgang von Goethe, and one by Alexey Pleshcheev of a poem by Moritz Hartmann. Of these, it is Tchaikovsky's setting of Goethe's 'Nur wer die Sehnsucht kennt' (better known in English as 'None but the Lonely Heart') that rapidly became the most popular, not just of this set of songs, but of all of the songs he ever wrote. Detached from its original context in Goethe's novel *Wilhelm Meisters Lehrjahre* (Wilhelm Meister's Apprenticeship, 1795–6), where it is sung by the strangely asexual foundling Mignon, it represents a tempting invitation for performers and listeners to project their own fantasies onto its melancholy sentiments.[32]

Inspired by the success of these early works, Tchaikovsky turned regularly to the song genre throughout the rest of his life. Alongside a small body of individual numbers, a further set of six followed in

1872 (Opus 16), followed by three more sets in 1875 alone (Opuses 25, 27 and 28). Many were dedicated with gratitude to the singers who performed in his stage works and often sound like miniature arias. Others, by contrast, were written on the more intimate scale of the salon romance and explore a vein of sentimentality that found a ready appeal among audiences, if not always with critics. The allure that his songs held is evident from a commission to write four further numbers – two each in 1873 and 1875 – for the popular music journal *Nuvellist*, another means by which he could create an impression of domestic intimacy with the growing audience for his works. Nikolay Bernard, the publisher of *Nuvellist*, would capitalize on this relationship when he commissioned Tchaikovsky to write twelve characteristic pieces for piano in 1875. These would be published as *The Seasons* the following year and constitute one of the composer's most adroit fusions of mercantile and artistic imperatives. Indeed, so successful were the works commissioned by Bernard that Jurgenson took over the rights for *The Seasons* in 1885, having previously refused to let Tchaikovsky accept a further commission from Bernard for six more piano pieces in 1882 (publishing them himself as *Six morceaux*, Op. 51). Tchaikovsky often complained about such commissions, treating them with an attitude of workmanlike duty rather than romantic inspiration, yet they were some of his most well-crafted, successful and appealing works.

It is, however, Tchaikovsky's three numbered string quartets that represent the high point of his early interest in chamber and instrumental music. Although quartet playing had some history in nineteenth-century Russia, the available repertoire was still predominantly foreign. The members of the Kuchka actively despised the form; Borodin was the only one of the group to be drawn to it, much to the disgust of Musorgsky and Stasov. Hence, when Tchaikovsky's String Quartet No. 1 was premiered in Moscow on 16 March 1871, it represented an audacious attempt to establish a native tradition, as well as a declaration of its composer's adherence to academic principles (it is significant that the second and third quartets date from early 1874 and the summer of 1876 respectively, a period when Tchaikovsky was beginning to distance himself from the influence of the nationalists). If the early symphonies are arguably uneven in their achievements, then the quartets arrived as fully fledged examples of their composer's ability to bring together his spontaneous melodic gift, facility for motivic development and interest in long-range form.

The success of the String Quartet No. 1 is all the more surprising when one considers that its composition was largely a pragmatic affair. Finding himself short of money, Tchaikovsky was encouraged to put on a benefit concert consisting solely of his own works; engaging an orchestra would have wiped out any profits to be made, but a quartet could be played by his friends from the Moscow Conservatory. Structured in four well-proportioned movements, the Quartet No. 1 represents the acme of classical form, as Laroche noted in his review of its premiere:

> This work is distinguished by that charm of succulent melodies, beautifully and interestingly harmonized, by that noble tone, devoid of the commonplace, by that somewhat feminine softness that we are used to encountering in this gifted composer; needless to say there are beautiful effects of sonority in it . . . but beyond all these qualities I found in his new quartet such a command of form . . . as found in none of his prior compositions . . . All the more precious for criticism are those rare compositions in which interest of content is joined with maturity of form.[33]

It was, though, the quartet's local colour that most guaranteed its popular success. Its slow second movement is based on a folk song that Tchaikovsky had heard in Ukraine; arranged as a stand-alone piece for string orchestra and a number of instrumental ensembles (the composer himself made a version for solo cello and string orchestra in 1888), it soon became one of his most widely performed works. And it was not just popular audiences who found themselves susceptible to its charms; when Tchaikovsky met Tolstoy in 1876, it was this *andante cantabile* that the writer heard with tears in his eyes. Even in the most concentrated, abstract form of the quartet, Tchaikovsky's music always found a way to speak to its listeners.

The popularity of the Quartet No. 1 has rather overshadowed Tchaikovsky's two other exercises in the genre. Written on a much larger scale than the first quartet, they have tended to strike critics as more obviously 'Beethovenian', and therefore somehow less characteristic – perhaps less 'Russian' even – than the Quartet No. 1. Their formal abstraction has likewise proved a challenge to those critics set on finding autobiographical elements in every work (even the sombre third movement of the Quartet No. 3, played on muted strings and explicitly entitled *andante funebre et doloroso, ma con moto*, impresses as much by its concentrated use of a limited range of rhythmic and melodic motifs as by its expressivity as such). Certainly they explore a more densely chromatic and intricately worked musical language than Tchaikovsky's other compositions at this time, and if they have no immediate successors in his output of chamber music, then this may be because their lessons fed into the later symphonies and orchestral works instead. Yet the Quartets No. 2 and No. 3 are not just inventive compositional exercises, but are outward-looking works too, whose aesthetics are in part shaped by the needs and expectations of contemporary audiences and institutions. The Quartet No. 2 was published almost immediately in a version for piano duet, suggesting how Tchaikovsky's works were disseminated and appreciated by talented amateurs as well as professional performers. And in its dedication to Ferdinand Laub, the Quartet No. 3 honours both a close personal friend and a musician who did much to foster the performance of chamber music in Russia (the Czech-born Laub had been the leader of the Russian

Musical Society's Moscow quartet and played in the premieres of the first two quartets). It is this fusion of public and private that makes Tchaikovsky's songs, chamber and instrumental music such important documents in the fashioning of his growing celebrity.

The String Quartets No. 1 and No. 3 were among the first major works that Tchaikovsky did not subject to a prior process of consultation with and approval by friends and colleagues (the second went down badly with Anton Rubinstein, but Tchaikovsky went ahead and had it performed anyway). They are characteristic of a period in the composer's life when he felt increasingly confident enough to pursue his own artistic vision despite potential objections and misunderstanding. A number of works dating from between 1874 and 1876 – above all the Piano Concerto No. 1, the Symphony No. 3 and *Francesca da Rimini* – show Tchaikovsky intuitively grasping the possibilities of new forms and ideas and putting into practice all those lessons he had learned since his graduation.

Vakula the Smith, a setting of Nikolay Gogol's short story 'Christmas Eve' (1832), showed progress of a different sort. Its libretto was originally prepared by Yakov Polonsky for Alexander Serov, who had died in 1871 before beginning work on the opera. Thereafter, the Petersburg branch of the Russian Musical Society took over the libretto, using it as a pretext for a competition that would bring its winner a prize of 1,500 roubles and performances at the Mariinsky Theatre. Constantly strapped for cash, and equally keen to make his name as an opera composer, Tchaikovsky was unable to resist the temptation to engage in underhand dealings. Not only did he submit his opera well before the official deadline of August 1875 (he completed the entire score in almost a single stretch during the summer of 1874), but he corresponded with members of the jury, arranged for the score to be published in advance of the planned production and even saw to it that its overture was performed in concert. Even if they did not recognize his handwriting, few members of the jury could have been unaware that it was Tchaikovsky who hid behind the slogan under which the score was eventually submitted: *ars longa, vita brevis* (art is long, life is short).

Notwithstanding the promise of official recognition and financial reward, it is possible that Tchaikovsky would have found his way to Gogol anyway. Tchaikovsky always included him in his list of favourite writers, and he was particularly drawn to his romanticized depictions of Ukrainian folklore, which appealed to contemporary audiences in the Russian capitals in much the same way as Walter Scott's Highland fictions had seduced metropolitan English readers. As with the String Quartet No. 1 and the Symphony No. 2, *Vakula* also offered Tchaikovsky the chance to draw on folk songs as a way of providing both local colour and lyric charm. But more than that, Gogol offered a way out of the dead-end of historical melodrama into which *The Voevoda* and *The Oprichnik* had led him. To be sure, *Vakula* contained little of the psychological depth that he had begun to explore in these works, and which would come to the fore in *Eugene Onegin* a few years later. Yet it was full of a charm and playfulness that were wholly characteristic of Tchaikovsky as a man, as well as a composer, and which promised to appeal directly to the nation's opera-going public. Its plot is a rather convoluted one and its charms lie in its telling, rather than its retelling. Put simply, it involves a dashing lad, Vakula, and his attempt to win the hand of his fair beloved, Oxana. Various improbable impediments are placed in his way: his mother, a witch by the name of Solokha, is involved in a liaison with the Devil; a trio of local dignitaries – the village mayor (Pan Golova), the church deacon and Oxana's father (Chub) – somehow find themselves hidden in sacks, which Vakula carries off with barely a complaint; and finally, Oxana herself demands that Vakula bring her the tsarina's ceremonial footwear, which he does by enlisting the Devil to fly him to St Petersburg and the court of Catherine the Great. Vakula returns home to find that Oxana would have married him anyway; virtue, constancy and character prevail, and as the opera ends, the young lovers look set to marry.

Rehearsals suggested that Tchaikovsky could look forward to both critical and popular success. Even Cui – who was often highly critical of Tchaikovsky's works in the press – spoke warmly of the new work. The Kuchka had a particular fondness for Gogol, whose works inspired Musorgsky's unfinished *Marriage* (1868) and *The Fair at Sorochintsy* (1874–80), as well as Rimsky-Korsakov's *May Night* (1880) and *Christmas Eve* (1895) – the latter being a setting of the same text that originally formed the basis of Tchaikovsky's own opera. When *Vakula* opened on 24 November 1876, however, audience reaction was mixed, as its composer reported to Taneev:

> The first two acts passed off in deathly silence, with the exception of the overture and the first duet, which were applauded. In the scene with *Pan Golova* and particularly the *Deacon* there

Tchaikovsky at the piano surrounded by his relatives, including his brother Nikolay, brother-in-law Lev, sister Alexandra and brother Anatoly (all seated around the table), and his brothers Modest and Ippolit (standing behind the piano), St Petersburg, 1874.

was a lot of laughter, but there was no applause and no curtain calls. After the third and fourth acts . . . I took many curtain calls, but there was a lot of hissing from a significant part of the audience. The second performance went a little better, but all the same, one can confidently say that the opera is not liked and will barely survive for more than five or six performances.[34]

Tchaikovsky's fears were, in fact, unfounded, and the opera ran for a total of seventeen performances by 1881. Audiences quickly grew accustomed to the fact that it was as much a lyric work as it was a comic one, and soon settled down to enjoy its many charms.[35]

Tchaikovsky was excessively frank about what he saw as the failings of *Vakula*, to which he returned repeatedly in his correspondence. Part of the problem may have been the enormous expectations he had of the new opera. He was all too aware of Russia's nascent operatic canon and was keen to win a place in it for himself. Around the time he was working on *Vakula*, he consulted the scores of two very different works – Musorgsky's *Boris Godunov* and Anton Rubinstein's *The Demon* (1871) – and although he found the first distasteful ('I send Musorgsky's music to the devil with all my soul; it's the most vulgar and base parody of music') and the second full of extraneous padding ('there are some charming moments, but a lot of ballast'),[36] he could barely claim to have found an operatic voice of his own. As with *The Voevoda* and *The Oprichnik*, Tchaikovsky felt that he was still wedded to a conception of opera that was fundamentally symphonic rather than dramatic (something for which he would later fault Wagner's operas). Moreover, the fussy libretto and his preference for lyrical rather than declamatory word-setting meant that the stage action lacked the kind of crisp good humour that Gogol's tale demands. Nonetheless, Tchaikovsky was fonder of *Vakula* than of almost any other of his works, and he revised and simplified it thoroughly in 1885 for a new production in 1887, giving it the new title *Cherevichki* (sometimes translated as *The Little Shoes* or *The Tsarina's Slippers*).

No such equivocations surrounded the Piano Concerto No. 1, the first reference to which comes in a letter written to Tchaikovsky's brother Modest towards the end of October 1874, not long after the completion of *Vakula*.[37] By Christmas the new work was complete, and Tchaikovsky played it through to his colleague and mentor, Nikolay Rubinstein. The devastating effect on Tchaikovsky's morale of Rubinstein's verdict can be seen from the fact that it took him more than three years to recall the event in detail:

> R.'s eloquent silence was full of portentous significance. It was as if he was saying to me: 'My friend, how can I say anything about individual details when the whole thing is objectionable to me!' I armed myself with patience and played to the end. Again silence. I stood up and asked: 'So, what then?' At this point a flood of words poured forth from N[ikolay] G[rigoryevich], quiet at first, then shifting ever more into the tone of Zeus the Thunderer. It turned out that my concerto was good for nothing; it was impossible to play it; that some passages were so trite, awkward and clumsy that there was no way to correct them; that as a composition it was bad and vulgar; that I had stolen this from one place, and that from another; that there were only two or three pages that could stay, and the rest had either to be thrown out or completely rewritten.[38]

Tchaikovsky's defiant response – '"I won't change a single note," I replied to him, "and I'll publish it exactly as it is now!"'[39] – may not literally be the case (revisions were made in each edition of the work published during the composer's lifetime), but it amply expresses just how far he had come since his graduation in 1865.

To be fair to Rubinstein, the concerto is an eccentric work, although excessive familiarity may have blinded modern audiences to its inventiveness. First, it is very oddly proportioned; at around twenty minutes in length, its opening movement runs to nearly twice the length of the ensuing slow movement and finale put together and is longer than any other orchestral movement Tchaikovsky had written before. There is the famous introduction too, which – in defiance of all musical logic – contains musical material that is never obviously heard again in the rest of the work. And then there is the puckish freneticism of the *Allegro vivace assai* that rather unexpectedly interrupts the otherwise limpid and introverted slow movement (*Andantino semplice*). There was certainly plenty here to perplex Rubinstein, and it was left to others to intuit Tchaikovsky's impressive sense of how to involve an audience in the work's dramatic dialogue between soloist and orchestra. The first performance of the new concerto was in fact given by the German pianist Hans von Bülow in Boston on 25 October 1875 (n.s.), the very first time a work by Tchaikovsky had been premiered abroad (Russian performances followed in November and December of that year in St Petersburg and Moscow, with Rubinstein himself conducting the second of these). Bülow's advocacy is significant for other reasons too. The previous year he had reviewed a production of *A Life for the Tsar* that was given in Milan in May 1874, and alongside his comments about the opera, he cited Tchaikovsky's String Quartet No. 1 and *Romeo and Juliet* as works that could withstand comparison with Glinka himself.

Like the Piano Concerto No. 1, the Symphony No. 3 was the product of a short and sustained burst of confident inspiration and similarly challenges the principles of the genre to which it nominally belongs. Written on the summer estates of Shilovsky and Kondratyev, its five movements – rather than the usual four – suggest the possible influence of Beethoven, Berlioz and Schumann, whose Symphony No. 6 (the so-called 'Pastoral', 1808), *Symphonie fantastique* (1830) and Symphony No. 3 (the so-called 'Rhenish', 1850), respectively, had been similarly structured. But to talk of influence in this one-off work is misleading, as it

Tchaikovsky (far right), with (from left to right) his brother Modest, Nikolay
Kondratyev, and his brother Anatoly, Moscow, 1875.

follows neither the precepts of the established Austro-German
symphony nor those of the nationalist experiments of the
Kuchka. Even its unofficial nickname, 'The Polish', is deceptive;
dating from a performance in London in 1899, it refers solely to
the finale, marked *Alla polacca*, and in suggesting some kind of
nationalist subtext, distracts from the work's innovative qualities.
Part of the symphony's charm lies in the delicate textures of its

middle three movements, which breathe the summer air of the estates on which it was composed (its sylvan qualities may also hark back to the incidental music that Tchaikovsky had written for a production of Ostrovky's play *The Snow Maiden*, which opened in Moscow in May 1873). But it is also full of allusions to eighteenth-century forms and comes closer to a classical divertissement than a full-fledged nineteenth-century symphony.[40]

Perhaps the most engagingly abstract of the symphonies, the Symphony No. 3 shows Tchaikovsky's delight in the play of form for its own sake. If the string quartets constitute a creative laboratory in which Tchaikovsky could address issues of musical structure whose solutions would feed into the last three symphonies, then the Symphony No. 3 looks forward not to its nominal successors but to the four orchestral suites that he would write between 1878 and 1888. Tchaikovsky was always rather wary of the limitations that literary and visual programmes might impose on musical argument, and it was dance that showed the way to a highly expressive form of language based on gesture rather than image or narrative. Indeed, the work's ludic, rococo aesthetic is as much a part of its composer's make-up as his self-dramatizing Romanticism, and it is no surprise that all the last three symphonies contain substantial sections – and even whole movements – that evoke the spectacle of the ballroom.

As the first of the symphonies not to be subjected to any subsequent revision, the Symphony No. 3 certainly deserves better than the benign neglect that seems to be its modern fate, whether in performance or criticism. Yet audiences may be more familiar with the work than is often realized, as George Balanchine used all but its first movement as the score for the third act of his ballet *Jewels* in 1967. And the dance-like qualities of the symphony are far from coincidental. In May 1875 Tchaikovsky had been commissioned to write a new ballet for Moscow's Bolshoi Theatre – evidence of the increasing regard in which he was held in the city's artistic world. The first two acts of what would become *Swan Lake* were completed that August, and the whole ballet was ready the following April, with the first performance given on 20 February 1877.

If Tchaikovsky was excessively aware of tradition when it came to opera, then the same can barely be said of his attitude to ballet at this time, and this may be just one of the reasons that *Swan Lake* proved to be such an unusually inventive and pioneering work. Indeed, when he first heard Léo Delibes' score for *Sylvia* in Vienna in late 1877, he was ecstatic at its discovery – and despondent about his own attempts in the same genre:

> I *heard* Delibes' ballet *Sylvia*; and I mean *heard* it, because this is the first ballet in which the music constitutes not just the main, but the sole interest. What charm, what grace, what melodic, rhythmic and harmonic richness. I was ashamed. If I had known this music earlier, then of course I would not have written *The Lake of Swans*.[41]

Tchaikovsky is too modest here, for his score has an almost symphonic sense of musical architecture, both within each act and across the ballet as a whole, as well as a dramatic intensity born of his experience in the opera house. Despite the fact that the identity of the author of its libretto is uncertain, *Swan Lake* certainly tapped into something deep within its composer's psyche. Whether in the form of Prince Siegfried's confrontation with the demonic Baron Rothbart or the black-and-white doubling of Odette/Odile as the object of Siegfried's love, the plot plays out the themes of destruction and damnation that so frequently appealed to Tchaikovsky elsewhere.

Unlike *Vakula*, which Tchaikovsky discussed extensively and repeatedly in his letters, neither the composition nor the staging of *Swan Lake* elicited much by way of commentary from its composer. Moreover, the paucity of material relating to the production has led many to assert that *Swan Lake* was not a success. Nonetheless, despite some lukewarm reviews of the performance and the by now standard criticism that Tchaikovsky's music was too symphonic, it survived in the Bolshoi Theatre's repertoire until early 1883, receiving 41 performances in three different productions.[42] Perhaps the real reason for the story of the work's initial failure was that it was one of the first of Tchaikovsky's works to be rediscovered after his death, albeit in a form that was rather different from its original conception. In 1894 Modest made a number of revisions to the libretto (as directors and choreographers continue to do to this day). More damagingly, when this new version opened at St Petersburg's Mariinsky Theatre on 15 January 1895, with choreography by Marius Petipa and Lev Ivanov, it also included some new music in the form of some of Tchaikovsky's late piano pieces as orchestrated by the conductor Riccardo Drigo, and it is this hybrid version that is still widely used around the world today.[43]

Francesca da Rimini, the tone poem that marks the end of Tchaikovsky's first decade in Moscow, also attests to new and productive influences, albeit very different ones from the classicism of the Symphony No. 3 or the gestural language of *Swan Lake*. August 1876 found Tchaikovsky attending the first Bayreuth Festival, which he was covering for a Moscow newspaper. Tchaikovsky was certainly familiar with Wagner's music, having heard him conduct in St Petersburg in 1863 and seen productions of *Lohengrin* and *Tannhäuser* in the same city, yet he was unprepared for the impact of seeing *Der Ring des Nibelungen* onstage for the first time. His reactions were largely negative, as he wrote to his brother Modest:

> Maybe the *Nibelungen* is a very great work, but it is probable that there has never before been anything more boring and tedious than this rigmarole. The accumulation of the most

complicated and refined harmonies, the colourlessness
of everything that is sung on the stage, the endlessly long
dialogues, the total darkness in the theatre, the absence
of anything interesting and poetic in the plot – all of
this exhausts one's nerves to the utmost degree.[44]

The criticisms he voiced to Nadezhda von Meck were substantially
the same, yet they contained an interesting equivocation too.
Wagner, he claimed, was 'a symphonist by nature . . . endowed with
a talent of genius', but nowhere in his scores was there 'a single
broad, well-rounded melody, not once is the singer given complete
freedom'.[45] Referring to a performance of *Lohengrin* he had heard in
1879, he returned to this point:

> *Wagner's* orchestra is too *symphonic*, too *plump* and *heavy*
> for vocal music. And the older I become, the more I become
> convinced that these two genres, i.e. *the symphony and the opera*,
> are in all respects the complete opposite of each other.[46]

Such statements ultimately tell us more about Tchaikovsky's
views of his own operas than about his understanding of
Wagner. Reviews of *The Voevoda*, *The Oprichnik* and *Vakula* had
all suggested that Tchaikovsky's writing was too symphonic to
allow the dramatic action to unfold effectively and that the detail
of the score compromised the lyric expression of the singers.
These were criticisms that Tchaikovsky made of himself, too, and
they may explain his resistance to both Wagner's theories and
his methods. Yet Tchaikovsky was too sensitive and responsive
a musician to let Wagner's influence go untapped, and it is in
Francesca da Rimini that his experience of listening to the *Ring*
is most palpable. Whether or not he was struck by parallels
with the story of the *Ring*, especially the incestuous love of
Siegmund and Sieglinde in *Die Walküre*, or the relationship

between Siegfried and Brünnhilde in *Siegfried*, *Francesca da Rimini* is certainly full of echoes of Wagner's orchestral writing.

But what is most impressive about *Francesca da Rimini* is not solely the intensity of its emotional register, whether this derives from Dante, Wagner or even Gustave Doré (whose illustrations of the *Divina Commedia* Tchaikovsky knew), but equally its enormous sense of control. At around 25 minutes, it is the longest of Tchaikovsky's tone poems and longer than any single movement in the symphonies too. It is sustained in part by a detailed literary narrative appended to the score, which charts Dante's descent into the second circle of Hell, his encounter with the damned lovers and Francesca's own account of her fate.[47] But beyond that, Tchaikovsky achieves coherence through the use of a broad ternary structure in which Francesca's narrative is flanked by music depicting the storm of souls writhing in eternal torment. The continued repetition of a limited range of musical motives adds to the mood, simultaneously imposing a formal logic as tightly productive as Dante's *terza rima*. It is the product not just of raw inspiration, but of formidable discipline. Writing to Modest in October 1876, Tchaikovsky pointed to the effects of a new regimen on his productivity:

> I don't know whether I have told you that I have started taking cold baths every morning . . . You cannot imagine what an *excellent* effect this has had on my health. Never before have I felt so well . . . as I do now. This development has had and will have an influence on my works. If there is something fresh and new about *Francesca*, then to a great extent this is due to *water*.[48]

A feverish imagination and a well-ordered lifestyle were not paradoxical, contradictory features of Tchaikovsky's personality; they were the very preconditions for his creativity itself. In his first decade as a professional musician, he produced a substantial corpus of major works, including three symphonies, three operas and a full-length ballet, as well as three string quartets and any number of songs, piano pieces and occasional works. The volume and quality of Tchaikovsky's output at this time is remarkable enough when one considers his heavy and increasingly disagreeable teaching load and the fact that he was without a permanent home of his own. It is all the more remarkable when one considers the emotional upheaval that he was about to experience.

3

'For the Sake of *Qu'en-dira-t-on*'

If *Francesca da Rimini* was a product of Tchaikovsky's visit to
Bayreuth, then its feverish atmosphere and dramatic storyline may
be linked to developments in its composer's personal life too. At
the time he was working on the symphonic fantasia, he penned a
number of frank letters to his brother Modest, which set in motion
a series of events that were to alter the course of his life. The first
was written on 10 September 1876:

> I have given a great deal of thought . . . both to me, to you
> and to our future. The result of all this contemplation is that
> from this day on I seriously intend to enter a state of lawful
> matrimony with anybody at all. I find that our *inclinations* are
> for us the greatest and most unsurmountable impediment to
> happiness, and we must fight our nature with all our strength.

Tchaikovsky's decision seems to have stemmed from the intense
feelings he experienced for Nikolay (Kolya) Konradi, an eight-
year-old deaf-mute boy to whom Modest had been engaged as
tutor earlier that year. Worried as much for Modest as for himself,
Tchaikovsky saw marriage as the only way to repress such troubling
emotions:

> I love you very much, and I love Kolya too, and truly wish
> that, for the good of you both, you may never be separated,

Tchaikovsky (left) in Montpellier, July 1876, with his brother Modest, Modest's pupil Nikolay Konradi and Nikolay's governess, Sofya Ershova.

but the condition *sine qua non* of the durability of your relations must be that you are no longer that which you have been up until now. This is necessary not for the sake of *qu'en dira-t-on* [the opinion of other people], but for you yourself and for your peace of mind. A man who, after parting with his own child (he can be called your own), finds himself in the embraces of the first rogue he comes across cannot be the teacher that you want to and should become.[1]

Tchaikovsky's resolve was not as strong as he had hoped. A few weeks later, he confessed to Modest that 'the realization of my plans is nothing like as imminent as you think. I am so fixed in my habits and tastes that it is impossible to cast them aside all at once like an old glove', before going on to give an account of a recent trip to a friend's estate, which he described as 'nothing but a pederastic bordello' and where he 'fell in love like a cat with his coachman!!!'[2]

This was not the first occasion on which Tchaikovsky had found himself contemplating marriage. Back in 1867 he had spent the spring in the Baltic resort of Haapsalu, where he encountered Vera Davydova, the sister of his sister's husband, who had long nurtured romantic feelings for him. His sister, Sasha, seemed keen to promote the match, but Tchaikovsky resisted:

> weariness makes me too lazy to establish any new conjugal relations, too lazy to become the head of a family, too lazy to take upon myself the responsibility for the fate of a wife and children. In a word, marriage is unthinkable for me.[3]

The following year saw a yet closer brush with matrimony. That March, the Belgian mezzo-soprano Désirée Artôt arrived in Moscow, and it seems that Tchaikovsky fell in love with her – or at least with the idea of her. By December, he was writing to his father about a possible wedding, yet within a month she had married the Spanish baritone Mariano Padilla y Ramos. The intensity of Tchaikovsky's emotional involvement with Artôt is hard to gauge. In a letter to Modest, his attitude to the affair was wry:

> The business with Artôt has resolved itself in the most amusing manner; in Warsaw she fell in love with the baritone *Padilla*, who was the object of her ridicule here – and is now marrying him! What sort of woman is this? You need to know the details of our relationship to have any idea how funny this dénouement is.[4]

To his father, he offered a rather different explanation for the failure of their relationship – one that sheds light on both the attitudes of his closest male friends and the precarious situation of a professional musician in mid-nineteenth-century Russia:

> my friends, and Rubinstein in particular, are employing the most energetic means to prevent me from carrying out my plan to marry. They say that once I become the husband of a famous singer I shall have to play the extremely miserable role of my wife's husband; that is, I should have to travel with her to every corner of Europe, live at her expense, give up and no longer have the chance to work. In a word, as my love for her cools just a little, I will have nothing left but the torment of vanity, despair and ruin. It might be possible to avert the possibility of this misfortune if she undertook to leave the stage and live with me in Russia, but she says that despite all her love for me, she simply cannot give up the stage, to which she is so accustomed and which affords her fame and wealth . . . Just as she simply cannot give up the stage, I in my turn am hesitant about sacrificing my entire future for her, as it cannot be doubted that I should lose the opportunity of making my own way in the world if I blindly followed her.[5]

Whether Tchaikovsky's infatuation with Artôt was the result of erotic attraction or, as seems more likely, a fatal instance of diva worship, their affair left a musical trace in the charming Six Mélodies, Opus 65, which he wrote for her when they met again some twenty years later, in 1888.

Tchaikovsky's attitude to marriage was more pragmatic than enthusiastic, and certainly had more to do with pleasing his family than providing for his own immediate emotional needs. Writing to his father in November 1872, for instance, he claimed:

> As far as marriage is concerned I can tell you that I too sometimes think about weighing myself down with a little companion, as plump and kindly as your little pudding [Tchaikovsky's affectionate nickname for his stepmother] – only I am afraid lest I should repent afterwards. Although I earn well enough (around 3,000 roubles a year), my disorderliness means I am always in a tricky situation. This is all well and good when you live alone, but how about with a wife and small children?[6]

This idea of marriage as a practical, even economic way of regularizing his rather unsettled and often impoverished existence continued for some time, as his friend Nikolay Kashkin suggested:

> Tchaikovsky began to dream of the ideal of family comfort, for which he needed the presence of a woman – not, however, a servant, but an educated companion capable of understanding his fervent aspirations and of being his trustworthy companion in life, freeing him from, among other things, all domestic cares. The thought of marriage to a middle-aged woman or widow began to enter his head – someone with whom he might have a mutual understanding without pretence to ardent passion.[7]

Certainly Tchaikovsky would not have been the first gay man to marry for convenience and comfort, and such arrangements could often be companionable and contented, as he would have known from a number of examples within his own social circle.

Ultimately, however, Tchaikovsky's homosexuality posed too great an impediment to marriage, and alongside his well-documented relationships with a series of potential brides, there is also a large body of evidence that demonstrates the extent and nature of his attraction to members of his own sex. Such involvements went back to his student years in St Petersburg, and on moving to Moscow he continued to move in circles frequented predominantly by other men. Through the singer Konstantin de Lazari he was introduced to Konstantin Begichev, an official in the Imperial Theatre Directorate, whose wife, Mariya Shilovskaya, was a singer, amateur composer and prominent salon hostess. She had two sons by her first marriage; the first of these, Konstantin, was to assist with the libretto for *Eugene Onegin*, but it was the younger, Vladimir, who became Tchaikovsky's pupil and, later, intimate friend. Theirs could be a tempestuous friendship, it is true, but the two young men were close enough to travel regularly to Europe in each other's company (always at Vladimir's expense), as well as spend time together at Shilovsky's country estate at Usovo.

Relationships with artistically minded younger men recurred throughout Tchaikovsky's life. In 1871 he found himself involved with Eduard Zak, whose suicide two years later remained one of his most painful memories. The intensity of the composer's feelings is agonizingly clear from a diary entry of September 1887:

Thought about and recalled *Zak* again. How amazingly vividly I remember him: the sound of his voice, his movements, but in particular the unusually wonderful expression of his face at times. I cannot imagine that he is *no longer* here *at all* now. Death – that is, *his* complete non-existence – is more than I can comprehend. It seems to me that I have never loved anyone so intensely.[8]

In early 1877, four years after Zak's death, Tchaikovsky fell passionately in love with the young violinist Josef Kotek, as he confessed to Modest on 19 January:

I am in love in a way that I have not been for a long time. Can you guess with whom? He is of average height, with fair hair and wonderful, brown eyes . . . I have known him for six years already. I have always liked him and have already fallen in love with him a little bit on a number of occasions. These were like a trial run for my love. Now I have gained full speed and fallen head over heels in love with him in the most decisive manner. I cannot say that my love is completely pure. Whenever he caresses me with his hand, whenever he rests his head on my chest and I play with his hair and secretly kiss it, whenever I hold his hand in mine for hours on end and exhaust myself in the struggle against the urge to fall down and kiss his little feet, so delicate and refined, passion rages within me with unimaginable force, my voice quavers like that of a youth, and I utter all kinds of nonsense. However, I am far from desiring bodily contact. I feel that if that occurred my feelings towards him would cool. It would be repellent to me if this wonderful youth stooped to intercourse with an aged and pot-bellied man. How ghastly this would be and how vile I would become to myself![9]

Something of the bittersweet pleasure of the entanglement with Kotek comes through in the works which Tchaikovsky wrote at this time. The Valse-Scherzo, Op. 34, for violin and orchestra is dedicated to Kotek (it may even have been orchestrated by him);[10] a five-minute burst of bravura virtuosity, it is testament both to its dedicatee's skill as a performer and to the feelings

ФОТОГРАФІЯ Н.И.БОРИСОВА

ВЪ МОСКВѢ, ГАЗЕТНЫЙ ПЕРЕУЛОКЪ Д. ФУЛЬДА.

Tchaikovsky with the violinist Josef Kotek, Moscow, 1877.

that he stirred in its composer. Likewise, the *Variations on a Rococo Theme*, Op. 33, for cello and orchestra are full of the same delicious playfulness as the Valse-Scherzo (although, as they were begun in December 1876, they slightly pre-date the involvement with Kotek). Tchaikovsky's love of the eighteenth century was profound; first announced in the Petersburg scenes in the final act of *Vakula the Smith*, with its depiction of the hero's reception at the court of Catherine the Great, it shaped the terpsichorean conception of the Symphony No. 3 and now found full expression in the *Variations*. The ludic evocation of the eighteenth century in so many of his works bespeaks not just his infatuation with Kotek but a profound love of order, discipline, proportion, charm and delicacy that is very different from the tortured emotional tenor of *Francesca da Rimini*, but equally integral to Tchaikovsky's musical self.

In his biography, Modest notes the introversion that beset his brother around this time. A letter written in December 1872 gives some sense of Tchaikovsky's prevailing moods:

> I don't suffer particularly from spleen, but it is true that there are sometimes moments when I am overcome, as before, by melancholy and misanthropy. This is partly a result of my nerves, which become irritated for no obvious reason, and partly because of the current state of my work as a composer, which gives me little comfort.[11]

As to the source of such moods, it has often been assumed that they stemmed primarily from his feelings about his sexuality. Tchaikovsky himself was capable of suggesting as much, as in this letter, written to his brother Anatoly in January 1875:

> I am very, very lonely here, and were it not for constant work, I should simply surrender myself to melancholy.

It is also true that my damned buggermania creates an
unbridgeable abyss between me and the majority of people.
It imparts to my character a sense of alienation, a fear of
people, immoderate shyness, mistrustfulness – in a word,
a thousand traits which make me ever more unsociable.[12]

Elsewhere, however, Tchaikovsky could be relatively sanguine
about his sexuality. Fundamentally, what seems to have troubled
him most was not some pathological sense of self-hatred, but
a sense of its potential consequences for his everyday life and
public reputation, as well as its effect on those closest to him.
Indeed, rather than trace his volatile emotional state to a sexuality
which he was capable of treating with relative equanimity, it
may be equally productive to trace his mood swings to his life
and vocation as a creative artist. (Kay Jamison has tentatively
identified Tchaikovsky as one of those composers who may have
suffered from manic depression, although she provides no further
evidence for her claims, and this line of enquiry may be as fraught
with essentializing assumptions as those which seek to establish
a causal link between the composer's works and his sexuality).[13]
   Whatever the causes of his precarious emotional state (and
there are simply too many letters missing from this period to
be absolutely sure), by the summer of 1877 Tchaikovsky was a
married man. The story of his marriage is both starkly simple
and unfathomably complex. Tchaikovsky claimed that he knew
nothing of his bride, Antonina Milyukova, until she wrote to him
in late March that year, yet he was certainly aware that she had
family connections with one of his friends from the School of
Jurisprudence (as he himself pointed out in a letter to Anatoly).[14]
He may also have known her from the Moscow Conservatory,
where she was a student. He responded to her initial letter, and
a brief correspondence ensued. The couple did not actually meet
until 20 May; three days later, Tchaikovsky proposed. Barely

a week later he left for a friend's estate, returning to Moscow less than a week before the wedding. The ceremony itself took place in Moscow on 6 July and was witnessed by just four other people: Tchaikovsky's brother Anatoly and his close friend Kotek, plus two of Antonina's friends. Anatoly had been told of his brother's engagement as recently as 23 June (the same day Tchaikovsky's father was also informed); Modest, Sasha and her husband Lev learned of it only on the eve of the ceremony itself.

After they were married, Tchaikovsky and his new wife set off for St Petersburg, and already his letters from that time show a sense of anxiety, if not yet foreboding. Just two days later, he wrote to Anatoly,

> I should be guilty of a great lie if I tried to assure you that I am already entirely happy and entirely accustomed to my new situation, etc. After a day as terrible as 6 July, after this endless moral torment, it is impossible to recover immediately.[15]

That same day, he wrote to Modest: 'I cannot say yet that I love her, but I already feel that I shall love her as soon as we grow accustomed to each other.'[16] He survived the difficult experience of introducing Antonina to his father and stepmother (it is not clear whether he was more troubled by his father's all-too-evident joy or his stepmother's equally apparent understanding of the complexity of his true emotions) and by 13 July was doing his best to assure Anatoly of his composure:

> Today I awoke for the first time without a sensation of despair and hopelessness. My wife is not at all repugnant to me. I am already beginning to treat her as any husband does who is not in love with his wife. But most importantly, I no longer feel awkward with her today, do not distract her with small talk, and I am completely calm. Starting from today the terrible crisis

Tchaikovsky with his wife, Antonina, Moscow, 1877.

has passed. I am recovering. But the crisis was terrible, terrible, terrible; were it not for my love for you and those close to me, a love that has supported me amidst *unbearable mental torments*, it might all have ended badly, that is with illness or madness.[17]

On returning to Moscow, Tchaikovsky then set off – alone – for his sister's estate at Kamenka, where he spent an agreeable summer with his family. He returned to Moscow in early September, spending a brief period in the new flat that his wife had arranged for them and introducing her to his circle of friends. By October, however, he had fled to St Petersburg – and then to Berlin, Geneva and the small Swiss town of Clarens. Thereafter, Tchaikovsky and his wife would never live together again. Neither would they divorce, although this had more to do with Antonina's refusal to agree terms than with any scruple on the part of her legal husband. The three children she had by her common-law husband, Alexander Shlykov, in 1881, 1882 and 1884 were all placed in orphanages and died tragically young. Antonina herself was eventually committed to an asylum, where she died in 1917.

The story of a young woman naively presenting herself to the hapless composer is certainly an appealingly poetic fantasy, but it in no way accounts for Tchaikovsky's motivations in leading her on and finally making a proposal of marriage. Although Antonina could be a difficult personality, she was not without her sympathizers. Initially at least, even Tchaikovsky's sister was inclined to side with his abandoned wife. Writing to Modest, she wrote damningly about her brother's character and sexual inclinations:

> his treatment of Antonina Ivanovna is very ugly. He is no longer a youth and could have understood that there is not a trace of the makings of a tolerable husband in him. To take any woman at all, to try to make her a screen for his own debauchery, and then to project on to her the hatred that should befall his own conduct – this is unworthy in such a developed human being.[18]

Although Sasha would soon tire of Antonina and come to take her brother's side entirely, her indignation is not entirely misplaced.

By contrast, Antonina's account of her marriage is remarkably generous to a man who repudiated his wife just months after marrying her, who wrote to his brothers of the repugnance he felt when it came to his failed attempts to consummate their relationship, and who could barely bring himself to name her in correspondence, preferring circumlocutions such as 'a certain personage' or even outright abuse ('reptile' was a particular favourite). Quite what Antonina knew about Tchaikovsky's sexual preferences is uncertain, but her account of his proposal suggests that she understood only too well that theirs would be no conventional marriage:

'I have thought everything through and this is what I have to say to you. Never in my life have I loved a single woman and I already feel myself too old to experience ardent love. I shall never feel it for anyone. But you are the first woman whom I like very much. If you can be content with a quiet, calm love, more like the love of a brother, then I make my proposal to you.'
Of course, I agreed to these conditions.[19]

The main target of Antonina's ire was, in fact, what she saw as a cabal of her husband's male friends and family members, who conspired to separate two individuals who might have made a go of such a seemingly unpropitious relationship. Certainly, Modest and Anatoly were heavily implicated not just in getting Tchaikovsky away from Russia, but in convincing him to abandon Antonina in the first place, and in this they were willingly abetted by Jurgenson and Rubinstein too. And in doing so, their concern may not just have been for Tchaikovsky as a human being, aware as they were that psychological disposition was unlikely to withstand marriage much longer. They were equally certain that Tchaikovsky's creativity might be imperilled by the kind of family and domestic concerns in which life with Antonina threatened to involve him. Tchaikovsky's status

as Russia's leading composer was at stake; the Artôt affair
had repeated itself, only in much more dramatic fashion.

That Tchaikovsky could give up his duties at the Conservatory
at all was due to another woman who made a sudden and dramatic
appearance in his life at this time, Nadezhda von Meck. The wealthy
widow of a railway magnate, she first approached Tchaikovsky in
late 1876 with a request for some trifling arrangements for violin
and piano for consumption at home. By 15 February 1877, however,
von Meck was intimating, 'there is much, much that I should like to
tell you about my fantastical attitude to you':

> All I can say is that this attitude, however abstract it may be,
> is as dear to me as the best and most elevated of all those
> feelings of which human nature is capable, and for this
> reason, Pyotr Ilyich, you may call me a fantasist if you wish,
> even a crank, but do not laugh, because all of this would
> be funny, were it not so sincere and so deep-seated.[20]

Two days later she revealed that, having been overwhelmed
by hearing his overture on *The Tempest*, she had endeavoured
to find out as much about him as possible. As a result of such
enquiries, she now felt 'happy that in you the musician and the
man are so beautifully, so harmoniously united, that one can
yield completely to the delight of the sounds of your music'.[21]
Tchaikovsky was more cautious in his reply, suggesting that
'on closer acquaintance with me, you would not find that
correspondence, that complete harmony between musician and
man, of which you dream.'[22] By mutual agreement, they were
never to meet (although they accidentally ran into each other
on a handful of occasions), something that perhaps explains the
remarkable intimacy and intensity of their correspondence, in
which each party constructed an ideal and idealized image of
the other.

Tchaikovsky's patron Nadezhda von Meck.

Although Tchaikovsky was later to worry that von Meck's attitude to him might change if she found out about his homosexuality, it seems barely credible that she did not already know about it by the time they first began to correspond. They had many friends and acquaintances in common, and their correspondence should be read against the background of the large amount of unspoken information that they would have had about each other from other sources. Indeed, von Meck's own personal life was as scandalous as Tchaikovsky's, if not more so (although Tchaikovsky probably knew nothing of this). According to a particularly piquant family legend, the youngest of von Meck's eleven surviving children, Lyudmila, was the result of a passionate extramarital affair with one of her husband's employees. When, four years later, her husband discovered the truth, he had a heart attack and died. Von Meck's lover, meanwhile, had married her eldest daughter.[23] Despite the fact that both Tchaikovsky and von Meck had reason enough to be suspicious of the family as a social institution, they nonetheless conspired to link their two families through marriage; after extended discussions, von Meck's son Nikolay married Tchaikovsky's niece Anna Davydova in 1884.

Between 1876 and 1890, Tchaikovsky and von Meck would exchange well over a thousand letters. Tchaikovsky referred to his side of their correspondence as 'my diary' and 'a chronicle',[24] and his letters do indeed provide valuable information about his emotional life and daily affairs; they also illuminate his views on music, literature, art, aesthetics, society, current affairs and religion. Writing on 22 January 1878, von Meck aptly summed up the tenor of their correspondence:

I have long been struck and continue to be amazed by that unusual sympathy, that supernatural oneness of the thoughts and feelings that are expressed in almost every letter between us; such an affinity between two natures is seldom found even in the closest of blood relations.[25]

Von Meck's role as Tchaikovsky's confidante, especially in the second half of the 1870s, would be enough to guarantee her a place in any biography, but the most crucial role she performed was a practical one. Already on 1 May 1877 he had begged her for a loan of 3,000 roubles to pay off his existing debts; on 15 July, he requested more money to deal with the expenses he had incurred as a result of his marriage.[26] Then, once he had fled both Antonina and Russia, he wrote with a further request for money (von Meck was fully informed about the breakdown of the relationship not just by Tchaikovsky himself but by Nikolay Rubinstein, with whom she liaised closely throughout the whole saga). Her reply of 17 October included a brief but highly significant postscript in which she undertook to pay him a regular stipend of 1,500 francs a month.[27] Until 1890 she would not only pay him this allowance (and other occasional sums too) but arrange for his hotel accommodation when in western Europe, grant him use of her Moscow house when she was away and invite him to spend extended periods on her Ukrainian estates at Brailov and Simaki.

To Tchaikovsky, von Meck was everything that Antonina was not: rich, cultured, sympathetic and – most of all – absent. Her financial support may have allowed Tchaikovsky to devote himself fully to composition, yet it came at the cost of a certain emotional dependency on von Meck's part. Writing on 14 September 1879, for instance, she allowed herself the following extraordinary confession about the nature of her feelings for him:

I do not know whether you can understand the jealousy I feel with regard to you, given the lack of personal relations between us. Do you know that I am jealous of you in the most unbecoming fashion, just as a woman is jealous of her beloved;

do you know that when you married, it was *awfully* difficult for me, it was as if something had been torn from my heart; I became ill and embittered; the thought that you were in the company of this woman was unbearable to me; and do you know that I am such a base person that I rejoiced when things did not go well for you with her; I reproached myself for this feeling, and it seems as though I gave you no occasion to notice it, but nonetheless I was unable to destroy it – a person cannot summon up feelings to order, and I hated this woman for making your life with her *difficult*, but I should have hated her a hundred times more had things gone *well* for you with her; it seemed to me as though she had taken from me that which might be *mine* alone, that to which I *alone* am entitled, because *I love you* like no one else, I value you more than anything in the world.[28]

By this point, Tchaikovsky was used to von Meck's effusions and was well able either to ignore them or reply to them with some florid piece of non-committal *politesse*. Yet what sometimes did offend him was her meddling in the management of his professional life. Von Meck may have sustained his career and facilitated his personal and artistic freedom, yet she also represented a form of support for the arts that was redolent of Russia's past, when musicians had little social status other than as hired servants. Such patronage remained crucial in Russia for some time (the flourishing of the arts around the turn of the century is unthinkable without such merchant patrons as Pavel Tretyakov, Sergey Shchukin, Savva Mamontov, Savva Morozov, Alexey Bakhrushin and Mitrofan Belyaev), and Tchaikovsky was certainly only too happy to benefit from von Meck's largesse (just as he would later enjoy the privilege of an annual pension from Alexander III). Alongside von Meck's support, however, Tchaikovsky was keen to explore other ways of asserting his artistic and financial worth. While Russian culture was still dependent on models of patronage inherited from the eighteenth century, it was also moving towards a more mercantile, proto-capitalist form of economy, in which artists were dependent on a growing market for financial security and even prosperity. Von Meck's subsidy was certainly imperative to Tchaikovsky's daily survival, but he also enjoyed an independent income as a musician, first as a professor at the Moscow Conservatory and then through a near-exclusive and mutually beneficial contract with Jurgenson, who negotiated astutely on his behalf both in Russia and abroad (the latter was particularly crucial at a time when Russia was not yet a signatory to embryonic international copyright agreements).

When in March 1879 von Meck discovered that Tchaikovsky had approached Jurgenson for money, she wrote to express her indignation; yet the composer's justification of his actions was equally firm: 'You reproach me for not approaching you directly *when I was in need* of money. But as a matter of fact, I *had no need*, as Jurgenson already has my money, money that I have earned and on which I rely.'[29] Then, in early 1880, Tchaikovsky and von Meck found themselves in disagreement about her financial support for a concert of his music in Paris. Tchaikovsky had, in fact, been only too happy for her to underwrite a performance of his Symphony No. 4 that was conducted by Édouard Colonne on 25 January (n.s.) that year. But when she proposed to repeat the endeavour, he reacted with prickly *amour propre*: 'I am indescribably grateful to you for writing to Colonne about my new works, but I will tell you openly: it would be *offensive and unpleasant* to the highest degree if you were once again to thank him materially for his interest in my works.'[30] Tchaikovsky was ostensibly worried that news of von Meck's financial involvement might be reported in the Russian press, and he was clearly also anxious that her patronage might give a misleading impression of his real standing among critics and audiences. As he put it bluntly,

> either he really finds my music worthy of his concerts,
> and in which case he should refuse any payment whatever,
> apart from what he receives from the public; or else he is
> not sincere when he tells you that he loves my music.[31]

More than any other artist, Tchaikovsky encapsulates this sense of Russia's economic doubleness in the second half of the nineteenth century; his correspondence with von Meck should be read alongside that with Jurgenson in order to get a fuller sense of how he fashioned a viable sense of his own personality as a creative artist.

The emotional and physical upheavals that followed Tchaikovsky's rash decision to marry make the fact that he composed some of his most successful and famous works during this period all the more remarkable. Partly, of course, this was down to the timely intervention of his friends and family, but his creative output in 1877 and 1878 also testifies to his prodigious work ethic, as well as to an ability to translate traumatic personal experiences into expressive artistic form. In fact, work on the Symphony No. 4 and *Eugene Onegin* was begun before his marriage, and the seeming rapidity of his recovery can be seen from the fact that he resumed the orchestration of the opera as early as 17 October, claiming in a letter to Modest, 'generally speaking, I am fully myself again.'[32] In fact, once free of Antonina and away from his duties at the Conservatory, he seems to have felt a renewed sense of confidence in his creative abilities. In a long letter to Sasha, he begged her to inform his wife that he could never return to her, before making a powerful statement of his overwhelming personal confidence:

> I am an artist, who can and should bring great honour to his homeland. I feel in myself great creative powers. I have not yet achieved one tenth of what I am capable of achieving. And I want to achieve this with all the powers of my soul.[33]

The four movements of the Symphony No. 4 were almost fully sketched by the end of May 1877; the orchestration was begun on Sasha's estate that summer and was completed in December and early January in Venice and San Remo. Its melancholy, not to say fatalistic, tone may reflect Tchaikovsky's mood that year; yet to attribute its gestation entirely to his psychological state as he contemplated marriage is to underestimate its sheer formal daring. Its first movement lasts around twenty minutes and is almost as long as the other three movements put together. Like the opening movement of the Piano Concerto No. 1 or *Francesca da Rimini*, it is one of those huge canvases on which Tchaikovsky demonstrated the viability of fashioning symphonic structures out of melodic gestures. This emphasis on lyric expansion can be seen in the use of three subjects in the exposition section (two was standard in most symphonies at the time), as well as in a number of repetitions of the opening 'fate' motif that interrupt the normal unfolding of the movement.[34] Lyricism, albeit of a more conventional, delicate kind, predominates in the second movement too. Effectively a series of iterations of a song-like tune (the movement is called *Andantino in modo di canzona*) with a contrasting middle section that seems like a faint echo of the love theme from *Romeo and Juliet* or the heroine's 'confession' in *Francesca da Rimini*, it exposes how much can be achieved through the repetition of melodic material against a background of changing orchestral sonorities. The third movement scherzo similarly privileges surface texture, this time by the extensive use of pizzicato strings set against contrasting sections played by woodwind and brass alone. Tchaikovsky's ability to 'play' the orchestra like an instrument, to use colour and texture to create satisfying structure, is exploited fully in the finale: a set of variations on a Russian folk song ('In the field a birch tree stood') that is brought to a sudden conclusion by the interruption of the original 'fate' theme from the opening movement.

Throughout the symphony, the rapid juxtaposition of often incongruously contrasting themes gives the impression of emotional instability, yet this is achieved by a command of form that is unprecedented in Tchaikovsky's output so far. In correspondence with Taneev, he was keen to defend the coherence and integrity of his new symphony, not least against his colleague's criticism that 'in each movement there is something that recalls ballet music.'[35] Tchaikovsky's reply was confident and revealing:

> I simply do not understand what you mean by ballet music and why you cannot reconcile yourself to it. By ballet music do you mean any cheerful melody with a dance rhythm? In which case you should not be able to reconcile yourself to the majority of Beethoven's symphonies, in which one comes across such melodies at every turn . . . Indeed, I simply cannot understand why there should be anything at all *reprehensible* about the expression *ballet music*! After all, ballet music is not always bad; there can be good ballet music too (here I might point to Léo Delibes' *Sylvia*) . . . I must therefore assume that the *balletic* passages in the symphony which displease you do so not because they are *balletic*, but because they are poor. You are quite right, perhaps – but I still cannot grasp why a dance melody cannot appear episodically in a symphony, if only with a deliberate shade of vulgar, coarse humour. Once again I cite Beethoven, who resorted to this effect more than once.[36]

Coming in the wake of *Swan Lake* and the Symphony No. 3, Tchaikovsky's interest in dance genres should come as no surprise, but his invocation of Beethoven – a figure who otherwise tended to leave him cold – is more significant, and shows how, as a Russian composer, Tchaikovsky was able to assess his own achievements against a supposedly universal standard, while confidently asserting his own voice at the same time.

Taneev's other criticism was that the symphony felt like a piece of programme music (especially its opening movement) and had 'the appearance of a symphonic poem to which three movements had been randomly appended'.[37] Tchaikovsky did not disagree:

> My symphony is, of course, programmatic, but the programme is such that there is no possibility of expressing it in words. This would give rise to ridicule and would seem comic. But is this not what a symphony – that is, the most lyrical of all musical forms – should be? Should it not express everything for which there are no words, yet for which the soul longs and which itself cries out for expression?

Once again making a comparison with Beethoven (here, his Symphony No. 5, with its equally famous opening 'fate' motif), he expressed confidence in the 'legibility' of both his own work and that of the model on which it was based: 'in my naivety, I imagined that the thought behind the symphony would be clear and that the general outline of its meaning would be accessible even without a programme.'[38]

The question of the symphony's programme is, however, more complicated than this rather straightforward account suggests. On 1 May 1877 von Meck had written to ask Tchaikovsky to write for her a piece for violin and piano, with the title 'Reproach', that would be 'the expression of an unbearable emotional state, one that can be summed up in the French expression: *je n'en peux plus!*'[39] She even provided a detailed programme in the kind of overblown prose so characteristic of her letters. Tchaikovsky delicately, yet firmly, declined the proposal, offering instead something altogether grander: 'I am now engrossed in a symphony that I began to write last winter, and which I should very much like to dedicate to you, since it seems to me that you will find in it echoes of your own innermost feelings and thoughts.'[40] Von

Meck attended the symphony's first performance in Moscow on 10 February 1878, subsequently enquiring whether it had any particular programme, and on 17 February the composer replied with a detailed account of the work's 'meaning'. It is, to be sure, a curious interpretation, which professional musicologists have on the whole shunned in favour of the more sober account of the work that Tchaikovsky gave to Taneev. Dismissed by one biographer as 'silly and unrelated to the music',[41] it certainly contains more than its fair share of poetic obfuscations. The first movement, for instance, expresses the notion of fate as 'that fateful force which prevents the urge towards happiness from achieving its aim, and which is jealously on guard lest well-being and peace should be complete and cloudless'. In the second movement, we hear

> that melancholy feeling that comes of an evening when, tired from work, you sit alone and pick up a book, but which slips from your hands. Memories come in waves. It is both sad that so much has *been and gone*, yet pleasant to recall one's youth.

The 'capricious arabesques' of the scherzo suggest 'ephemeral images which flit past in the imagination when you have had a little wine to drink and you are experiencing the first phase of inebriation'. And the finale suggests nothing more than 'a picture of ordinary people celebrating at a festival'.[42]

This was just the sort of narrative designed to please von Meck; yet to scorn it as naive, unsophisticated or even opportunistic is to overlook how important programme music was for Tchaikovsky as a means of engaging with an audience little able to distinguish between first and second subjects, let alone expositions, developments and recapitulations. When, regarding his new symphony, he expressed his pleasure that von Meck had 'experienced the same feelings which filled me when I was writing it',[43] he had in mind not some facile correspondence between his particular authorial intention and her corresponding emotional response, but something closer to the emphasis on sincerity and even emotional infection that characterizes Tolstoy's later writings on aesthetics. Von Meck's letters showed him the kind of physical, embodied, imaginative responses that his music could stir in its listeners, and his programme for the Symphony No. 4 represents not so much a hidden inspiration or pre-existing narrative as a tentative way of putting the experience of such listening into words. If Tchaikovsky aspired to establish himself as a successful professional composer who lived on the income from his works, he would need to find a musical language that spoke not just to his rich and impressionable patron but to an audience that would pay to hear his works in concert halls and opera houses, and would buy his sheet music to play at home.

Between completing the first draft of the Symphony No. 4 and embarking on its orchestration, Tchaikovsky turned his attention to a very different work – and one that was as seemingly associated with Antonina as the symphony was with von Meck. Sometime in mid-May 1877, the singer Elizaveta Lavrovskaya suggested that Pushkin's *Eugene Onegin* might make an ideal libretto for an opera. Work began on Shilovsky's estate that June, continued at Kamenka in August and was completed during the winter that Tchaikovsky spent in Switzerland and Italy. Already by 18 May, in an excited letter to Modest, he had sketched a scenario that was to be little changed thereafter, as well as suggesting both the charms and challenges of the project:

How glad I am to be rid of Ethiopian princesses, pharaohs, poisonings and all manner of stilted gestures. What depth of poetry there is in *Onegin*. I am not deluded; I know that there will be few scenic effects and little action in this opera. But the general poeticism, humanity and simplicity of plot, along with a text of *genius* will make up for these deficiencies many times over.[44]

If *Onegin* represents Tchaikovsky's distaste for the alien conventions of grand opera, it also constitutes his response to hearing Bizet's *Carmen* in Paris in 1876 ('this is music without pretention to depth, but so charming in its simplicity, so alive, uncontrived, and so sincere that I have learned it almost by heart from beginning to end'),[45] as well as his own homage to Mozart, whose music he had loved since childhood. It also represents an extraordinarily fluent and original response to what many then regarded – and indeed still regard – as a literary masterpiece that resists all attempts at adaptation.

Tatyana Larina is a solitary, bookish girl who falls for Eugene Onegin when he pays a visit to her family's country estate only because he corresponds to the romantic stereotypes she has encountered in her reading. She pens a confession of love made up of sentimental clichés, which he rejects in a pompous, if well-intentioned, manner. At her name-day party, Onegin flirts with Tatyana's sister, Olga, provoking Lensky – his own best friend and Olga's betrothed – to challenge him to a duel. They fight, and Lensky is killed. After a number of years travelling abroad, Onegin returns to Russia, where he encounters Tatyana again, this time as the society wife of an elderly general. He confesses his love, but Tatyana rejects him, pledging fidelity to her marriage vows. If the plot of Pushkin's *Eugene Onegin* is simple, not to say trite, then the manner of its telling is altogether more original. Written in verse and employing a fixed stanza of fourteen lines, it is a self-conscious and playful work that contains a series of knowing allusions to eighteenth- and nineteenth-century literature: Tatyana is straight from the pages of a novel by Samuel Richardson, Onegin is a mock-Byronic hero and Lensky represents a parody of a German Romantic poet. Its main character is not, in fact, any of the named characters, but the narrator himself, who intervenes to comment on the action and frequently addresses the reader directly.

Tchaikovsky's opera has frequently been criticized for its failure to deal adequately – indeed at all – with the sophisticated irony of Pushkin's narrative style. This much is, of course, true. Two of Pushkin's most virtuoso parodies – Tatyana's letter to Onegin and the poem that Lensky writes before the duel scene – become, in Tchaikovsky's treatment of them, fully embodied confessions of sincere emotion and dramatic verisimilitude. In Pushkin, we read these texts in the company of the knowing narrator; in Tchaikovsky, we see and hear these characters unmediated and respond directly to their predicaments. Yet the opera has its moments of calculating self-consciousness, too. Tchaikovsky knew full well that his *Onegin* was neither an opera in the conventional sense, nor a faithful reading of Pushkin, and in subtitling the work 'Lyric Scenes', he intimated something of its unconventional genre. This sense of the opera's unconventionality can be perhaps best grasped in Tatyana's letter scene, in which psychological realism and narrative sophistication are brilliantly fused. For all its popularity in concert performance (a habit of which Tchaikovsky disapproved), it is avowedly not an aria in any usual sense. Rather, it is made up of four separate sections that not only chart the evolution of Tatyana's psychological state, but evoke the musical language of the parlour romances that were so popular in the 1820s and 1830s, the era of the novel's composition.[46]

It is Tatyana's name-day party, however, that is the most extraordinary compositional tour de force in the whole opera. Composed as a sequence of old-fashioned dances redolent of the Larins' provincial mores, it intertwines these with Monsieur Triquet's cod verses in praise of Tatyana's beauty, Onegin's flirtation with Olga, Lensky's challenge and a whole gamut of society gossip. One early critic faulted the scene, in which the composer saw 'in the words and action only a pretext for his creative ardour as a symphonist'.[47] Though designed to wound Tchaikovsky, who was always sensitive to the accusation that his operas were insufficiently dramatic, this comment is in fact entirely apposite.

The scene is a glorious piece of through-composed stage action that subtly and unexpectedly brings all of Tchaikovsky's skill as a master of complex symphonic structure to the operatic house. It is here that one hears the lessons learned during the composition of the Symphony No. 4; not until Act III of Chekhov's *The Cherry Orchard* – a similar scene of tense expectation that takes place in the context of a series of dances – would another Russian artist produce anything so architecturally satisfying for the stage.

At the very time Tchaikovsky was writing *Eugene Onegin*, he was also courting Antonina, whose situation struck him as poignantly similar to that of Tatyana. Unlike Onegin, however, Tchaikovsky resolved not to dismiss a naive and vulnerable young woman, and it was this decision to read life through the prism of art that was to have such painful consequences. This was not, in fact, the first time that Tchaikovsky had confused life and art; in 1868 he had looked back on his non-affair with Vera Davydova as 'an entire abyss of various psychological subtleties which surely only a Tolstoy or a Thackeray could analyse'.[48] Now, however, he himself was portraying the emotional predicament of Pushkin's characters with all the psychological insight and delicacy characteristic of a Turgenev novel.[49] Yet the greatest emotional weight in the opera is carried not by any of Pushkin's named characters, but by a role that Tchaikovsky was forced to invent. In Pushkin, we know nothing of Tatyana's husband other than that he is a 'fat general'; he has no name, no history, and serves only to embody Tatyana's stoicism, fidelity and glittering success in St Petersburg high society. By contrast, Tchaikovsky not only gave him a name ('Gremin'), but wrote for him some of the most ardent and unfeigned music in the whole opera.[50]

Gremin's Act III aria not only expresses a fictional character's touching confession of late and unexpected love, but seems to articulate Tchaikovsky's own aspirations for the kind of loving and sustaining relationship that he himself would never enjoy. Confected from various fragments of the novel and a number of strategic poetic additions, the words of Gremin's aria reveal the disjuncture between Tchaikovsky's life and his art at this time. The stage action is suspended for a moment, and during this moment of stasis the audience steps outside the immediate confines of the opera's action to inhabit another configuration of time and space. Running contrary to the rest of the opera, the scene is not just a scenic coup but an emotional necessity. When Onegin sings of his love to Tatyana, he does so in music unconsciously borrowed from her own letter scene; he has no expressive means of his own. Gremin, by contrast, has music that belongs to him alone, and the poignancy of the scene derives from Tchaikovsky's empathetic ability to evoke in art something he could only imagine in life.

Structured around three leads – Onegin, Gremin and the mature Tatyana – the whole of Act III explores contrasting facets of Tchaikovsky's character. Acts I and II may contain the opera's most expressive lyric moments – the young Tatyana's letter scene and Lensky's farewell aria – but it is the final act that best sums up its emotional significance. Onegin is the fictional version of the man Tchaikovsky feared becoming by spurning Antonina, and his final outburst – 'Ignominy! Anguish! O, my pitiful fate!' – suggests something of the composer's own emotional volatility.[51] Gremin expresses the very thing Tchaikovsky most longed for, yet would never achieve. It is Tatyana, though, who best illustrates that path that Tchaikovsky would take once he had survived the failure of his marriage. In the opera's opening scene, Tatyana's mother and nanny look back on the past, remembering how youthful love affairs give way to the acquiescence of adulthood:

Habit is sent us from above
In place of happiness.
Yes, that is how it is:
Habit is sent us from above,
In place of happiness.

This is the lesson that Tatyana learns by the end of the opera, as she chooses loyalty to Gremin over the love she still so painfully feels for Onegin. It was also the lesson that Tchaikovsky learned during the course of 1877. As he wrote to von Meck from Kamenka on 30 August, still somehow hoping to make his marriage work,

> It will be difficult for me to leave here. After the disquiet that I have experienced, I have so enjoyed the peace here. In any case, I shall leave here a healthy person, who has gained sufficient strength for the struggle with *fate*. But the main thing is that I do not cherish false hopes. I know that there will be difficult moments, but afterwards habit will come along, something that, as Pushkin says,
>
> > . . . is sent us from above,
> > In place of happiness!
>
> After all, I grew accustomed to my classes at the conservatory, which once seemed to me the greatest of disasters.[52]

In the end, habit could never reconcile him to a life as Antonina's husband. But habit, routine, discipline and hard work would help him through the ensuing crisis, constituting some kind of substitute for a happiness that all too often eluded him.

The score of Eugene Onegin was completed in San Remo in early 1878, and although the score, excerpts and arrangements of individual numbers were published swiftly afterwards and sold well, stage performances were slower in coming. Tchaikovsky immediately understood that his new opera posed an unusual challenge to current stage conventions, writing to Modest in June 1877:

My opera may not be fit for the stage and there may be too little action in it, but I am in love with the image of Tatyana, I am enchanted by Pushkin's verses and I am setting them to music because I do nothing else.[53]

His distaste for the Imperial theatres was equally evident in a letter he wrote to Karl Albrecht that December: 'what I need here is not the grand stage with its *routine and conventionality, with its talentless directors and its senseless, albeit luxurious productions, with its signalling machines instead of conductors, etc., etc.*'[54] But if Tchaikovsky was critical of the musical establishment, he was far more positive about the public's receptivity to new ideas. Writing to Jurgenson, he provided an uncannily astute prediction of the opera's fate:

This opera will, it seems to me, soon enjoy great success in *homes*, and perhaps on the concert platform more so than on the main stage, and for this reason, the fact that it will be published much earlier than it will enter the repertoire of the main theatres is not unfavourable. The success of this opera should begin from below, and not from on high. That is to say, it is not the *theatre* that will make it well known to the public, but the opposite: that the public, having slowly become familiar with it, may fall in love with it, and then *a theatre* might stage the opera, in order to satisfy the demands of the public.[55]

At first, however, both public reaction and critical response were hesitant. A dress rehearsal of the first four scenes was given at the Moscow Conservatory on 16 December 1878, followed by a student performance of the complete opera at the city's Maly Theatre the following March. Extracts were also given at the St Petersburg home of the mezzo-soprano Yuliya Abaza that spring, as well as at concerts in January and March 1880, but it was not until 11 January 1881 that the complete opera received its first professional performance, at Moscow's Bolshoi Theatre. It was, however, the production at St Petersburg's Mariinsky Theatre in October 1884 that really established the opera in the repertoire (it had also been heard in Kharkov and Kiev by this point). Productions followed in Prague (1888), Hamburg (1892, where it was conducted by Gustav Mahler), London (1892) and, eventually, at New York's Metropolitan Opera (1920).[56]

This sense that critics and audiences were not yet ready to appreciate Tchaikovsky's subtle innovations also applies to the Violin Concerto, which was sketched, with a fluency that outstripped even that of *Eugene Onegin*, in just ten days in March 1878. Tchaikovsky was still in western Europe at this time, but his brother Anatoly, who had helped him flee Antonina the previous autumn, had by now returned to Russia. Since the composer was deemed still too fragile to be left entirely alone, Anatoly was replaced by a group of new and eminently agreeable companions: Modest (accompanied, of course, by young Kolya Konradi), his friend the violinist Josef Kotek, and his own devoted manservant, Alexey (Alyosha) Sofronov. Having played through the new work with Kotek, Tchaikovsky decided to write an entirely new slow movement; the resulting *canzonetta* was completed in a single day in late March, and the whole concerto was orchestrated in under a week.

The ease with which it was composed is evidence of how completely Tchaikovsky seems to have put the ordeal of his failed marriage behind him. As he wrote to Anatoly in February:

I woke up healthy. Today is the last day of our stay in San Remo. *Recapitulating* all seven weeks we have spent here, I cannot but come to the conclusion that they have done me a great deal of good. Thanks to the orderliness of my life, the often boring, but always uninterrupted peace, and above all thanks to time, which heals all wounds, I am completely recovered from *madness*.[57]

Tchaikovsky (far right) in San Remo, January 1878, with Nikolay Konradi, his brother Modest and his manservant Alyosha Sofronov.

The appeal of the concerto's melodic invention suggests something of the joy that Tchaikovsky continued to derive from artistic inspiration, as well as of the pleasure afforded by his new companions. Modest's pupil continued to delight him ('with each day I fall more and more in love with Kolya', as he wrote to Anatoly),[58] and if Kotek was no longer the object of the intense infatuation he had been the previous spring, his company was still more than agreeable. The earlier performance history of the concerto, however, was to be far less straightforward than the process of its composition. Its original dedicatee, Leopold Auer, refused to perform it on the grounds that it was unidiomatic and unplayable. Kotek, influenced by Auer, also declined to perform it, which led to a cooling in relations with the composer. Instead, it was left to Adolf Brodsky to premiere the work at a concert in Vienna in December 1881; yet even this performance was ill-starred.

Tchaikovsky's compositions had been heard more and more frequently in European concert halls during the 1870s. After its premiere in Boston in 1875, for instance, the Piano Concerto No. 1 was performed in London in 1876, and in Paris and Wiesbaden two years later; *Romeo and Juliet* was heard in London, Vienna and Paris in 1876; and Colonne conducted the French premiere of the Symphony No. 4 in January 1880. At this time, critics and audiences struggled to place Tchaikovsky's music properly. On the one hand, his conservatory training meant that he had a mastery of form and technique that made him thoroughly European in spirit; at the same time, enduring stereotypes about the Russian national character, as well as a tendency to compare him unfavourably to western European models, meant that he was frequently heard as barbaric, exotic and downright unruly. The Berlin premiere of *Francesca da Rimini*, for instance, was given alongside Brahms's Second Symphony, somehow setting up a rivalry between German and Russian repertoires that often worked to Tchaikovsky's disadvantage. Thus when the Violin Concerto was heard for the first time in Vienna, it was viciously attacked by the city's most influential critic, Eduard Hanslick. Concerned above all with the purity of the Austro-Germanic tradition and the defence of 'absolute' music against the rival claims of programme works and the innovations of Wagner and his followers, Hanslick proved himself unable to hear the classical dignity and elegant proportions of the concerto, which he infamously described – in words that its composer would recall by heart for the rest of his life – as 'music that stank'.[59] But all this was yet in the future in 1878. By the end of April that year, Tchaikovsky was back in Russia, first at his sister's estate at Kamenka and then at von Meck's estate of Brailov, where he would spend a happy and productive summer before being due to return to his position at the Moscow Conservatory in the autumn.

4

'I am a Free Man'

Writing to Anatoly on 13 February 1878, Tchaikovsky gave voice to a growing self-awareness that was allied with a newly found stoicism: 'Only now, particularly after the story of my marriage, am I finally beginning to understand that there is nothing more fruitless than wanting to be anything other than what I am by nature.'[1] This statement is often taken to refer to the composer's acceptance of his homosexuality, and from now on, Tchaikovsky would certainly be more relaxed about his erotic encounters with other men. Just under a week later, he offered Anatoly the following account of his recent life:

> An entire day of torment and indecision. This evening I had arranged a rendezvous . . . Finally I resolved to go. I spent a wonderful couple of hours in the most romantic setting; I was afraid, my heart sank, I took fright at the slightest sound; embraces, kisses, a lonely apartment far away and high up, sweet nothings, pleasure! I came home tired and exhausted, but with marvellous memories.

A few days later, Tchaikovsky was again on the lookout for adventure:

> After luncheon I hung about in the hope of meeting my delight, but without luck. However, another joy awaited me.

On the Lungarno I ran into some street singers and immediately enquired of them whether or not they knew our boy. It turned out that they did and they gave their word that he would be on the Lungarno this evening at nine o'clock.[2]

The figure referred to here is Vittorio, a Florentine street singer who crops up repeatedly in Tchaikovsky's letters at this time, and one of whose songs Tchaikovsky immortalized as 'Pimpenella', the final number of his Six Romances, Op. 38. Back in Moscow that September, he allowed himself to be introduced to a manservant by Nikolay Bochechkarov, one of the denizens of the city's gay demi-monde; although the encounter was unconsummated, Tchaikovsky was charmed by the young man's face and body, which he described to Modest as '*un rêve* – the incarnation of a sweet dream'.[3] It was abroad, though, that Tchaikovsky found the greatest sexual release; a letter to Modest written in Paris in early 1879 gives a long and detailed account of an affair with a young hustler, whose squalid garret briefly became 'the place where all human happiness was concentrated'.[4]

Yet Tchaikovsky's conviction that he could only really be happy by yielding to 'what I am by nature' encompasses more than simply an acceptance of his sexuality. The long letter in which he makes this statement was written to console and advise Anatoly, who was prone to bouts of despair at the slow advancement of his legal career, as well as at his perpetually complicated emotional life (he was at this time fruitlessly involved with the soprano Alexandra Panaeva, to whom the composer would later dedicate his Seven Romances, Op. 47, in 1880). Tchaikovsky's letter can equally be read as a cautionary tale about the perils of vanity and ambition, and about how he had slowly come to a pragmatic understanding of the consequences of his own talent:

This is what I wanted to explain to you: there is nothing more fruitless than those sufferings which are caused by immoderate vanity. I can say this because I myself have always suffered from this and was also never satisfied with the results that I achieved. Perhaps you will say that because people write about me in the papers, I am famous and should be happy and satisfied. But this is not enough for me *et j'ai toujours voulu péter plus haut que mon cul*. I wanted to be not only Russia's first composer, but of the whole world too; I wanted to be not only a composer, but also a first-class conductor; I wanted to be an *unusually* clever and colossally learned person; and I also wanted to be elegant and worldly and able to shine in salons; I wanted all of this so very much. Only little by little, at the price of a whole series of unbearable sorrows, did I come to understand my own true worth . . . It's amusing for me to recall, for instance, how much I suffered because I was unable to break into high society and be a society figure . . . How much time did it take me to realize that I was not a stupid person, but that I was certainly not one of those people with an outstanding mind. How many years did it take me to understand that even as a composer, I was simply a talented individual, and not some exceptional phenomenon.[5]

Tchaikovsky is certainly disingenuous about his own sense of self-worth here, and his seeming modesty hides a deep sense of ambition. Alongside coming to terms with his sexuality, the most important question that he faced at this time was how to arrange his professional life so that he could communicate with his audiences, while avoiding the kind of social interactions that were so capable of upsetting him. How to achieve this ideal state of affairs became the main focus of his life between 1878 and 1885, and he proved singularly adept at liberating himself from duties that would either impose intolerable social burdens or interrupt his creative life.

Already at the end of 1877, Tchaikovsky had turned down Rubinstein's invitation to represent Russia at the forthcoming World's Fair in Paris, which would have provided him with much-needed financial support, as well as a pretext for his prolonged absence from Russia. His decision – which he readily admitted was egotistical – spoiled his relations not only with Rubinstein but with almost all of his colleagues at the Moscow Conservatory too; yet Tchaikovsky was unrepentant, claiming rather dramatically, 'I would rather undertake hard labour than go to Paris as part of the delegation . . . I am ill, I am mad.'[6] Unsurprisingly, he was equally reluctant to resume his teaching commitments at the Conservatory. His attitude was clearly shaped by his lack of pedagogical zeal, but his anxiety was heightened by insinuations that were published in a newspaper article in August 1878. As he wrote to Modest:

at one point the article refers to the professors' *amours* with young girls and adds at the end: '*amours of another variety also go on at the Conservatory, but for a very obvious reason, I will not speak of these*' etc. It is clear what is hinted at.[7]

The daily reality of teaching was just as depressing, as he confessed to Anatoly on 18 September: 'Moscow is absolutely repellent to me . . . I have a numb disgust for my male and female students and their labours.'[8] By 23 September he could bear things no longer and gave Rubinstein notice of his intention to resign that December.[9] Rubinstein put aside their former differences, despite the fact that this meant losing such a prestigious member of the Conservatory's teaching staff. On 7 October, Tchaikovsky at last wrote to von Meck: 'Yesterday I gave my last class . . . I am a free man. The realization of this freedom affords me inexplicable pleasure!'[10] After a number of social visits in the capitals and a brief sojourn to Kamenka to see his sister Sasha and her family, he made his way first to Vienna and then to Florence, where he was to spend the winter.

Tchaikovsky's freedom was not quite as absolute as he had hoped. Negotiations with Antonina, which were usually carried out via Anatoly or Jurgenson, dragged on for many years and were never entirely resolved to the satisfaction of either party. Even Kamenka, which had long been a refuge, slowly became a source of anxiety. Sasha was often unwell and eventually developed a serious morphine addiction. Tchaikovsky's niece, Tanya, could be capricious and wilful, and in April 1883 she gave birth to a child as a result of an affair with her music teacher, Stanislav Blumenfeld. Tchaikovsky and Modest conspired to take her to Paris for the final months of the pregnancy and arranged for her son, christened Georges-Léon, to be fostered by a French family (three years later, he was adopted by Tchaikovsky's older brother Nikolay and his wife, Olga, who were childless). Tchaikovsky's itinerant life meant that he came to rely more than ever before on his manservant, Alyosha, when it came to arranging the practical details of his daily life. Indeed, Tchaikovsky seems to have been unusually devoted to Alyosha, and the intensity of his feelings towards him has led some to posit that the two men were lovers. Such a cross-class relationship would certainly not have been unusual at the time, when coachmen and bathhouse attendants often worked as unofficial prostitutes for highborn clients, and even after the abolition of serfdom in 1861, quasi-feudal relations between master and servant would often shade into sexual ones too, whether homosexual or heterosexual.[11]

Professional concerns disrupted Tchaikovsky's independence as well. Some of these were the inevitable result of getting his works performed; seeing an opera produced in Moscow or St Petersburg took a great deal of face-to-face diplomacy. Artistic disputes took up valuable time too. When, for instance, Nikolay Rubinstein died in 1881, Tchaikovsky found himself caught up in the complicated question of who exactly was best placed to take over the running of the Moscow Conservatory, as well as of the local branch of the

Russian Musical Society. Even von Meck's commitment could seem uncertain. By 1881 her financial situation was precarious, and although Tchaikovsky's brother-in-law Lev Davydov looked into her accounts, Lev was unable to come up with a solution; Brailov was sold that summer, followed in December by von Meck's Moscow house.[12] Although von Meck continued to reassure Tchaikovsky of her ongoing support, he could not but worry about the conditions that sustained both his artistic freedom and his material comfort. Moreover, just as he was the beneficiary of patronage, he likewise found himself in demand as a source of financial support. Not only were there family members to look after, such as his niece Tanya and his brother Modest, who was then trying to establish a career as a playwright; there were also any number of strangers who approached him for help, including the gloomy and depressive Leonty Tkachenko, whom Tchaikovsky attempted to set up as a provincial music teacher in the early 1880s, not to mention students at the Conservatory whom he supported through their studies.

To an extent, such demands were offset by growing support from the Imperial household. Already in 1880 Tchaikovsky had been commissioned to write *The Year 1812* (popularly known as the *1812 Overture*) to mark the consecration of the Cathedral of Christ the Saviour during a joint exhibition of industry and the arts that was to be held in Moscow in 1882. The fact that the new work was premiered that August as part of a concert consisting solely of his works – including *The Tempest*, the first Russian performance of the Violin Concerto, the *Capriccio Italien* and various songs – shows the extent to which he had rapidly become a symbol of both the nation and its ruling dynasty.[13] In fact, following the accession of Alexander III in 1881, official commissions became all the more frequent. Back in 1866, Tchaikovsky had been commissioned to write the *Festival Overture on the Danish National Anthem* for the marriage of the then Grand Duke Alexander Alexandrovich to Princess Dagmar of Denmark. In the 1880s he wrote a march to be performed during Alexander's coronation festivities of 1883, as well as a substantial cantata – *Moscow* – that was premiered at the Bolshoi Theatre that May, although neither work gave him much creative satisfaction. Such official commissions necessitated a degree of time-consuming socializing, too. When, on the occasion of the St Petersburg premiere of *Mazepa* in February 1884 the Tsar expressed his displeasure that its composer had not been present, Tchaikovsky was obliged to dash back from Paris (that he was awarded the Order of St Vladimir, Fourth Class, on this occasion suggests that the faux pas was not altogether ruinous).

Other Imperial connections were more agreeable. In March 1880, Tchaikovsky was introduced to Grand Duke Konstantin Konstantinovich Romanov. As well as being an influential member of the ruling dynasty (he headed the Izmailovsky and Preobrazhensky regiments of the Imperial Russian Army and later became president of the Academy of Sciences), he was an accomplished poet who published under the none-too-subtle cryptonym of KR. Whether Tchaikovsky was aware of Konstantin's guilt-inducing sexual encounters with other men is not known, but he was certainly drawn to one of the more sensitive and learned members of Russia's ruling dynasty.

Many critics and biographers have seen the works that came directly after the Symphony No. 4, *Eugene Onegin* and the Violin Concerto as representing something of a decline in terms of inspiration, if not of effort. Tchaikovsky may have recovered from his failed marriage with seeming rapidity, yet the psychological traces took much longer to heal, as suggested by the almost pathological sense of shyness that many noted in him around this time. The anxieties caused by family concerns and his growing official status also took their toll on his physical and psychological well-being. Tchaikovsky's own attitude to his works at this time can sometimes come across as one of opportunistic professionalism rather than creative satisfaction. Thus, writing to his friend, the cellist Karl Albrecht in the summer of 1878, he catalogued his recent output:

> I have just finished a whole series of various non-orchestral works and am very glad that I can now do nothing for a while. I have written a piano sonata, three violin pieces, twelve small pieces for piano, twenty-four little piano pieces for children, six romances, and an entire Liturgy of St John Chrysostom for mixed voices. Our poor Pyotr Ivanovich! That's some work I've given him.[14]

A week letter he invoiced Jurgenson (the same Pyotr Ivanovich referred to in his letter to Albrecht) for his recent compositions:

> Here is the fee that I'd like to receive for all of this:
>
> 1) for the Sonata – 50r
> 2) for the twelve pieces at 25 each – 300r
> 3) for the children's album at 10 each – 240r
> 4) for the six romances at 25 each – 150r
> 5) for the violin pieces at 25 each – 75r
> 6) for the liturgy – 100r
>
> In total – 915r,
> or a round sum of 900r, but in view of the fact that I have written so much all at once, I will let you have it all for 800r.[15]

Here, composition becomes a rudely economic transaction whose rewards are determined by the tastes of the contemporary market. Songs and instrumental miniatures sold well and therefore fetched a higher price than the more challenging sonata that would have been beyond the technical reach of Russia's growing caste of amateur musicians. But the transaction between Tchaikovsky and Jurgenson was more than just a financial exchange between composer and publisher; it was also a way of quantifying the emotional debts that Tchaikovsky had run up over the previous decade, when Jurgenson's belief in him was one factor that allowed him to dare to become Russia's leading composer. As Tchaikovsky wryly noted in December 1877, 'I know perfectly well that my creations will fill your shelves, but not your pockets'.[16]

Yet all the works that Tchaikovsky completed at this time have a claim to be taken seriously in other terms. The Grand Sonata for Piano, Op. 37, is generally thought to be the weakest of them (one critic calls it 'a strong candidate as the dullest piece Tchaikovsky ever wrote'),[17] and suggests that despite his ability to fashion long-range architectural structures in his symphonic and orchestral works, the motivic discipline required to hold together an ambitious work for a single instrument failed him. Like the sonata he wrote while still a student (and published posthumously in 1900), it nods in the direction of Schumann, yet never quite lives up to its ambitions. The miniatures are consistently better, however, and both the Twelve Pieces, Op. 40, and *Children's Album*, Op. 39, are ideally pitched for the kind of enthusiastic domestic music-making that supported Tchaikovsky's reputation outside the cultural and official elites of the capitals (the former set is described as being 'of moderate difficulty' and the second is an explicit homage to Schumann's earlier *Kinderszenen* of 1838). They also encode the friendships and relationships that sustained him throughout this period; the Twelve Pieces are dedicated to Modest and the *Children's Album* – composed partly while staying at Kamenka – was conceived for Tchaikovsky's young nephew Vladimir (who was to play such a decisive role in his life several years later). Both sets also make use of melodies that Tchaikovsky heard in Florence, suggesting that the image of Vittorio still haunted his imagination. The Six Romances, Op. 38, were dedicated to Anatoly in return for his help in looking after Tchaikovsky in late 1877: whether their theme of love and its torments refers to the scandal of Pyotr's marriage or Anatoly's perpetually broken heart, the songs surely encapsulate the wry sense of collusion that existed between the two brothers.

It is, however, his setting of the *Liturgy of St John Chrysostom*, Op. 41, that reveals most fully the extent of Tchaikovsky's artistic curiosity at this time. Writing to von Meck from Vienna in late 1877, he articulated the fusion of aesthetic and spiritual motivations that lay behind his rather fluid and undogmatic sense of religious faith:

> I very often attend Eucharist; the Liturgy of St John Chrysostom is, in my opinion, one of the greatest of all works of art. If you follow the service attentively, trying to fathom the meaning of each ritual, it is impossible for your spirit not to be moved when present at one of our Orthodox services. I also love the all-night vigil very much. To head off on Saturday to some ancient little church, to stand in the semi-darkness, filled with smoke from the incense, to withdraw into oneself, and to search for answers to eternal questions: *why? when? whither? for what purpose?*, and then to be stirred from one's pensiveness as soon as the choir begins to sing: '*From my youth up many passions have warred against me*', and to yield to the fascinating poetry of this psalm, to be imbued with some kind of quiet delight when the doors of the icon screen are flung wide and '*Praise the Lord from the heavens!*' rings out – oh, I love it all terribly, it is one of my greatest pleasures![18]

The *Liturgy* was written early the following summer, but despite Tchaikovsky's affection for Orthodox services, it immediately ran into problems with the ecclesiastical authorities. The director of the Imperial Chapel claimed that the work infringed the chapel's monopoly on the composition and publication of religious music and promptly had the plates confiscated. Concert performances only exacerbated matters, as did a successful legal appeal against the seizure of the plates (although Jurgenson clearly relished the publicity the whole affair provoked).

With the monopoly overturned, Tchaikovsky went on to explore the field of religious music yet further. In addition to his Nine Sacred Pieces of 1884–5, he produced a setting of the *All-night Vigil* (Vesper Service), Op. 52, in 1881–2, which was partly influenced by his conversations with the village priest at Kamenka, where he liked to attend services with his sister and her family. In both cases, his interest was as much professional as it was personal; the mid-century saw extensive discussion of the contemporary state of Russian church music, with historical research suggesting that its original, Byzantine roots had been overlaid with incongruous Italianate influences from the eighteenth century onwards. As Tchaikovsky explained to Modest, his settings of the *Liturgy* and the *Vigil* embodied a wish to write in a way that was more respectful of tradition, while retaining a strong element of his own creative individuality: 'I want to sober church music up from excessive Europeanization, not so much *theoretically* as on the basis of my own *intuition* as an artist.'[19] Jurgenson's interest in this repertoire was less high-minded; he was clearly aware that if the repertoire could be successfully reformed, he would stand to benefit from the resulting demand for new scores. Accordingly, he commissioned from Tchaikovsky an edition of the sacred concertos of Dmitry Bortnyansky, an eighteenth-century composer of Ukrainian origin whose works – for all their European borrowings – still formed a substantial part of the modern liturgical repertoire. Tchaikovsky's exasperation at having taken on this task is clear from a letter he wrote to von Meck in August 1881:

> Bortnyansky was a person with a modest talent and very productive. He left behind a vast body of works, of which only a few are worth any attention. All the rest is either average or totally bad and vulgar.[20]

Nonetheless, Tchaikovsky's labours in this field were not entirely in vain, as subsequent generations of Russian composers also began to view the composition of sacred church music as a worthwhile creative activity; in particular, Rachmaninoff's *Liturgy of St John Chrysostom* (1910) and *All-night Vigil* (1915) are direct acts of homage to his pioneering work in the field.

Following the disappointing failures of his earlier historical operas, Tchaikovsky nonetheless returned to the genre in *The Maid of Orleans* (1878–9) and *Mazepa* (1881–3). It was as if the inspired rejection of the conventions of grand opera in *Eugene Onegin* had been a temporary eccentricity, although because this opera had yet to establish itself with audiences and critics, Tchaikovsky could have had little sense of how successfully its innovations would eventually work on the stage. In other ways, however, neither *The Maid of Orleans* nor *Mazepa* would have been possible without the discoveries that he had made in the intervening years. *Onegin* left its mark on all of Tchaikovsky's later operas; where *The Voevoda* and *The Oprichnik* can seem impersonal and schematic, his newer works on historical themes were to contain roles that were far more psychologically and dramatically convincing. In a letter to Modest, he gave a clue as to the importance that *The Maid of Orleans* held in his artistic evolution: 'Absolute simplicity of style. Its forms are to be readily understandable. In a word, it will be a sharp contrast to *Vakula*.'[21]

The new operas were shaped by pragmatic considerations, too. When, back in 1876, Tchaikovsky had met Tolstoy, the elder writer had counselled him to give up writing operas, which he believed were trivial works for society consumption, as well as being aesthetically mendacious in their powerful ability to make audiences suspend their rational disbelief. Tolstoy had depicted these very features in a famous scene in *War and Peace*, where the young Natasha Rostova attends the opera and is promptly induced to abandon her fiancé, Andrey Bolkonsky, in favour of the rakish Anatole Kuragin. Tchaikovsky had no time for Tolstoy's literalism, however, always preferring what he referred to as 'the depth of *artificial* truth'.[22] And it was precisely this sense of artifice that made opera such a powerful social institution, especially for a composer so determined to win artistic fame, even while he shunned society itself. As he wrote to von Meck in late 1879, just after he had completed *The Maid of Orleans*, 'opera has the great advantage that it gives one the opportunity of addressing *the masses* through the language of music.'[23] Tchaikovsky returned to this idea at the end of 1883, again in correspondence with von Meck: 'one cannot but admit that opera has the great advantage of allowing one to influence the musical feelings of the *masses*, whereas the symphonist must deal with an elite audience that is small in number.'[24] Tchaikovsky felt that, unlike the more recondite forms of chamber and symphonic music that potentially required a degree of technical understanding and aesthetic cultivation, opera was ideally placed to reach as many people as possible, thus allowing him to fulfil his social role as a Russian artist and simultaneously providing for his not inconsiderable material needs.

Tchaikovsky read Vasily Zhukovsky's translation of Friedrich Schiller's *Die Jungfrau von Orleans* while in Kamenka in the autumn of 1878.[25] In many ways, it was an astute choice for a libretto: the German dramatist's plays had long served as the source for some of Europe's most compelling operas, including Rossini's *Guillaume Tell* (1829), Donizetti's *Maria Stuarda* (1834) and Verdi's *Don Carlos* (1867). Work began as soon as Tchaikovsky was back in Europe in late 1878, first in Florence and then in Clarens and Paris, where he could consult additional historical sources, as well as an earlier opera on the same subject by the French composer Auguste Mermet (1876), which was itself based on a play by Jules Barbier (1873). The opera was drafted with incredible speed, not to say haste; Tchaikovsky completed the score by mid-February 1879, orchestrating it when back in Russia in the late spring and summer. Yet practical considerations meant that by the time *The Maid of Orleans* opened in St Petersburg at the Mariinsky Theatre on 13 February 1881, it had undergone a number of significant revisions. Originally, the role of Joan of Arc had been conceived for a dramatic soprano, but complications over casting meant that Tchaikovsky had to rewrite the part for Mariya Kamenskaya, a mezzo-soprano (this necessitated a number of fiddly changes to the orchestration as well). Further modifications were made in 1882, leading to a certain confusion about how the role should be performed; even in its revised form, it has a challenging tessitura that is beyond all but the most accomplished vocalists (this is perhaps one reason for the opera's comparative obscurity). Additionally Eduard Nápravník insisted on a number of cuts to the opera's long and frequently unwieldy score, just as he had with *Vakula*; it is testament to the conductor's tact and good sense that Tchaikovsky dedicated the opera to him all the same.

Although resources were limited (sets and costumes were reused from other productions, for instance), the new opera went down well on its opening night. Act I was especially warmly received, and rightly so, for it achieves a strikingly successful fusion of lyric intimacy and public drama. In many ways, it recalls both the atmosphere and structure of Act I of *Onegin*. In both cases, a young girl finds herself at odds with her family and community; seized by a strong and strange emotion – romantic love in the case of Tatyana, political and religious conviction in the case of Joan – both heroines sing an aria in which they commit themselves to the unknown consequences of their precipitate action (Joan's 'Farewell, ye valleys' beautifully links the physical setting of the heroine's childhood with her inner psychological landscape). Thereafter, the impression is more mixed, and it is strange to see Tchaikovsky – who had so decisively turned against the clichés of grand opera in *Eugene Onegin* – embrace them once again so heartily. To be sure, the depiction of Charles VII as a cowardly, lovelorn ruler who has lost sight of his regal vocation gives Act II a sense of private anguish, although the ballet numbers performed by his retinue of gypsies, dwarfs, clowns and tumblers fatally undermine the dramatic tension at a crucial moment. Thereafter, the interaction between lyric scenes and public tableaux is never as well handled as it is in Verdi's operas (Tchaikovsky claimed to dislike Verdi's own *Giovanna d'Arco* of 1845), and the tension between Joan's sacred visions and her profane love for Lionel, a Burgundian knight, is never adequately resolved. Too much off-stage action has to be reported indirectly, the crowd scenes are overblown, and the sprawling range of geographical settings – Joan's village of Domrémy, Charles' court at Chinon, the battlefield, Reims Cathedral, a wood, a square in Rouen, not to mention the evocation of Heaven by means of an off-stage chorus of angels – undercuts the heroine's psychological interiority. With *Eugene Onegin*, Pushkin's original was so familiar to Russian audiences that they could readily fill in the details that are missing from it in Tchaikovsky's opera. In *The Maid of Orleans*, by contrast, a canonical historical narrative is undone by sketchy characterization and dramatic inconsistency.

The main problem, however, was that *The Maid of Orleans* was never given a chance to establish itself in the repertoire. On 1 March, barely two weeks after the opera opened, Alexander II was assassinated by members of the Narodnaya Volya (People's Will), a revolutionary organization that had already made a number of unsuccessful attempts on his life. Theatres were closed for the rest of the season; *The Maid of Orleans* was briefly revived that autumn, and again in the winter of 1883–4, but after that it was not heard again during the composer's lifetime. It was also staged in Prague in 1882, becoming the first of Tchaikovsky's operas to be heard outside Russia – although this was not necessarily a sign of its exportability. Bohemia was then a centre for pan-Slavic patriotism; the performance of a Russian opera dealing with a nation's struggle against a foreign oppressor would certainly have nurtured the kind of anti-German sentiments that were prevalent there and which certainly struck Tchaikovsky during his successful visit to Prague in 1888.

Many of the issues that Tchaikovsky had faced in *The Maid of Orleans* resurfaced in his next opera, *Mazepa*. Based on a narrative poem by Pushkin, it deals with the historical character of Ivan Mazepa, who ruled Ukraine on behalf of Peter the Great until he betrayed the Tsar in favour of the Swedes at the battle of Poltava in 1709. Having fled with Charles xii of Sweden after Peter's victory at Poltava (the battle gives Pushkin's poem its title), he died in exile the following year. Whereas with *The Maid of Orleans* and *Eugene Onegin* Tchaikovsky had adapted an existing source text himself, with *Mazepa* he took a pre-existing libretto that had originally been written by Viktor Burenin for the cellist and composer Karl Davydov (although in a much later letter to Jurgenson, Tchaikovsky claimed to have adapted Burenin's text liberally).[26] Work progressed fitfully at first, but by 1882 Tchaikovsky began to write with greater fluency, completing the opera that September (the orchestration was ready by April 1883). Pushkin had written *Poltava* in 1828–9, attempting to ingratiate himself with Nicholas i by advocating a conservative and nationalist reading of Russian history, and indeed the story of Mazepa's treachery and Charles xii's defeat made for excellent official propaganda. Little wonder, then, that Tchaikovsky's operatic version was lavishly staged in both Moscow and St Petersburg, with productions opening at the Bolshoi Theatre on 3 February 1884 and at the Mariinsky Theatre just three days later. Unlike *The Maid of Orleans*, it rapidly established itself in the repertoire of Russia's opera houses, where it featured regularly right up until the outbreak of the First World War.[27]

Part of this success can be attributed to Imperial politics (*Mazepa* was staged in the Georgian capital, Tbilisi, in November 1885, for instance), yet the opera's achievements go beyond the merely circumstantial. Throughout it, Tchaikovsky downplays the historical and political context; the Battle of Poltava itself happens off-stage and is represented by the symphonic tableau that opens Act III. Instead, Tchaikovsky concentrates on the emotional predicament of his characters. The elderly Mazepa is in love with the young and beautiful Mariya, daughter of Kochubey. She, in turn, is loved by a young Cossack, Andrey. When Kochubey discovers that Mazepa and Mariya are in love, he denounces them. They elope, and in revenge Andrey and Kochubey denounce Mazepa. The Tsar does not believe their accusations, and has Kochubey delivered to Mazepa to be tortured; Mariya arrives too late to save her father from execution. After Mazepa's defeat at Poltava, he is attacked by Andrey, whom he fatally wounds in self-defence. Mariya, now out of her mind, appears; as Mazepa flees, she sings a lullaby to the dying Andrey.

Mazepa's great achievement is to distil the complex personal and political motivations that characterize Pushkin's original characters into the kind of heightened melodramatic action that can work so effectively on the operatic stage. The ensemble work is compelling, giving rise to a series of brilliant dramatic confrontations and credible, if extreme, emotions. The addition of a tenor role for Andrey heightened the opera's psychological conflict yet further, and alongside the four main leads, there is a major part for Mariya's mother, Lyubov. In addition to restoring a number of Pushkin's original verses, Tchaikovsky also commissioned Vasily Kandaurov to write the words for a new aria for Mazepa in Act II that would make it clear that his love for Mariya was sincere. He also changed Burenin's original ending, in which the deranged Mariya takes her life, witnessed by a crowd; in a daring theatrical coup, the opera now ended *pianissimo*, to the haunting sound of her tragic lullaby for the dying Andrey. Part of the success of the opera surely also lay in the quality of the first performances; four of the Six Romances, Op. 57 (1884) were dedicated to the singers who had created the roles of Mazepa (Bogomir Korsov), Lyubov (Alexandra Krutikova), Mariya (Emiliya Pavlovskaya) and Andrey (Dmitry Usatov) in the Moscow production that Tchaikovsky himself supervised.

Given its emotional concentration and heightened musical language, *Mazepa* can make for exhausting listening and viewing. It was an exhausting opera to compose, too, and Tchaikovsky was offended at the sum offered by Jurgenson for the score:

> Now something completely repellent has happened; the sum you propose for *Mazepa* bears *absolutely* no relationship to fairness, and I cannot leave matters without protesting. If I am not mistaken, even for *The Maid of Orleans* I received more than 1,000 roubles from you . . . But that was four years ago. How can it be that my price has not increased by a single penny in all this time? . . . When you were beginning to engrave *The Maid*, a production was still in doubt and her fate was not yet certain. Now, when both theatres in the capitals are anxious to receive the parts and scores for *Mazepa* from you, you name the sum of 1,000 roubles for an opera to which I dedicated two years and three months of painstaking work.[28]

Arguing that other publishers would have offered more, and that Jurgenson's fee was barely what he would have earned for a handful of songs or piano pieces, he demanded 2,000 roubles for the rights to the work, plus an additional 400 roubles for preparing the piano score and proofreading the parts. Jurgenson replied immediately and with the tact of both a true friend and an astute businessman:

> I have never liked the role of putting a price on your compositions, and I am very glad to see you taking advantage of your right to name the honorarium due to you. This is a thousand times more agreeable to me.[29]

Negotiations with the Imperial theatres were more complicated, with the official administration insisting on paying Tchaikovsky the fee for a three-act opera, despite his insistence that *Mazepa* was equal to a four-act work. This news was, however, offset by an offer of 10 per cent of the box-office receipts: more than the 8 per cent that was usual in such cases.[30]

The highly strung heroines of *The Maid of Orleans* and *Mazepa* have led some critics to read them as somehow indicative of Tchaikovsky's psychological make-up. Joan's inability to decide between love and duty leads to her destruction; and as Mariya's godfather, Mazepa's love borders on the incestuous in a way that echoes the earlier evocation of doomed and transgressive love in *Francesca da Rimini*.[31] Certainly Tchaikovsky showed a particular affinity with his tragic female characters, writing some of his most ardent music for them. This artistic empathy for the plight of his operatic heroines was matched by a more playful and self-conscious habit, employed in intimate correspondence with Modest, of referring to himself in the kind of grammatically feminine terms that are available in Russian, as well as sometimes disguising the gender of his sexual partners in similar fashion.[32]

But to insist too strongly on a supposed link between homosexuality and femininity is to subscribe to precisely the kind of reductive psychoanalytic readings of human identity that have been so detrimental to the composer's reputation. Tchaikovsky was certainly able to translate intense personal emotional into forceful musical expression, but alongside this was an equally significant engagement with genre. Turning to the instrumental works that Tchaikovsky wrote after the Symphony No. 4, one sees a fertile series of experiments in sonority and form above all. Moreover, although they sometimes have immediate biographical stimuli, they are more often than not abstract in conception. It is striking how few programmatic works Tchaikovsky wrote at this time; it is really only *The Year 1812* that conforms to this description, and this was written to an Imperial commission (the *Italian Capriccio*, Op. 45, of 1880 evokes something of the pleasures of his life in western Europe, as well as nodding to Glinka's Spanish-themed *Jota Aragonesa* and *Recollection of a Summer Night in Madrid*).

Whereas Tchaikovsky's operas were often based on important texts of European Romanticism (Pushkin's *Eugene Onegin* and *Poltava*, Schiller's *Die Jungfrau von Orleans*), his orchestral works are more emblematic of his long-standing interest in the eighteenth century. Take, for instance, the Piano Concerto No. 2, which he wrote in the autumn of 1879. Having finished the proofs of *The Maid of Orleans*, he was keen to indulge in a bout of what he referred to to von Meck as *dolce far niente* (idleness), yet soon found inspiration taking over.[33] More delicately scored than the Piano Concerto No. 1 (like the *Variations on a Rococo Theme* and the Violin Concerto, it does without trombones), it is also a more formal and elegant piece of musical rhetoric. Its opening gestures suggest a stylized version of some rococo serenade, and thereafter its constructional principle is sectional and contrastive, rather in the manner of a baroque *concerto grosso*. The inclusion of prominent solos for violin and cello in the slow movement harks back to the kind of lyric expressivity that Tchaikovsky adored in Mozart, and the interplay throughout the concerto between the pianist and various orchestral instruments heightens the sense that this is a *concertante* work, albeit one cast in grand, nineteenth-century style.

The concerto was dedicated to Nikolay Rubinstein, who had by now revised his poor opinion of the Piano Concerto No. 1. He died, however, before he could play the new work, so it seems entirely fitting that the composition that Tchaikovsky wrote to honour his memory should take the form of a trio for violin, cello and piano – the very sonority that he had explored in the 'Andante non troppo' of the concerto. Rubinstein died in Paris in March 1881, and despite the personal and professional disagreements that could occasionally mar their relationship, Tchaikovsky remained devoted to him. The death of Tchaikovsky's father in January 1880 had saddened, but not overwhelmed him; now, however, the death of a powerful father-figure brought forth a work of chamber music that was written on an ambitious, even symphonic, scale. Dedicated, rather tactfully, not to Rubinstein directly, but *À la mémoire d'un grand artiste*, it consists of just two substantial movements – an opening *Pezzo elegiaco* followed by a *Tema con variazioni* that alone takes half an hour to perform – which recall the bipartite form of Beethoven's final Piano Sonata No. 32 (1821–2).

Yet alongside the more obviously mournful and Romantic elements that frame the trio (it finishes with a funeral march marked *lugubre*), the Piano Trio also looks back to aspects of the eighteenth century in both form and tone, just at the Piano Concerto No. 2 had done. The variation technique that structures the long second movement allows Tchaikovsky to explore a series of more subtle textures, especially in the two dance movements – a waltz and a mazurka (there is also a more well-behaved fugue that pays tribute to the academic training on offer at the conservatory that Rubinstein headed). The playfulness of much of the trio may seem out of place in a work designed to mourn a recently deceased friend, yet in its use of old-fashioned genres, it delicately evokes the social milieu of the composer's early professional life in Moscow. Although the trio was dedicated to Rubinstein, Tchaikovsky conceived the individual parts for some of his most important living friends in Russia's second city: Jan H□ímal (violin), Wilhelm Fitzenhagen (cello) and Sergey Taneev (piano). The eighteenth century and its forms represented not just delight, but nostalgia too.

Tchaikovsky found the instrumental combination of violin, cello and piano a particularly unpleasant one and worked hard to 'orchestrate' his trio in a way that was agreeable to his inner ear. This process is one that can be heard in the other substantial orchestral works that Tchaikovsky wrote after the Symphony

No. 4: the three suites for orchestra (a fourth dates from 1887 and consists of arrangements of four pieces by Mozart) and the Serenade for Strings. To many, these works – especially the suites – have seemed trivial and occasional pieces that lack the emotional intensity and artistic inspiration of the symphonies or orchestral tone poems; even to Modest, Tchaikovsky admitted that he began work on what was to become the first of the suites out of a wish 'to say farewell to symphonic music for a long time'.[34] Yet this diffident claim is disproved by the very significant role that they played in his creative evolution and underestimates their considerable inherent interest too. Just as the three string quartets that he wrote between 1871 and 1876 helped him to work through issues of form and structure in his early career, so too do the orchestral suites represent a kind of creative laboratory for the works of his maturity. Although Tchaikovsky's letters and diaries of this time often complain of creative barrenness, the genesis of the suites shows just how attentively he listened to the dictates of form; while frequently setting out to write what he thought would be a new symphony, he would find his inspiration taking him in wholly unexpected directions, and he responded accordingly.[35]

The sense of creative renewal that was offered by the suites also applies to the Serenade for Strings, Op. 48, composed in late September and early October 1880. It certainly makes an interesting counterpart to the work that was to follow directly afterwards, *The Year 1812*, although as Tchaikovsky cautioned in a letter to von Meck, the circumstances of a work's composition often had little bearing on its quality:

First of all I must divide my works into two types, which is very important for an understanding of the process of composition.

1) Compositions which I write on my own initiative, as a result of spontaneous inclination and overwhelming inner compulsion.
2) Compositions which I write as a result of an external

impulse, at the request of a friend or a publisher, *to order* – such as happened, for instance, when I was commissioned to write a cantata for the opening of the Polytechnic Exhibition or was commissioned to write a march (Serbo-Russian) for a concert that the Russian Musical Society planned to hold in aid of the Red Cross, etc.

I should immediately qualify my comments. I know from experience that the quality of a composition does not depend on the type to which it belongs. It often happens that a work belonging to the second group, despite the fact that the initial impulse for its composition came from outside, has turned out entirely successfully, and by contrast, a work which I dreamed up myself has, for unrelated reasons, been less successful.[36]

Tchaikovsky was certainly well able to work within the constraints of an official commission; to some extent, in fact, his genius was as attuned to the discipline of form as it was to the lure of self-expression. Nonetheless, the Serenade is a work that shows him listening carefully to the dictates of his inner musical intuition. Having initially felt the work would be another symphony, he soon came to realize that his material was taking him in a very different direction.[37] As he wrote to von Meck in the summer of 1881, the Serenade soon became an act of homage to the eighteenth century: 'In the first movement I paid homage to my love of Mozart; this is a deliberate imitation of his manner, and I should be happy if you found that I was not too far from my chosen model.'[38]

Certainly, Tchaikovsky was under the particular spell of Mozart in the early 1880s, savouring performances of *Don Giovanni* in Moscow in 1882 and *The Magic Flute* at the conservatory there two years later.[39] Yet the Serenade has a deeper significance than merely revealing something of its composer's artistic tastes. Its beguiling melodic surface marks a sophisticated treatment of musical

Tchaikovsky aged 43, Moscow, 1884.

form and exemplifies just how intricate the relationship between European traditions and the Russian school was for Tchaikovsky. As he wrote to Taneev just before he began work on the Serenade,

> If, thanks to Peter the Great, we have *fatefully* found ourselves at the tail end of Europe, then we shall remain there forever. I appreciate very much the wealth of material which the *grubby and suffering people* produce, but we – that is, those of us who employ this material – will always develop it in forms borrowed from Europe, since although we are born as Russians, we are at the same time much more European, and their forms have been so profoundly and resolutely adopted and assimilated by us that in order to tear ourselves from them it would be necessary to commit acts of great violence and force, and from such violence and force nothing artistic can come.[40]

Despite the use of two folk tunes in its finale, there is nothing narrowly 'national' about the Serenade, just as there is nothing 'national' about the suites, other than their determination to demonstrate that Russian music had just as much right to consider itself part of the European mainstream as any other repertoire.

Looking back on his output from the perspective of the Suite No. 3 of 1884, Tchaikovsky explained the genre's significance to von Meck: 'This form is extremely appealing to me, since it offers no constraints at all and does not require me to subject myself to any traditions or rules.'[41] Even the genre of 'suite' was a potentially ambiguous one. Partly, it expressed his love of the eighteenth century; yet it looked forward, too, prefiguring aspects of early twentieth-century modernism with its emphasis on matters of form and surface texture (Igor Stravinsky, for example, was just one of Tchaikovsky's most evident heirs in this regard). The Suite No. 1, Op. 43, proved to be the most troublesome of all. Begun in the late summer of 1878, it was not completed until April the following year, and even then Tchaikovsky was uncertain about its overall shape, adding a further movement in August 1879. Its individual movements – *Introduzione e fuga, Divertimento, Intermezzo, Marche miniature, Scherzo* and *Gavotte* – allude to a number of eighteenth-century genres, with a particular emphasis on dance forms (the *Marche miniature* and *Scherzo* were originally entitled 'March of the Lilliputians' and 'Dance of the Giants' respectively). Yet if the suite is retrospective in form, its sound world is entirely contemporary. It is as if the kind of simplification that had characterized his operas after *Vakula the Smith* had created a concomitant need to explore more complex forms and sonorities in his purely orchestral works (at its first performance in Moscow in December 1879, Rubinstein complained that it was too difficult for the players). Much the same can be said about the Suite No. 2, Op. 53 (sometimes also known as the *Suite charactéristique*). Written in the summer of 1883 at Podushkino, Anatoly's dacha near Moscow, and orchestrated that same year at Sasha's estate at Verbovka, it takes the first suite's emphasis on instrumental colour to an entirely new level. Its first movement is explicitly entitled *Jeu de sons* (Play of sounds), and it is indeed the juxtaposition of different sounds that one hears most of all, both here and in the other four movements (Tchaikovsky even included optional parts for four accordions in the *Scherzo burlesque*).

The first two suites are charming, decorous works whose retrospective abstraction in matters of form and surface brilliance in matters of orchestral colour suggest that not all of Tchaikovsky's compositions should be read psychologically. By contrast, the Suite No. 3, Op. 55, is constructed on an altogether larger scale and has a strange, if inconclusive, connection with its composer's inner life. By 1884 he was beginning to think of writing a full-scale symphony again; yet, as he confessed to Taneev, 'I intended to write a symphony – but it didn't come off.'[42] The suite is certainly ambitiously conceived, taking almost as long to perform as any of the four symphonies that Tchaikovsky had written so far, and its emotional tone is darker than the other works with which it shares its nominal designation; the first movement is described as an *Elégie* and the second a *Valse mélancolique*. The *Dies Irae* is even quoted in the concluding *Tema con variazioni*. Written at Kamenka during the summer of 1884, it may owe something of its reflective quality to the tales he heard there from his sister's mother-in-law.[43] Alexandra Davydova was the widow of Vasily Davydov, a contemporary of Pushkin who had taken part in the failed Decembrist Revolution of 1825 that had sought to replace Russia's autocracy with some kind of constitutional form of government. Although Tchaikovsky's own politics were far from revolutionary, he was proud of his family's connection, through Pushkin (who had stayed at Kamenka in the 1820s), to a key moment in Russia's history. In all of Tchaikovsky's orchestral suites, the use of inherited musical genres becomes a way of encapsulating such historical continuities and of showing the presence of the past in the here and now.

The Suite No. 3 is also one of those rare works for which there exists a relatively comprehensive compositional history, as Tchaikovsky's diary for the summer of 1884 is one of the few such documents to have survived. Alongside satirical vignettes of the residents at Kamenka and an account of the composer's reading, card-playing, English lessons and long country walks, it traces the evolution of the suite in considerable detail. More tantalizingly, it also chronicles the composer's feelings for his twelve-year-old nephew, Vladimir (known affectionately within the family as Bob). Tchaikovsky had previously dedicated the *Children's Album* to his young nephew in 1878. Now, however, he was struck by a far more intense set of feelings. The first mention of Bob's charms comes some two weeks into Tchaikovsky's stay at Kamenka, on 24 April: 'All day, Bob captivated my glances; how incomparably sweet he is in his little white suit.' Nearly a month later, on 22 May, Bob's hold over Tchaikovsky had become total: 'As soon as I stop working or go out for a stroll (and that is also work for me), I begin to long for Bob and grow melancholy without him.'[44] The diary also includes a number of cryptic references to feelings referred to as X and Z; long held to allude to Tchaikovsky's homosexuality, these are now believed to indicate the dissatisfaction he felt at his excessive gambling, as well as his lack of gratitude for his family's hospitality.[45]

Read as a whole, the diary is a strange and fragmented document, more of an aide-memoire than an exercise in self-analysis. Yet whatever secrets the Suite No. 3 contains, it does not seem unreasonable to suggest that it might indeed owe something of its charm and wistfulness to the complex emotions that its composer experienced in the summer of 1884. And once again, Tchaikovsky's ability to translate personal predicaments into artistic form paid off; on its first performance in St Petersburg in January 1885, the suite was greeted with real enthusiasm by audience and critics alike. Tchaikovsky's pleasure is clear from the account of the concert that he gave to von Meck:

> A secret presentiment told me that my suite ought to please and entrance the audience . . . But reality far exceeded my expectations. Never before have I experienced such a triumph; I saw that the entire mass of the audience was moved and grateful to me. These moments are the finest adornments of an artist's life. Thanks to them it is worth living and labouring.[46]

The success of the first performance was repeated a week later in Moscow, with the suite becoming something of a calling card for its composer thereafter. He included the finale in concerts that he conducted in Hamburg, Prague, Paris and London in 1888 and subsequently gave the whole work on numerous occasions, including at New York's Carnegie Hall during his 1891 American tour (as Tchaikovsky noted in a letter to Jurgenson: 'My 3rd suite is, I think, the most *gratifying* of all my orchestral works for foreign audiences').[47] The Suite No. 3 had demonstrated, once again, that despite his personal shyness, Tchaikovsky's musical persona was one that vividly appealed to audiences.

5

'Where is My Home to Be?'

Between 1877 and 1885, Tchaikovsky lived an itinerant life, utilizing
von Meck's subsidy to support his extended sojourns in western
Europe during the winter and staying on the estates of friends and
relatives during the rest of the year. Yet such freedom brought with
it its own problems, not least a sense of homesickness when abroad.
He wrote to Modest from Paris in late 1884: 'somehow or other I
must have a *home* . . . it is becoming barbaric and strange to live
like a wandering star . . . Where is my home to be?'[1] Accordingly,
in early 1885, he took the decision to return to Russia permanently,
placing an advertisement on 1 January in a local newspaper that ran:
'Single person seeks dacha with estate for rent.'[2] By February he had
settled in the village of Maidanovo in the first of a series of homes
he would rent just outside Moscow (he would later live in Frolovskoe
and Klin as well). At this time, he also agreed to serve as director of
the Moscow branch of the Russian Musical Society, a position that
brought with it practical tasks such as examining and organizing
concerts, as well as the challenge of overseeing the management of
the Conservatory and negotiating with the Imperial administration.
From now on, Tchaikovsky was to become one of Russia's leading
public figures, and for a man whose nervous temperament was well
known to those closest to him, he proved himself surprisingly adept
at managing the burden of his growing fame.

Evidence of just how well known Tchaikovsky had become
came in the summer of 1886, when a certain Marie Lipsius (writing

Tchaikovsky standing in front of his house at Frolovskoe, 1890.

under the pseudonym of 'La Mara') approached Jurgenson for a copy of a letter she might include in an anthology of musicians' correspondence she was then compiling. Tchaikovsky's reply to Jurgenson is so revealing that it is worth quoting in its entirety:

> Dear friend,
> I well understand the difficulty of your situation. You are asked for some letter or other of mine to print; you have several hundred of them – yet there is not a single one which would be suitable in the given situation. This is understandable: our correspondence has always been either too practical or too intimate. But how can I assist you in your misfortune? Can I not, for the pleasure of appearing in Mme *La Mara*'s book, commit an act of forgery, that is write a letter especially for her collection, and take advantage of this convenient occasion to display myself as a musician, thinker and man in the most favourable light? Such a sacrifice on the altar of European fame sickens me, although on the other hand, I should be guilty of telling a lie if I tried to assure you that I was

Tchaikovsky aged 50 at Frolovskoe, 1890.

not at all flattered by Mme *La Mara*'s desire to add me to the
number of eminent musicians of our time. On the contrary, I
am very touched and flattered by the attention of this famous
author and admit with complete sincerity that I should be happy
to appear in the company of Glinka, Dargomyzhsky and Serov.
Had there been enough time, it would have been possible to
approach one of my musical friends, *Laroche*, for example, who

has a number of my letters with detailed outpourings of my musical delights and displeasures – in a word, letters where I express myself with complete sincerity as a musician. But there is no time, and Laroche is far away. Is it not curious that it appears to be so difficult to find a letter from a man who has conducted and still conducts a vast correspondence, such as only a person engaged in artistic labour, and not in enterprise and industry, can conduct? I conduct a constant written correspondence with my four brothers, my sister, several cousins, and a multitude of friends and acquaintances, and in addition to this I have a vast casual correspondence with people who often I do not know at all. Frequently I am so burdened by the necessity of giving over too great a portion of my time to correspondence that I inwardly curse all the postal organizations in the world. The post very often causes me painful moments, but it also brings me the greatest of joys. There is an individual who has played a pre-eminent role in the story of my life for the last ten years; this individual is my guardian angel, and I am obliged to her for my entire good fortune and for the fact that I can devote myself entirely to my beloved work – and yet I have never seen her, never heard the sound of her voice, and all my relations with her are exclusively postal. So in general one might say that I flood the entire world with my correspondence, and yet still I cannot extricate you from your difficulty.

There remains but one thing to do: to send to Mme *La Mara* my present letter. If it gives no sense at all of my character as a musician, then at least it will allow you to satisfy this author's desire, so flattering to me, to include my person among the eminent.

Goodbye!

Your

P. Tchaikovsky[3]

One can imagine Lipsius's delight at receiving this letter, which is not just an engaging literary document in its own right, but an acute analysis of modern celebrity. Tchaikovsky is at once intimate and unknowable here; he alludes to details of a private life that remain confidential between himself and his publisher, while also revealing how his public persona is constructed through networks of correspondence and publication. Even von Meck – whose patronage he had long struggled to keep secret – is referred to in a manner that simultaneous breaks and keeps intimate personal confidences.

The circumstances of Tchaikovsky's everyday life at this time mapped on to a shift in his aesthetics too. The composer's eventual recovery after his marriage had occasioned a series of orchestral works that favoured abstract questions of form and sonority over apparent self-dramatization. Now, however, in his *Manfred* symphony, he returned to programme music as a powerful means of translating his inner emotional experiences into artistic form, while simultaneously engaging with contemporary audiences through suggestive musical narrative. The libretto for *Manfred* was initially written by Vladimir Stasov, who offered it to Balakirev and Berlioz as early as 1867, although both composers turned it down. In the intervening years, Balakirev had undergone a spiritual and artistic crisis, withdrawing from public life to work as a railway clerk. By the 1880s, however, he was back on the musical scene in St Petersburg, and in the autumn of 1882 he wrote to Tchaikovsky with a detailed literary narrative suitable for musical treatment. Initially, at least, Tchaikovsky equivocated; after the Symphony No. 2 and *Vakula the Smith*, his relations with the Kuchka had become more distant, and in any case the arch-Romanticism of Byron's tale was out of keeping with the stylized classicism that he was then exploring in the orchestral suites and the Serenade for Strings. By October 1884, however, Tchaikovsky had begun to think seriously about *Manfred*; work on the new symphony took place between April and September the following year – the first product of his new life at Maidanovo.

Tchaikovsky's own programme for *Manfred* describes its hero as 'wearied by the fatal questions of existence, tormented by hopeless longings and the memory of past crimes'.[4] The reference to 'past crimes' has led some to read autobiographical significance into the symphony. Indeed, the plot of Byron's original poem, with its suggestion of an incestuous affair between the hero and his beloved, Astarte (itself based on Byron's own rumoured involvement with his half-sister, Augusta), might be taken by some to be a covert narrative of homosexual psychopathology. Yet such interpretations distract from the work's other, more pertinent biographical traits. Tchaikovsky, now settled in his new home, might well have seen Manfred's wanderings through the Alps as somehow redolent of his own itinerant years, just as the work's setting may have recalled his visits to Switzerland in late 1884, where Josef Kotek, once a close friend, was confined to a sanatorium in Davos (he died there in early 1885). Yet once again, what is most significant about *Manfred* is not so much its confessional aspect, as its extraordinary formal inventiveness. In his first four symphonies, Tchaikovsky had shown ever greater confidence in adapting the inherited structures of the European classical symphony to his own imaginative ends. Now, he relied on his dramatic instinct, melodic ingenuity and flair for orchestral colour to create a vast structure that, at around an hour in performance, is longer than any orchestral work he had yet written – or would ever write again.

Superficially, it retains the four movements of the standard Austro-German symphony, but in tone it is closer to Berlioz's *Symphonie fantastique* (1830). Indeed, in the first movement, Tchaikovsky did without the conventional underpinnings of sonata form altogether; later on, when he had grown dissatisfied with the work, he suggested to Grand Duke Konstantin that he would like to recast the first movement as a symphonic poem in its own right, and this observation gives a clue to his practice in the symphony as a whole.[5] In *Manfred*, each movement is constructed as a series of tableaux that suggest individual scenes from Byron's poem yet do not follow its narrative directly. Such an innovative work was not without its risks. Writing to Taneev, Tchaikovsky worried about the work's potential popularity with audiences: 'When composing a programme symphony, I feel as if I am swindling the public like a charlatan; I am paying them not with sonorous coin, but with torn notes of credit.'[6] And to Jurgenson he expressed his anxiety that the work would not recoup the costs of its publication:

> *Manfred*, even if it is a work of genius, is the kind of symphony that because of its unusual complexity and difficulty can be played only once every ten years; for this reason, it cannot make any money for you . . . On the other hand, I value it very highly, but how can one put a price on such a thing in money?[7]

In fact, the work proved to be rather more popular than Tchaikovsky feared; it was warmly received at its premiere in Moscow in March 1886, and was heard three times in St Petersburg that same year, as well as in New York.

With its debts to Stasov and Balakirev, *Manfred* is a work profoundly shaped by the realist aesthetics of the 1860s. Likewise, the Symphony No. 5 also attests to the kind of extra-musical elements that had long been central to Russian music. Early sketches for the first movement contain the outline of a programme suggesting religious revelation:

> *Programme:* 1st movement of symph.
> Intr. Total submission before fate, or, which is the same thing, the inscrutable designs of Providence.
> Allegro. I) Murmurs, doubts, laments, reproaches against . . . xxx
> II) Shall I cast myself into the embrace of *faith*???
> A wonderful programme, if only it can be fulfilled.[8]

Tchaikovsky aged 46, Paris, 1886.

Although the direct relationship between this programme and the finished work is far from clear, the possibility of some kind of spiritual narrative seems at least feasible. Tchaikovsky's letters and diaries at this time attest to a rebirth of his religious feelings, even if his attitude to organized Christianity was always rather uncertain.[9] The musical journey charted by the symphony suggests some kind of movement from darkness to light; the lugubrious E-minor opening of the first movement is transformed into a radiant E major by the end, and the finale is characterized by a seeming optimism unsurpassed in any of the other symphonies.

Yet the Symphony No. 5 was equally the product of Tchaikovsky's engagement with the musical tastes of western Europe. Writing to Modest from Paris in May 1886, he noted the current vogue for Russian literature, recommending Eugène Melchior de Vogüé's *Le Roman russe* as 'this excellent book'.[10] He expressed similar sentiments to von Meck, wondering when music would have its turn:

> How pleasant it is to convince oneself with one's own eyes of the success that our literature is enjoying in France. All the étalages [displays] of the bookshops are adorned with translations of Tolstoy, Turgenev, Dostoevsky, Pisemsky, Goncharov. In the newspapers one is forever coming across enthusiastic articles about one or other of these writers. Perhaps it will soon be the turn of Russian music too![11]

Tchaikovsky was more prescient than he perhaps realized. César Cui's *La Musique en Russie* had already appeared in book form in 1880 (its individual chapters had been serialized in the *Revue et gazette musicale de Paris* between 1878 and 1880), and although his views on Tchaikovsky were distinctly partisan and often hostile, it nonetheless became an important source for Western audiences keen to learn more about Russian music.[12] Then, in 1885, Félix Mackar bought the rights to distribute Tchaikovsky's works in

France and Belgium for the impressive sum of 20,000 francs, split equally between the composer and his Russian publisher.[13]

These developments were not, on their own, enough to promote Tchaikovsky's works abroad. It was, above all, his role as a conductor of his own compositions that cemented his reputation, first in western Europe and then in America. He made his debut as a conductor with the premiere of *Cherevichki* (the revised version of *Vakula*) in January 1887, and news of this development led to ever more frequent offers to conduct his own works abroad. The first of these came in the summer of 1887, when Tchaikovsky received an invitation from the publisher Daniel Rahter (who held the rights to his works in the German-speaking world) to undertake an extensive concert tour early the next year that included Leipzig, Berlin and Hamburg, followed by Paris, London and Prague. In each city he was enthusiastically received by audiences and professional colleagues, yet critical responses to his compositions could be decidedly ambiguous; all too often, he was seen as some primitive and untutored embodiment of the 'Russian soul', something that went against his ingrained sense of discipline and well-honed command of musical technique. It would be some time before Western audiences began to see him as the thoroughgoing professional that he was.

Tchaikovsky found it easy enough to overlook the kind of hasty criticisms he found in the press, but an encounter with Theodor Avé-Lallement, president of the Hamburg Philharmonic Society, produced a very different reaction. Writing in his *Autobiographical Account of a Foreign Tour in 1888*, Tchaikovsky recalled his meeting with Avé-Lallement in Hamburg:

> Almost with tears in his eyes, he exhorted me to leave Russia and settle permanently in Germany, where classical traditions and conditions of the highest culture would not fail to correct my shortcomings, which in his view

Tchaikovsky aged 47, Hamburg, 1888.

could be easily explained by the fact that I was born and educated in a land still little enlightened and lagging far behind Germany as far as progress was concerned.[14]

Rather than take offense at such condescending views, Tchaikovsky replied by dedicating his Symphony No. 5 – composed between May and August that year – to his detractor. To be sure, it is a work full of characteristic touches, such as a recurrent fate motif, frequent dance-like passages in the opening movement, the languid melancholy of the slow second movement, the third-movement waltz and the manic energy of the finale, all of which might have been dismissed by German critics as stereotypically Russian. Yet the symphony is also a calculated response to Avé-Lallement's suggestion that Tchaikovsky should learn from the German tradition. Its four movements are handsomely proportioned and show little of the novel approach to form witnessed in his earlier orchestral works; in particular, the opening allegro has a densely worked motivic integrity that verges on Beethoven's practice, and the lyric writing for woodwind and horn in the second-movement andante is reminiscent of Brahms.

This suggestion of a parallel with Brahms is not accidental. The two composers met in December 1887, and Brahms arranged to attend a rehearsal of the Symphony No. 5 before its German premiere in Hamburg in February 1889 during another of Tchaikovsky's extended conducting tours of western Europe. Relations between the two men were respectful, if not exactly cordial, and although Brahms seems to have admired the new symphony, he had little time for the bombast of its finale. Tchaikovsky, by contrast, claimed to admire Brahms's technique, but found his music itself soulless and barren. As he wrote to Konstantin Romanov: 'In the music of this master (and mastery cannot, of course, be denied in him) there is something dry and cold that alienates my heart.'[15] Strikingly, the opening allegro of the Symphony No. 5 is described as being '*con anima*', as is the moderato central section of its second-movement andante. If the new work was in part a response to Brahms (or, rather, to the cult of Brahms's music that dominated much German criticism at the time), then in paying homage to his command of form, Tchaikovsky also insisted on the equal importance of emotional warmth.

Patronizing German attitudes to his music were always only one of the possible responses to Tchaikovsky's music; in Paris and London, his works were generally received with greater enthusiasm and understanding. Moreover, as he travelled, Tchaikovsky found himself exposed to other currents in contemporary music. French music had always appealed to him, and while in Prague in 1888 he met Antonín Dvořák, whose compositions charted a course midway between discipline and imagination, inherited form and local colour, which was not unlike his own practice. The music of Edvard Grieg also suggested that the geography of European music was subtly changing, as voices from the peripheries challenged the values of the supposed centre. Tchaikovsky met the Norwegian composer while in Leipzig in early 1888, striking up an affectionate relationship with him and his wife, Nina, and his description of Grieg's music reads rather like a version of what mattered to him most as an artist:

> Perfection of form, strictness and impeccable logicality in the development of themes . . . are not things that we will insistently seek in this famous Norwegian; but what charm, what immediacy and wealth of musical invention! How much warmth and passion there is in his singing phrases, what life pours forth in his harmony, how much originality and delightful individuality in his witty, piquant modulations, and in his rhythm, which is, like everything else, so interesting, new and distinctive! If we add to all of these rare qualities complete and utter simplicity, devoid of all preciosity and pretention to

unheard of depths and novelty . . . then it is no surprise that Grieg is so beloved and that he is popular everywhere.[16]

If Tchaikovsky, Dvořák and Grieg were composers who belonged to the same generation and could hence look on the older Brahms as a source of ambivalent inspiration, then a final encounter that took place during the tour of 1888 shows how Tchaikovsky's music was to point a way forward too. That January, he met a promising young conductor in Leipzig: Gustav Mahler. Mahler was to become an early exponent of Tchaikovsky's music abroad, conducting the German premieres of *Eugene Onegin* (January 1892) and *Iolanta* (January 1893); the Viennese premieres of *Onegin* (November 1897), *Iolanta* (March 1900) and *The Queen of Spades* (December 1902); and eventually the North American premiere of *The Queen of Spades* at New York's Metropolitan Opera in March 1910. He certainly knew Tchaikovsky's symphonies, too, and his own experiments in this genre owe not a little to the example of his Russian precursor. In copying, without ever entirely assimilating, existing models, Tchaikovsky would not just establish a Russian symphonic tradition but would create powerful examples for subsequent generations of European composers to emulate.

Tchaikovsky was all too aware that many of his previous stage works had been marred by fussy libretti and overly complex music; accordingly, his 1885 revision of *Vakula* had sought to rectify such perceived problems by simplifying the stage action and thinning the orchestral textures. However, *Cherevichki* (as it was now called) received just a handful of performances in early 1887 and thereafter was never to be heard again in its composer's lifetime. It is all the more ironic, then, that Tchaikovsky's next opera, *The Enchantress*, was to intensify the problems that had prevented the successful reception of his earlier operas. Work on the score extended over nearly two years, from September 1885 to May 1887, and was constantly interrupted by Tchaikovsky's frequent visits to Moscow and St Petersburg on official business, as well as by a number of trips abroad. Ippolit Shpazhinsky's original historical melodrama deals with the fate of a young widow, Nastasya, who runs a local hostelry. She is reputed to be a sorceress and is involved with both Prince Yury and his father Nikita. Nikita's wife has her rival poisoned; Nikita kills his own son out of jealous rivalry, and the opera ends with his descent into madness.

Superficially at least, the play seemed like a promising source of drama and conflict, and Tchaikovsky wrote with genuine enthusiasm. Yet Shpazhinsky found it difficult to adapt his original five-act stage play, and the libretto remained wordy and static. Tchaikovsky did his best, compressing the text where he could – even during the first dress rehearsals in September 1887. If *The Enchantress* works at all, it is because the music genuinely dramatizes the emotional predicament of its protagonists; yet Tchaikovsky ultimately realized that an opera could not rest on its music alone. Reaction to its premiere in October 1887 was muted, and Tchaikovsky knew exactly who was at fault: 'the blame lies with me', he wrote to his librettist's wife, Yuliya Shpazhinskaya,

and primarily with Ippolit Vasilyevich. He has an excellent understanding of the stage, yet is still insufficiently attuned to the demands of opera. There are too many *words* in him, *conversation* dominates the lyricism too much. And however much I shortened his text, whatever *cuts* I was obliged to make, the scenes generally came out too long. But for much I too am to blame.[17]

As well as revealing Tchaikovsky's ongoing struggles with the demands of operatic form, *The Enchantress* sheds significant light on his public status in Imperial Russia. For all the complexity involved in collaborating with librettists, performers and administrators, opera continued to appeal to him precisely because it enabled him to engage with a broad public that was essential to both his financial security and artistic fame. To von Meck, who expressed a preference for his orchestral works, Tchaikovsky offered the following defence of his stage works:

> there is something irresistible which draws all composers to opera: it is the fact that opera alone gives you the means to communicate with *the masses* of the public. My *Manfred* will be played once or twice and will then disappear for a long time, and no one, except a handful of connoisseurs who attend symphony concerts, will recognize it. Whereas opera, and opera alone, brings you closer to people, establishes a relation between your music and the genuine public, makes you the property not only of small individual circles but also, if conditions are favourable, of the whole nation.[18]

Alongside Tchaikovsky's interest in the 'genuine public', his involvement with opera was equally tied up with his relationship to the Russian court. As he wrote to von Meck in March 1885, he saw Russia's autocratic regime as the only one able to guarantee the nation's survival:

> There was a time when I was completely sincere in my belief that in order to remove capricious government and inculcate the rule of law and order we needed all sorts of political institutions like land gatherings, parliaments, councils, etc., and all one had to do was introduce something like this and everything would be wonderful and everybody would be happy. Now, it is not that I have gone over to the camp of the ultraconservatives, but I have at least begun to doubt the validity of such institutions . . . I have come to the conclusion that there is no ideal form of government and that people are condemned in this respect to feel disappointment

until the end of time . . . One might ask whether there is
someone we can rely on? I reply: yes, and that person is
the Tsar. He made a charming impression on me as an
individual, but regardless of these personal impressions
I am inclined to see in him a good ruler . . . I like the fact
that he does not court popularity, I like his blameless life
and in general, that he is an honest and kind person.[19]

Tchaikovsky's political views were undoubtedly shaped by
Imperial patronage, too. His Twelve Romances, Op. 60 (written
at great speed between 18 August and 9 September 1886) were
dedicated to the Empress, Mariya Fyodorovna. Similarly,
the Six Romances, Op. 63 (1887), set to the poetry of Grand
Duke Konstantin Romanov, to whom the set is also dedicated.
Tchaikovsky even aspired to dedicate *The Enchantress* to the Tsar
himself, and although nothing came of this audacious piece of
obsequiousness, on 31 December 1887, Alexander III decreed
that the composer should receive a life pension of 3,000 roubles
a year. Alongside the fees and box office receipts he received for
commissions from Russia's musical institutions, this annuity
became a welcome source of additional income for the composer.

The arts had always been central to how the Romanovs 'staged'
their claim as Russia's autocratic rulers,[20] and under Alexander
III and Nicholas II, Imperial support for opera, ballet and theatre
reached new heights. Funding for sets and costumes was lavish,
and leading singers, dancers, conductors and choreographers
were engaged to ensure the prestige of the Imperial institutions.
Tchaikovsky, as Russia's leading composer and one of the nation's
best-known and best-loved artists, was one of the most immediate
beneficiaries of this policy, especially after the retirement of
Léon (Ludwig) Minkus as resident ballet composer in 1886. Ivan
Vsevolozhsky – director of the Imperial Theatres from 1881 – had
already commissioned a new écossaise to be used in the final act of

the production of *Eugene Onegin* that was staged at the Mariinsky
Theatre in September 1885, thus restoring to Tchaikovsky's intimate
lyric drama some of the conventions of grand opera which it had
originally rejected. To those who remembered it, *Swan Lake* had
proved Tchaikovsky more than able to write ballet music of the
highest calibre too, and much of his symphonic and orchestral
music had employed gestures and genres borrowed from the world
of dance. It was therefore unsurprising when, in 1886, Vsevolozhsky
commissioned a new ballet from him, although his initial
suggestions for libretti – Flaubert's *Salammbô* and Fouqué's *Undine*
– came to nothing. Only in May 1888 did Vsevolozhsky propose
a scenario that seemed sure to pique the composer's interest:

> I have been thinking of writing a libretto on Perrault's fairy
> tale *La belle au bois dormant*. I want to stage it in the style
> of Louis XIV, allowing the musical fantasy to run high and
> melodies to be written in the spirit of Lully, Bach, Rameau,
> and such-like. If this idea is to your liking, why shouldn't you
> undertake to compose the music? In the last act there will
> be a quadrille made from all Perrault's fairy tales – Puss in
> Boots, Tom Thumb, Cinderella, Bluebeard, and such-like.[21]

Tchaikovsky was certainly taken with the idea, although work
on the new score was interrupted by his frequent performing
engagements. He set down his first ideas that October, before
conducting premieres of the Symphony No. 5 in St Petersburg,
Moscow and Prague (where he also gave the first foreign
performance of *Eugene Onegin*). He returned to the score in earnest
in January 1889, before once again leaving for an extensive
European tour that took in Berlin, Cologne, Frankfurt, Dresden,
Leipzig, Geneva, Hamburg, Paris and London. It was not until
May that he found himself back in Russia, and the score was
finally completed by early autumn.

In the case of *The Enchantress*, such hiatuses had fatally undermined the opera's dramaturgical coherence. With *The Sleeping Beauty*, however, this risk was counteracted by Tchaikovsky's fruitful collaboration not only with Vsevolozhsky, but with the ballet's choreographer, Marius Petipa. Previously, composers had been presented with a finished libretto in which the choreographer's demands were paramount; now, composer and choreographer worked closely with each other to produce a score that not only accommodated all the set-piece requirements of the genre but also had an inherent musical coherence of its own. Nonetheless, Tchaikovsky's new score – along with Petipa's evocative choreography – was not an immediate success. At its official dress rehearsal on 2 January 1890, audience reaction was respectful rather than enthusiastic and even Alexander III's reaction amounted to nothing more than a condescending 'very nice!!!'[22] Certainly the press showed itself unable to grasp what Tchaikovsky and Petipa had achieved in their synthesis of stage action and musical narrative. Yet the appeal of Tchaikovsky's music and the charisma of Petipa's choreography – abetted, no doubt, by the virtuosity of Mariinsky's dancers and the extravagance of Vsevolozhsky's sets – meant that the ballet did establish itself in the Imperial repertoire. Indeed, so familiar has *The Sleeping Beauty* become that it is hard for modern audiences to intuit the revolutionary nature of its original conception; if *Swan Lake* was a false start, only to be appreciated in retrospect, then *The Sleeping Beauty* represents a decisive moment in the history of modern ballet. It also proved how readily Tchaikovsky could write music of genius within the context of official commissions and – in the case of ballet – practical limitations on his creative freedom. In *The Sleeping Beauty*, his inspiration flowed with seeming spontaneity, showing how he could simultaneously identify with the self-dramatizing romanticism of Byron's *Manfred* and the affable luminosity of Vsevolozhsky's eighteenth-century pastiche.

Barely had *The Sleeping Beauty* opened than Tchaikovsky found himself in receipt of a further Imperial commission, this time for a new opera. The libretto for *The Queen of Spades* had originally been begun by his brother Modest for another composer, Nikolay Klenovsky, in 1887, although this particular collaboration came to nothing (Nikolay Solovyov also turned down the opportunity to set the libretto). Tchaikovsky took Modest's draft with him to Florence in January 1890, completing the score at extraordinary speed by early March (it was orchestrated by the end of May). More than the swiftness of its composition, *The Queen of Spades* impresses by the conviction of its dramatic form and shows just how acutely Tchaikovsky had learned from the unhappy experience of *The Enchantress*. Writing to Mikhail Ippolitov-Ivanov, he gave notice of a new direction in his compositional practice:

> For a long time I imagined that there was no need to think about the *dramatic side*, and that the music would fend for itself despite all the deficiencies of the libretto. Experience has now taught me that for an opera to be successful in the long run, one must give the most careful consideration to the details of the drama.[23]

Accordingly, Tchaikovsky worked very closely with his brother on every detail of the libretto, demanding revisions, compressions, cuts and – occasionally – additional material as the opera took shape.

The source of the libretto is Pushkin's famous short story 'The Queen of Spades' (1834), in which a young officer, Hermann, seeks to make his fortune by extracting from an aged and wealthy countess a secret formula for winning at cards. Cynically courting her ward Lisa, he gains access to the countess's house. Once in her boudoir, Hermann threatens her with an unloaded gun; she dies, claiming that the secret was 'just a joke'.[24] After attending her funeral, Hermann is visited by the ghost of the countess, who reveals the secret: 'the three, the seven and the ace'.[25] He duly presents himself at a gaming house, winning with the three and the seven, but losing when he plays his final card – not the expected ace, but the queen of spades. Hermann goes mad and is confined to an asylum; meanwhile, Lisa makes an advantageous marriage, as well as acquiring a ward of her own.

What makes the literary 'Queen of Spades' so special – just like *Eugene Onegin* before it – is the sophistication of its construction and playfulness of its narrative tone of voice. Pushkin relates the events of the story in an ironic fashion that exemplifies his search for 'brevity' and 'precision' in prose fiction; its characters are literary archetypes and parodies rather than psychologically credible individuals, and the reader constantly hesitates in an attempt to adjudicate between real and supernatural interpretations of its meaning.[26] All of these facets are, it seems, lost in Tchaikovsky's version, with its emphasis on melodrama and emotional intensity. In the opera, Herman (his name is spelled with a single 'n') is truly in love with Lisa and hence finds himself caught between emotion and ambition; Lisa – now transformed into the countess's granddaughter and granted a high-society fiancé in the form of Prince Yeletsky – responds to his betrayal by drowning herself; when the secret fails to win him a fortune, Herman shoots himself.

Predictably enough, most criticisms of the first performance on 7 December 1890 focused on the shortcomings of Modest's libretto and its departures from Pushkin's seemingly untouchable original. Tchaikovsky's music was more warmly received, and productions rapidly followed in Kiev, Moscow, Kharkov, Saratov and Odessa, as well as in Prague and Hamburg. Yet the opera is a far more original and sophisticated treatment of Pushkin's original than has often been appreciated; just as Tchaikovsky's *Eugene Onegin* reads like a novel of the 1820s through the prism of mid-century psychological realism, so *The Queen of Spades* transposes a text from one era into the very different aesthetics of the present – this time, the *fin de siècle*.[27] At first glance this might seem like an eccentric view, since one of Vsevolozhsky's most idiosyncratic interventions had been to situate the action during the reign of Catherine the Great in the second half of the eighteenth century in order to allow for the inclusion of a pastoral interlude, *The Faithful Shepherdess*, in Act II. This interlude – which holds up the action in an opera that is otherwise terse and brooding – can seem at best an eccentricity and at worst a craven acquiescence to the kind of pageantry required by the Imperial stage. Yet for all its apparent dramatic redundancy, it signals a crucial facet of the opera: its haunting temporal ambiguity, which is present not just in Tchaikovsky's Act II Mozartian pastiche, but in almost every other scene too. In Act I, Lisa and her friend Polina sing stylized salon romances with words by the early nineteenth-century poets Vasily Zhukovsky and Konstantin Batyushkov, which, in fact, post-date the opera's ostensible action. In Act II, the countess recalls her glittering youth by singing an aria from André-Ernest-Modeste Grétry's *Richard Coeur-de-lion*; yet since this particular work dates from 1784, it cannot be anything but contemporary with the action of Tchaikovsky's opera.[28]

Pushkin's original derives much of its impact from the way in which it parodies existing literary forms; it adroitly fuses elements of the society tale, the gothic story, the folk tale and even elements of nascent realism to produce a work that is truly *sui generis*. This sense of stylization extends to the self-conscious treatment of the literary origins of the main operatic characters too. At the opening of Pushkin's story, the reader suspects that Lisa's fate will be the same as that of her namesake in Nikolay Karamzin's sentimental tale 'Poor Lisa' (1792), in which the peasant heroine, rejected by her noble suitor, drowns herself in a lake. Tchaikovsky's libretto cleverly restores the sentimental eighteenth-century archetype that Pushkin himself had originally suppressed.

But it is the figure of Herman who most completely embodies the opera's sense of synchronicity. A brooding and demonic outsider (Pushkin describes him as having 'the profile of Napoleon and the soul of Mephistopheles'),[29] he is conspicuously out of place in Vsevolozhsky's eighteenth-century world; rather, he steps from the pages of a Dostoevsky novel, bringing with him the atmosphere of the city of St Petersburg as it had been depicted in the works of a whole host of nineteenth-century writers after Pushkin. The Tchaikovsky brothers even managed their own covert homage to Pushkin's interest in numerology, the presence of which in *The Queen of Spades* has long stretched the inventiveness and credulity of critics. Cast in three acts and seven scenes, the opera encodes the countess's secret in its very structure, as do Herman's oft-repeated three-note mantra ('*tri karty, tri karty, tri karty*' in Russian) and a striking number of phrases made up of three and seven syllables.[30] Little wonder, then, that *The Queen of Spades* appealed so much to a new generation of artists – and one, moreover, who was to prove so decisive in the development of Russian modernism. The artist Alexandre Benois – who had already hailed *The Sleeping Beauty* as the ultimate *Gesamtkunstwerk* (Wagner's term for a single dramatic work that synthesized all of the arts) – adored the new opera, as did other members of his circle, for whom the eighteenth century was a presentiment of their own era.[31] Sergey Diaghilev, even before he thought to dazzle Paris audiences with his evocations of exotic Russian barbarism, was fascinated by the rococo, staging a major exhibition of portraits unearthed from Russian country houses in 1905.[32]

That Tchaikovsky was able to evoke the spectral world of Pushkin's Petersburg in *The Queen of Spades* while resident in Florence is testament both to the intensity of his creative imagination and his profound identification with the emotional world of its main characters. He was moved to tears as he penned Herman's final scene; here, it was a male character who stirred the composer's compassion, rather than an ill-fated operatic heroine. Yet, if *The Queen of Spades* is pervaded by the half-light of Russia's northern capital, Tchaikovsky's Italian sojourn nonetheless found an outlet elsewhere. On completing his opera, he set about recording his impressions of the last few months in the form of a four-movement string sextet, the *Souvenir de Florence*, completed during the summer of 1890 and revised the following winter. As a composition, it does not yield to any particular biographical reading; it is certainly not a diary of his day-to-day life in the Tuscan city. Yet it does evoke something of the sunlit mood of the south in its radiant, open textures and unfeigned and spontaneous sense of joy. Equally, it attests to Tchaikovsky's profound and ongoing interest in issues of form and sonority, harking back to the three string quartets of the 1870s, as well as the orchestral suites and Serenade for Strings that followed them. The sextet may also be read as a contribution to the development of Russian music more generally; written at the request of the St Petersburg Chamber Music Society, it shows Tchaikovsky adding to the still very slim body of Russian chamber music in existence at the time (as well as perhaps nodding in the direction of Brahms, whose first string sextet was a work that he knew and – somewhat exceptionally – tentatively admired).[33]

Something of the luminosity of the *Souvenir de Florence* can be sensed in Tchaikovsky's next opera too. Based on *King René's Daughter* (1845) by the Danish playwright Henrik Herz, *Iolanta* was commissioned by Vsevolozhsky in December 1890 as part of a double-bill to include a new ballet, *The Nutcracker*. As with *The Queen of Spades*, the opera's libretto was prepared by Modest, and the draft score was written between July and September 1891 (the orchestration was finished by December). Conceived in a single act, *Iolanta* is Tchaikovsky's shortest opera and has a simple, allegorical plot that takes place in fifteenth-century Burgundy (Iolanta is the Russian version of the French name Yolande). Though blind since birth, Iolanta is ignorant of her condition. A Moorish physician, Ibn-Hakia, insists that she will be cured only when she learns of her blindness, yet her father, King René, refuses to act on his advice. Meanwhile, Iolanta's betrothed, Prince Robert, hopes to be released from his vow, as he is in love with another. He comes to the castle with his friend Count Vaudemont, who immediately falls in love with Iolanta. When Vaudemont realizes that she is blind, he innocently explains the meaning of sight to her. The force of his love as well as Iolanta's own desire to see cure her.

Iolanta is, to be sure, a strange work on first encounter, yet its strangeness is also the source of its fascination. Though it may lack obvious dramatic tension, it makes up for this by means of an expressive intensity that is more often than not the result of Tchaikovsky's extraordinary delicate and inventive orchestration (as well as, of course, of his bountiful melodic gift). More a series of lyric tableaux than a carefully elaborated piece of drama, *Iolanta* subtly delineates the inner world of its protagonists. Some might interpret Iolanta's blindness as a metaphor for Tchaikovsky's homosexuality; for others, it might equally represent a commentary on the possibility of an inner emotional life, rich in ways that the conventional world cannot fathom. More profitably, perhaps, it can be interpreted as a commentary on Tchaikovsky's own romanticism, which by the 1890s was no longer a belated aesthetic inherited from the early nineteenth century. Instead, it had come to represent a nascent form of symbolism that rejected the realist association between the object and its representation in favour of a more nebulous, intuitive mode of cognition. When Vaudemont exposes to Iolanta the fact of her blindness, he does so with a degree of unthinking pity that fails to account for the ways in which her understanding of the world is already profoundly and self-consciously sensual. Her response is ardent and impassioned in its defence of her own experience:

Can one see the chirrup of birds
In the rose bush,
Or the sweet gurgling

Of the swift rivulet on the sands?
Can one see in the sky
The distant roll of the thunder,
Or the trilling of the nightingale,
The crystalline sound of ringing bells,
Or your voice, or your words?
No, I have no need of light, my knight,
To know the beauty of the universe.

Throughout his life, Tchaikovsky rejected the search for literal, naturalistic truth in favour of a more indirect form of artistic truth that sometimes went against the conventions of realism, and *Iolanta* is one of his most important works in this regard. Its medieval setting may suggest a retrospective, even conservative, aesthetic, yet it also feels like a work written in an age that witnessed the rise of psychoanalysis. It is perhaps not insignificant that in early 1883 Tchaikovsky's niece Tanya was treated by the pioneering French neurologist Jean-Martin Charcot, who not only influenced Sigmund Freud's theory of hysteria but trained Nikolay Dahl, famous for curing Sergey Rachmaninoff after his nervous breakdown in 1897.[34] Only *Iolanta*'s finale disappoints; a paean to the Creator, it seems forced and overblown, sacrificing the static interiority of the preceding scenes. Nonetheless, if *Iolanta* is shaped by certain residual conventions of nineteenth-century Russian opera, it also looks forward, to Debussy's *Pelléas et Mélisande*, Dukas' *Ariane et Barbe-bleue* and even Bartók's *Bluebeard's Castle*.

Both *Iolanta* and *The Sleeping Beauty* are narratives of emotional maturation and even erotic liberation; their heroines are awakened from sleep and released from blindness to face an adult world of recognition in a way that is very different from Tchaikovsky's earlier stage works, where his heroines are undone by an implacable and destructive destiny. The same can be said of *The Nutcracker* too, although its canonization as a fairy-tale work piously performed each Christmas for generations of young balletomanes has perhaps numbed our sense of its captivating strangeness. Tchaikovsky drafted the score in the first half of 1891, before turning to the composition of *Iolanta*; he orchestrated it only in early 1892 and often found work hard-going and uninspiring. On account of their content and the circumstances of their composition, both the ballet and the opera deserve to be read – and perhaps also heard and seen – in tandem. Both feature an exotic and slightly unsettling outsider who defies conventional parental authority: in *Iolanta*, Ibn-Hakia challenges King René to tell his daughter about her blindness; in *The Nutcracker*, it is Clara's godfather Drosselmeyer who brings eccentric and even slightly alarming gifts on Christmas Eve (including the eponymous toy nutcracker in the form of a soldier). These outsiders presage the arrival of figures embodying a Romantic ideal: Vaudemont in *Iolanta* and the handsome prince in *The Nutcracker*.

There are, of course, some obvious differences in tone between the opera and the ballet: *Iolanta* is emotionally expansive and scenically static, whereas *The Nutcracker* flashes by in a series of fleeting and inventive vignettes whose decorative and self-conscious superficiality delights the ear and enratures the eye in equal measure. Yet Tchaikovsky's genius is in transforming the frivolous plot of *The Nutcracker* into something not only delightful but at times profound too. The music inventively articulates outrageous moments in the libretto that defy obvious practical realization on stage, such as the moment when the family Christmas tree grows in size, the transformation of the house into a pine forest, the scene were a sugar house melts in the rays of the sun, or the final apotheosis featuring a giant beehive. Here, Tchaikovsky conjures up the realm of the imagination and dreams in a way that only music can; but he is also profoundly sensitive to deeper human emotions, as in the music for Clara and her prince, which harks back to works such as *Romeo and Juliet* in its expansive lyric warmth. It is also worth remembering that *The Nutcracker* is based on a story by the German Romantic author E.T.A. Hoffmann, whose work was also the inspiration for Delibes' *Coppélia*. Like *Coppélia*, *The Nutcracker* features an automaton which, when brought to life, transforms the world around it; and, like *Coppélia*, it clothes its evocation of the fantastic power of magic with deceptive humour. Hoffmann's Romanticism is never entirely superficial or merely enchanting; it always entails something unsettling, uncanny even. Petipa's libretto may have purged Hoffmann's original tale of much of its original darkness, but Tchaikovsky was always alive to its ambiguous charms.

By the time *Iolanta* and *The Nutcracker* opened on 6 December 1892, Tchaikovsky was not just Imperial Russia's leading composer but one of its most prominent celebrities. Since he had given up his nomadic existence in Europe, his life had become a busy round of administrative commitments for the Russian Musical Society, conducting engagements at home and abroad, and prestigious official commissions. For the first time in his life, he could also count himself a relatively wealthy individual; in addition to his pension from the Tsar, he could rely on fees and honoraria from his publishers in Russia and western Europe, as well as generous revenues for his conducting engagements. Already in 1889, in a letter to Yuliya Shpazhinskaya, he had observed the transformation in his lifestyle and personality:

> I cannot recognize myself! Some six or seven years ago I was a complete anchorite, I was unsociable and entirely taken up with work. Now I am one of the links in the social whirl. I must admit that my former way of life was much more agreeable to me. But I do what I consider to be my duty.[35]

If Tchaikovsky derived little personal pleasure from his newfound status, this was in part due his own highly strung nature. When *The Queen of Spades* was removed from the stage

after just thirteen performances, he wrote to Vsevolozhsky
to express not just his indignation but his apprehension that
the Tsar's attitude to him had begun to cool. Vsevolozhsky
reassured him that this was not the case (the real reason
for the withdrawal of the opera from the repertoire was the
pregnancy of the female lead, Medea Figner, and her husband's
refusal to sing with any other soprano), and sensitively
identified the underlying cause of the composer's anxiety:

> You have a strange and unhappy character, dear Pyotr Ilyich!
> You have a desire to torment and torture yourself with empty
> apparitions. Everyone knows your worth. To be precise, you
> are a Russian talent – real, not hollow – therefore you do
> not possess over-confidence but excessive modesty.[36]

Yet Tchaikovsky's often gloomy frame of mind at this time was
not simply the result of 'empty apparitions'; he frequently had good
reason to feel harried by fate, and this could sometimes blind him
to his equal good fortune. The single most shocking blow came in
September 1890, when von Meck wrote to say that she was ruined and
could no longer pay his regular stipend. Superficially, Tchaikovsky
could afford to be sanguine about the immediate financial
consequences, as he confessed to his erstwhile patron directly:

> Of course, I should be guilty of telling a lie if I were to say
> that such a radical reduction in my budget would have no
> effect upon my material well-being. But its effect will be much
> less than you probably think. The fact is that in recent years
> my income has greatly increased and there is no reason to
> doubt that it will not continue to grow at a rapid rate.[37]

The psychological cost was much higher, however, and Tchaikovsky
suffered enormously at the loss of an individual who had saved

him financially and emotionally in 1877 and allowed him to
devote himself wholeheartedly to composition thereafter.
Tchaikovsky's subsequent letters to von Meck went unanswered,
and he suspected that his correspondence was simply not
passed on by her secretary, Władysław Pachulski (who was in
addition her son-in-law). Beyond the simple facts, it is hard
to understand what caused the rupture and whether it could
have been healed by means of greater efforts and diplomacy on
both sides. The end of the relationship between composer and
patron reveals just how complicated the motivations of both
parties had always actually been; for all their protestations, their
friendship always had its price, both financial and emotional.

Neither did Tchaikovsky's family life offer the sort of comfort it
once had. His niece Tanya – who had given birth to an illegitimate
child in Paris in 1883 – continued to live a wild and wilful life;
addicted to morphine, she died suddenly at a costume ball in St
Petersburg in 1887. But most of all it was the death of his beloved
sister Sasha that struck Tchaikovsky most forcefully. Long unwell
and by now addicted to both morphine and alcohol, she had been
badly shaken by the premature deaths of two of her seven children
(her second daughter, Vera, had died in 1888). Tchaikovsky learned
of Sasha's death on 28 March 1891 while in Le Havre awaiting his
passage to America, where he had been engaged to conduct at the
celebrations marking the opening of New York's Carnegie Hall.
Although his relations with Sasha had cooled somewhat by this
time, he remembered fondly the time when the Davydov estate at
Kamenka represented a refuge from the pressures of his personal
and professional life, as well as a source of artistic inspiration. Grief
almost led him to cancel his tour, but financial considerations – as
well as Modest's encouragement – persuaded him to continue.

It was not just family members who died around this time. In
the summer of 1887, Tchaikovsky spent a number of tortured weeks
in Aachen attending to his intimate friend Nikolay Kondratyev,

Tchaikovsky with the cellist Anatoly Brandukov, Paris, 1888.

who was dying of syphilis. Tchaikovsky's traumatized responses
to this event are recorded in a number of detailed diary entries
at this time, and he expressed something of his sadness in the
Pezzo capriccioso (Op. 62) for solo cello and small orchestra that
he composed on his return to Russia that August (although its
dedication is to the young cellist Anatoly Brandukov, whose
playing and personality Tchaikovsky admired in equal measure).

Tchaikovsky aged 50, photographed in New York by Napoleon Saroni, 1891.

Little wonder that Tchaikovsky's letters and diaries of the late 1880s and early 1890s are full of references to ageing, mortality and death. The enormous artistic and financial success of his American tour in 1891, which took in not only New York but Niagara Falls, Baltimore, Philadelphia and Washington, DC, was somewhat offset by the fact that the local newspapers described him as much older than his 51 years. He noted, not without indignation, a report in one newspaper that described him as 'a tall, grey, well-built interesting man, *well on the way to sixty*.'[38] On his return to Russia that June, he wrote ironically to his nephew Bob:

No! The old man is obviously in decline. Not only is his hair thinning and white as snow, not only are his teeth falling out and refusing to chew his food, not only are his eyes weakening and becoming easily tired, not only are his feet beginning to drag rather than walk – but even his one and only gift for any sort of activity is failing and evaporating.[39]

That autumn, Tchaikovsky made a will, providing for those surviving members of his family for whom he felt greatest affection – or at least greatest responsibility. Alongside his brother Modest and nephew Bob, he left legacies for the young Georges-Leon, his manservant Alyosha and estranged wife Antonina. Photographs taken at the summer estate of Nikolay and Medea Figner the previous summer show the composer looking weary and withdrawn, an impression corroborated by one contemporary:

The last photographs of Tchaikovsky represent his appearance accurately. Of medium height, refined, with regular and handsome facial features, he was not remarkable for his youthful appearance but rather, appeared older than his years. His eyes had already lost their glitter . . . he had lost one of his front teeth and he sometimes lisped as a result of this.[40]

Tchaikovsky with Nikolay and Medea Figner at the Figners' estate at Lobynskoe, near Tula, in the summer of 1890. The Figners were to star in the premiere of *The Queen of Spades* that December.

In the summer of 1892 he headed to Vichy, where he took the waters in an attempt to alleviate the symptoms of the stomach catarrh that had plagued him for so long. The first and only lifetime portrait of the composer reflects something of his physical and psychological state at this time. During a hugely successful festival of his music held in Odessa in January 1893, Tchaikovsky sat for the painter Nikolay Kuznetsov; the resulting canvas, with its rapid brush strokes and stark contrast between dark and light tones, depicts his focused, penetrating gaze in a manner that suggests profound, even tragic, introspection.

Given the events of Tchaikovsky's life in the years running up to 1893, it would be surprising if mortality – both his own and that of others – did not inform the last substantial composition that he was to complete, the Symphony No. 6. The work we know today, however, was not the one he initially began to sketch during his trip to America in May 1891. Eventually written over the course of 1892, the projected symphony attested to his obsession with questions of life and death, as its draft programme suggests:

> The ultimate essence . . . of the symphony is *Life*. First part – all impulsive passion, confidence, thirst for activity. Must be short (the finale *death* – result of collapse). Second part love: third disappointments; fourth ends dying away (also short).[41]

By the end of the year, however, he had grown dissatisfied with the work, claiming in a letter to his nephew Bob that he had destroyed it. In fact, he reworked his sketches to create a new piano concerto, of which he managed to complete the opening movement by October 1893, as well as drafting the other two movements in rough outline.

The extent to which Tchaikovsky's Symphony No. 6 was directly inspired by elements of the abandoned work is uncertain, yet in a letter to his nephew written after his return from Odessa,

Tchaikovsky aged 52 with his nephew Vladimir ('Bob') Davydov, Paris, 1892.

he observed that the new composition did indeed have some sort of musical narrative:

> During the journey an idea for another symphony came to me, this time a programme symphony, but with such a programme as shall remain a riddle for everybody – let them try to guess, but the symphony will thus be named: *Programme Symphony* (No. 6); *Symphonie à Programme* (No. 6); *Programm-Symphonie* (No. 6). The programme itself is nothing if not shot through with subjectivity, and frequently during my travels, as I composed it in my head, I wept a great deal. As soon as I returned home, I began to make some sketches, and work was so impassioned and quick that in less than four days the first movement was completely ready, and the remaining movements are clearly outlined in my head.[42]

Nikolay Kuznetsov,
*The Composer Peter
Ilyich Tchaikovsky*,
1893.

Work on the symphony was indeed miraculously swift; it was
sketched in around six weeks between February and March 1893,
and orchestrated in around a month that summer (in the meantime,
Tchaikovsky paid a fleeting visit to Cambridge, where he was awarded
an honorary doctorate alongside Arrigo Boito, Max Bruch and his
old friends Camille Saint-Saëns and Edvard Grieg, although the latter
was unable to attend the ceremony due to ill health).[43] Tchaikovsky's
particular claim to have wept during its composition is borne out
by its expressive tone; its subtitle, *Pathétique*, suggests not so much
'pity' (as implied by the English 'pathos') as extreme emotional
intensity and even suffering. Once again, Tchaikovsky had managed
to produce a work that was extremely – indeed almost excessively
– expressive, yet he did so without an explicit programme, thereby
inviting audiences to engage in acts of speculative and imaginative
interpretation of their own.

Specific attempts to interpret the symphony as an allegory of the composer's growing sense of mortality have tended to rest on his claim that it encodes a secret programme, as well as on selectively quoted extracts from his correspondence in the final years of his life. Konstantin Romanov, for example, had suggested that Tchaikovsky might set Alexey Apukhtin's long poem 'Requiem' as a testament to the poet, who died in August 1893. Tchaikovsky demurred, but did admit that there was a certain similarity between Apukhtin's work and the new symphony, noting that the latter work was 'imbued with a mood very close to the one that also infuses the "Requiem"'.[44] A trip to see his old nanny, Fanny Dürbach, in the French town of Montbéliard in December 1892 may also have instilled in him a mood of reflection, not least because Fanny read him a number of his mother's letters, which he described to Modest as 'especially precious'.[45] And on 20 August 1893 – after the symphony was completed, admittedly – Tchaikovsky wrote to Jurgenson, observing how many of his former friends had died: 'As I write this letter, my comrade and old friend *Apukhtin* is being buried in St Petersburg. How many deaths among my old friends: Karlushka [Karl Albrecht], both Shilovskys, Apukhtin!!!'[46]

There is a degree of internal evidence for reading the Symphony No. 6 in terms of retrospection too. Broodingly cast in the key of B minor, the symphony includes a possible allusion to the Russian Orthodox service for the dead in its first movement and, unlike the other numbered symphonies, it ends in the minor, thus corroborating tragic interpretations of its musical trajectory. Audiences at its first performance in St Petersburg on 16 October 1893 certainly found the work sombre and melancholic, even downright unsettling, although whether this was due to the work itself or its composer's apparently rather stilted conducting of it, is hard to tell. Reporting on the premiere to Jurgenson, Tchaikovsky observed: 'It is not so much that people did not like it, but it

Tchaikovsky in Cambridge, June 1893, dressed in his doctoral robes.

did produce a certain degree of bewilderment. As far as I am concerned, I am more proud of it than of any other of my works.'[47]

Yet to see the *Pathétique* as a 'late' work – akin to the compositions of Beethoven's final deafness, or the sonatas and song cycles that Schubert wrote in the second half of the 1820s when he was already ill with the symptoms of tertiary syphilis – is to mishear both its musical language and the circumstances of its creation. Tchaikovsky was, after all, only in his early fifties when he wrote the *Pathétique*, and despite his often morbid feelings at the time, 1893 had been a year of considerable inspiration and productivity. The symphony itself had been drafted and orchestrated with remarkable rapidity and represents not so much a valedictory summing-up of everything he had achieved beforehand as a radically new departure in its composer's style. This impression of creative renewal is borne out by the other compositions from that year; the Eighteen Pieces for piano, Op. 72, and the Six Romances, Op. 73. Admittedly, the piano pieces can seem like just one more set of occasional miniatures, the likes of which Tchaikovsky had produced to order so many times before; he completed them in just two weeks that April, dismissing them as 'pancakes' in a letter to his nephew.[48] Yet this account belies the formidable range of genres, forms and textures that are explored in the set, and fails to account for the extraordinary sense of inventiveness and adventure they embody. Each is dedicated to a friend or colleague of the composer, but their technical complexity means that they belong more properly to the concert hall than the private salon.

Barely had Tchaikovsky completed the Eighteen Pieces than he turned his attention to the poetry of the then unknown Daniil Rathaus, who had sent some of his verses to Tchaikovsky the previous August. As if aware of the propensity of audiences to read his works autobiographically, Tchaikovsky wrote to the young poet:

> I hate it when people try to peer into my soul . . . In my music I claim extreme sincerity; I am on the whole inclined to sad songs, yet at the same time, like you, at least in recent years, I want for nothing and can generally consider myself a happy person![49]

Tchaikovsky aged 53, London, 1893.

Although this was not the first time that Tchaikovsky had composed a set of songs to a single poet (the Six Songs, Op. 63, feature lyrics by Konstantin Romanov), this is the first of his vocal works to feel as though it was conceived as a cycle, although it is too seldom performed as such. Completed by 5 May, it charts the evolution of a love affair from early optimism to its sad conclusion. The cycle's literary narrative is matched by its striking musical architecture too: all six songs are connected by means of a subtle and original set of harmonic relationships in which a single note in one song acts as a pivot into the next one; a number of recurrent melodic motifs cement this sense of structural coherence.[50]

'There will be much that is new about the form of this symphony', Tchaikovsky noted proudly in a letter to his nephew in February 1893. As he went on:

> The finale will not be a loud allegro but quite the opposite, a most protracted *adagio*. You cannot imagine what bliss I feel now that I am convinced that my time has not yet passed and that I can still work. Of course, I may be mistaken, but I do not think so.[51]

The decision to replace the traditional upbeat finale with something quieter and more introverted was an astute one; a criticism sometimes still levelled at Tchaikovsky's earlier symphonies is that their finales can be marred by a surfeit of bombastic cliché that undoes the subtle innovations of the preceding movements. But the slow finale of the *Pathétique* is only the most obvious instance of the score's inventiveness. While conforming to the principles of sonata form, its first movement turns its back on the kind of expansive melodic expressivity characteristic of the earlier symphonies, as well as on the detailed motivic development explored in the Symphony No. 5. Rather, it presents the listener with a series of stark and often unsettling juxtapositions of contrasting musical material that suggests a succession of intense and fluctuating emotional states. The second movement seems to be another of the composer's beloved waltzes, yet for all its poise (it is marked *allegro can grazia*), it too can be a disconcerting experience; each bar contains five beats, giving an uncanny impression of either excess or insufficiency, and Tchaikovsky's tendency to repeat rather than develop the already modest motivic material from which the movement is fashioned gives it an obsessive, skittish quality. The emotional range of the third movement – nominally a scherzo – is so comprehensively expanded that it begins to take on the quality of a triumphant finale, before giving way to the concluding lament. Throughout, Tchaikovsky makes use of improbably extreme dynamic markings – from *ffff* to *pppppp* – which push the orchestral players to their physical limits, test the endurance and perception of the audience and hint at a world beyond the work's immediate confines. Its title may allude to Beethoven's Piano Sonata No. 8, the *Grande sonate pathétique* (just as its stormy mood may recall the Piano Sonata No. 23, the so-called *Appassionata*), yet it is Beethoven's final symphony that might constitute the better comparison: just as the Symphony No. 9 had cast a long shadow over the whole of the nineteenth century, so too would the *Pathétique* prove decisive in the evolution of the symphony from the late nineteenth century and throughout the twentieth. One can hear its influence in Mahler and Sibelius, and even in Elgar (Tchaikovsky was all but inescapable in turn-of-the-century Britain), and it is the starting point for Shostakovich, too.[52]

Conclusion: 'Some Kind of Banal, Stupid Joke'

What transformed the *Pathétique* from a breakthrough work into an exemplary instance of late style was, of course, its composer's sudden and unexpected death on 25 October 1893, just nine days after its first performance. Having completed the orchestration of the symphony that August, Tchaikovsky embarked on a busy round of practical engagements, including the first foreign production of *Iolanta* in Hamburg in September and affairs at the Moscow Conservatory in early October. He arrived in St Petersburg on 10 October, staying at Modest's apartment. Six days later, he conducted the premiere of the *Pathétique*. On 18 October, he attended a meeting with Vladimir Pogozhev, an official in the St Petersburg branch of the Imperial Theatre Directorate, during which they discussed possible revisions to *The Maid of Orleans*. The next day, Tchaikovsky signed an agreement with the publisher Vladimir Bessel for a new edition of *The Oprichnik*. He also attended a dress rehearsal for a new production of *Eugene Onegin* (18 October), as well as a performance of Anton Rubinstein's opera *Die Maccabäer* (19 October) and Alexander Ostrovsky's play *An Ardent Heart* (20 October). That evening he dined at Leiner's restaurant with friends and family. Letters written during these days show Tchaikovsky making plans for concerts in Russia and abroad. This is decidedly not a portrait of a composer putting his affairs in order; it is a professional artist actively occupying himself with the future.[1]

The events that followed have been endlessly embroidered in memoirs and biographies ever since. On 21 October, a Thursday, Tchaikovsky fell ill with an upset stomach, although given his poor digestion, no one seemed particularly anxious. After a round of social and business calls he returned home that afternoon feeling much worse; his regular doctor, Vasily Bertenson, was called. Fearing for his patient's condition, Bertenson summoned his brother Lev, also a doctor, who diagnosed cholera. For the next three days, a number of standard treatments were applied: laxatives, injections of musk and camphor, and finally a hot bath. It was all to be in vain. Tchaikovsky died, early in the morning, on Monday 25 October. A lavish funeral was held on 28 October at St Petersburg's Kazan Cathedral, after which Tchaikovsky was buried in the Tikhvin cemetery at the city's Alexander Nevsky monastery. Attended by leading members of the Imperial institutions with which the composer was associated (including members of the royal family), as well as by fellow artists and a huge crowd of ordinary music lovers, the funeral was a remarkable moment of national coherence and personal grief. Few other figures at the time would have been mourned so ostentatiously and sincerely, especially during the increasingly tense reign of Alexander III. The closest parallel would be with the death of Lev Tolstoy in 1910, during the reign of the equally reactionary Nicholas II.[2] In both cases, it was art that brought the nation together where politics only divided.

The details of Tchaikovsky's final days were widely reported in the press, and during the most critical phase of his illness, bulletins about his worsening condition were posted on the door of his brother's apartment. Even before his funeral, newspapers carried tributes to the deceased composer, as well as various accounts of the events that had led up to his death, including an interview with Lev Bertenson that appeared in *The New Times* on 27 October. To some, however, it seemed impossible that such a high-placed member of the cultural elite should have contracted such a vulgar and avoidable illness as cholera, and questions were soon raised about the efficacy of his medical treatment. In a letter to *The New Times* on 7 November, Modest defended Lev and Vasily Bertenson and their assistants, but this did little to calm matters. To others, Tchaikovsky's most recently completed composition seemed to hold a clue to events. By a kind of circular logic, his death allowed the symphony to be read as a requiem, and the tone of the symphony seemed to justify subsequent claims that his death had been more than simply a misfortune. A second performance of the *Pathétique* on 6 November (followed by its Moscow premiere on 4 December) sealed its reputation as a work bordering on the autobiographical and even confessional, and the rest of Tchaikovsky's output was soon read in its retrospective light.

In the gossipy atmosphere of the capital, rumour soon began to mingle with the reported facts, and before long innuendo began to propose ever more lurid accounts of the composer's final days. Many were by supposed eyewitnesses to the events themselves, although when set against what is known of the documentary record or examined for internal consistency, they often turn out to be at best, misremembered and at worst, falsified. Take, for instance, Sergey Diaghilev's account of his supposed part in the events following Tchaikovsky's death:

> In despair I rushed out of the house, and although I realized Tchaikovsky had died of cholera I made straight for Malaya Morskaya, where he lived. The doors were wide open and there was no one to be seen. The place was upside down. In the entrance hall the score of the Sixth Symphony lay open on a table, and I noticed on a sofa the camel-hair skull-cap which Tchaikovsky wore all the time. I heard voices from another room, and on entering I saw Piotr Ilyitch in a black morning coat stretched on a sofa. Rimsky-Korsakov and the singer Nicolai Figner were arranging a table to put him on.

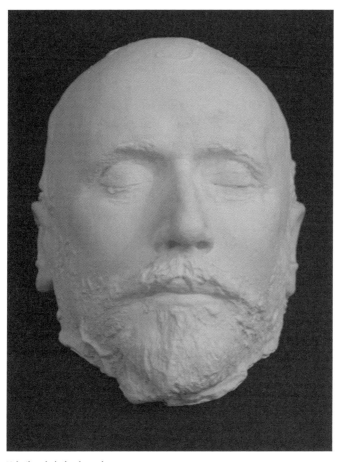
Tchaikovsky's death mask.

We lifted the body of Tchaikovsky, myself holding the feet, and laid it on the table. The three of us were alone in that flat, for after Tchaikovsky's death the whole household had fled. Piotr Ilyitch looked little different from when he was alive, and as young as ever. I went off to buy flowers. For the whole of that first day my wreath was the only one lying at his feet.[3]

Diaghilev was certainly in St Petersburg in late 1893 and was well connected in musical and artistic circles, but it is highly unlikely that he could have witnessed the events as they are described here, let alone participated in them. His is a highly poeticized account that tells us more about the turn-of-the-century Russian intelligentsia's interest in myth and self-fashioning that it does about the circumstances of the composer's death.

Ever since Tchaikovsky's death, official and unofficial accounts of his life and death have gone hand-in-hand, all of them attesting to his enormous critical importance and popular appeal. Modest's biography, rapidly translated from Russian into German and English, presented a sanitized version of his more famous brother's life that nonetheless remains useful for the vast amount of primary material and personal recollection it contains. Cultural politics immediately after the Bolshevik revolution of 1917 was characterized by an iconoclastic attitude to the legacy of the past, and Tchaikovsky, with his close connections to the court, cosmopolitan tastes and comfortable lifestyle, was frequently dismissed as a figure likely to be of little interest to proletarian audiences. Under Stalin in the 1930s, however, the Soviet Union witnessed a thorough rehabilitation of the past. Although Tchaikovsky's surviving diaries had been published as early as 1923, this volume was to remain a bibliographical rarity.[4] His voluminous correspondence with von Meck appeared in three volumes between 1934 and 1936 (the first volume of his correspondence with Jurgenson followed in 1938, followed by a second in 1952).[5] Then, in 1940, a volume of intimate letters to his family appeared.[6] Despite a number of censored passages these letters contained a number of unambiguous references to his personal life. Yet the volume was ill-timed and it was soon removed from libraries and placed beyond the reach of all but the most highly placed researchers.

The year 1940 marked the hundredth anniversary of Tchaikovsky's birth, and the authorities used the opportunity to promote a new, more socially acceptable version of the composer for Soviet audiences.[7] From now on, Tchaikovsky was sanctified as a national treasure. His works were officially promoted in concert halls and opera houses, the conservatories in both Moscow and Kiev were named after him, and a complete edition of his compositions, correspondence and other writings was launched. Running to over one hundred volumes and not completed until 1990, this edition – which removed all references to his monarchist sympathies, as well as occasional anti-Semitic comments and other politically unacceptable statements – was central to a new myth of the composer fit for consumption by Soviet audiences.

Yet these same audiences could read between the lines, or draw on folk memories that were very different from the state-sponsored biography to which they were officially exposed. According to one widely told joke, a listener calls into an Armenian radio station to ask whether it is true that Tchaikovsky's sexual tastes were unorthodox. 'Yes,' comes the reply, 'but that's not the only reason we love him.' It was in the West, however, where questions of Tchaikovsky's sexuality impinged most on both critical and popular attitudes to the composer. From the 1890s onwards, his orchestral compositions were played ever more frequently in concert halls in western Europe and North America, rapidly becoming some of the most popular works in the modern repertoire. The overwhelming intensity of these works troubled some commentators, such as the composer and teacher Hubert Parry. Writing in 1905, he argued that contemporary British interest in Russian music derived from its 'vehement emotional spontaneity, orgiastic frenzy, dazzling effects of colour, barbaric rhythm, and unrestrained abandonment to physical excitement which is natural to the less developed races.'[8] Above all, it was Tchaikovsky's *Pathétique* that was responsible for seducing impressionable audiences:

The public recognized the singular intensity of its emotional expression, ranging from the exaltation of rapture to the depths of almost comatose collapse. As a human document the work was unmistakable, and the interest generated by such a graphic study of the subjective states induced a desire for more of the same kind, and for a time the Russian composer became the central object of musical public interest.[9]

That Parry's distaste was as much to do with Tchaikovsky's sexuality as it was with his Russianness can be sensed from a reference in a later work to his 'abnormally sensitive nature'.[10] Such allusions were widespread in early twentieth-century writing on Tchaikovsky and show how speculation about his private life was an important factor in his reception, especially in the English-speaking world.[11] In the interwar period, modernist distaste for sentiment marginalized Tchaikovsky yet further; the major beneficiary of such a reaction was Jean Sibelius, whose ruggedly austere musical language and well-documented family life carried no implications of effeminacy.[12]

Discussion of Tchaikovsky's sexuality was not, however, always negative or dismissive. Around the turn of the century, a new field of enquiry was taking shape: sexology. In 1908 the socialist and gay rights activist Edward Carpenter published *The Intermediate Sex*, which contained a list of homosexual men and women (or 'Uranians', as he called them) who, he argued, had shaped human history for the good:

> Certainly it is remarkable that some of the world's greatest leaders and artists have been dowered either wholly or in part with the Uranian temperament – as in the cases of Michel Angelo, Shakespeare, Marlowe, Alexander the Great, Julius Caesar, or, among women, Christine of Sweden, Sappho the poetess, and others.[13]

Of all the arts, it was music that most ideally expressed this gay sensibility, as Havelock Ellis, another prominent figure in the field of sexology, observed: 'It has been extravagantly said that all musicians are inverts; it is certain that various famous musicians, among the dead and the living, have been homosexual.'[14]

Evidence for the extent to which Tchaikovsky's music was associated with same-sex desire can be found in E. M. Forster's posthumously published novel *Maurice* (1971). In order to understand his sexuality, its hero turns to a number of sources. As an undergraduate at Cambridge, Maurice reads the Greek classics, yet his lover at the time insists that their relationship remain chaste. Later on, he turns to medicine, initially consulting the family doctor, who suggests marriage as a cure, before seeking treatment from a hypnotist. But it is Tchaikovsky who finally provides the answer. Maurice first encounters his music at Cambridge, where a group of artistic male undergraduates play the second movement of the *Pathétique* on a pianola; later, he attends a concert in London at which he hears the whole of the symphony. Alerted to its composer's sexuality by a friend, he borrows a biography of Tchaikovsky from the library and his life is transformed; from now on, he will not seek to cure himself, but will eventually find love and happiness with another man.[15]

Other literary cultures experimented with the figure of Tchaikovsky too. Thomas Mann's *Death in Venice* (1912) contains a number of possible allusions to Tchaikovsky's biography that are as potentially significant as the parallels with the more recently deceased Mahler (Aschenbach contracts a fatal case of cholera that is somehow mysteriously linked with his infatuation with the Polish adolescent Tadzio). Mann's son, Klaus, was also to explore the creative potential of Tchaikovsky's life. His novel *Symphonie pathétique* (1935) is an account of the composer's final years that is not just a fictionalized biography but an apologia for a sexuality that Klaus himself shared.[16] Another product of the interwar years was Nina Berberova's *Tchaikovsky: Story of a Lonely Life* (1936). An elegant and intimate biographical novel that draws extensively on new publications from the Soviet archives, it is perhaps not too dissimilar to the 'new biographies' with which Lytton Strachey and Virginia Woolf had experimented in the 1920s, with an admixture of Russian émigré gossip.[17]

Yet imagined accounts of the composer's private life could be lurid and sensationalist too. Perhaps the most infamous instance of this particular trend is Ken Russell's film *The Music Lovers* (1970). Purportedly based on Catherine Drinker Bowen and Barbara von Meck's *Beloved Friend*, an account of Tchaikovsky's relationship with Nadezha von Meck that was first published in 1937,[18] it contains so many scenes of such boisterous bad taste (including the failed consummation of his marriage to Antonina in a violently rocking railway carriage and a demonic fantasy sequence to the accompaniment of *The Year 1812*) that it ought to be easy to dismiss it as a trivial and meaningless fiction. Yet the darker side of *The Music Lovers* is that its sensationalist emphasis on matters of sex above all undoubtedly played a role in promoting a fallacious sense of the composer's supposedly pathological personality. For a long time this view was limited to hearsay, yet in the 1980s, rumours achieved the status of supposed fact when a story about a sexual escapade with a young Russian nobleman and a 'court of honour' made up of the composer's former classmates from the School of Jurisprudence was promoted by Alexandra Orlova, who had recently emigrated from the Soviet Union.[19]

Many Western scholars have wanted to find Orlova's claims convincing, not least David Brown, the author of a substantial and otherwise sober four-volume critical study of Tchaikovsky's life and works. Yet, as Richard Taruskin has suggested, such accounts seem closer to the life and downfall of Oscar Wilde in late-Victorian England than to the documentary record of Tchaikovsky's life.[20] The available evidence suggests that, far

Tchaikovsky (standing, far left) during a visit to Tbilisi, April 1886. His brother Anatoly and sister-in-law Praskovya are seated directly in front of him. Ivan Verinovsky, with whom Tchaikovsky was possibly involved at this time, is standing, second from the right.

from risking his hard-earned public reputation by engaging in salacious love affairs in Russian high society, Tchaikovsky succeeding in arranging his personal life in a manner that was discreet and well ordered, especially after he settled outside Moscow in 1885. The closest he seems to have come to scandal was in 1886, when he spent the best part of April in Tbilisi, where his brother Anatoly was a state prosecutor (and later deputy governor). There he found himself caught up in what appears to have been an unresolved love triangle involving his sister-in-law Praskovya and a young officer by the name of Ivan Verinovsky. Aside from a few gnomic comments in his letters and diaries, the details of what transpired are far from clear, but Tchaikovsky was moved to tears when he learned of Verinovsky's suicide a few days after he had left for Paris (probably because he had failed his exams, rather than because of any emotional complications).[21]

Once in Paris, however, Tchaikovsky threw himself into the pleasures of living incognito in a city famous for its erotic pleasures. His diary entries from this time are full of passing references to its fleeting attractions:

[18 May] Near the *Café chantant* an unexpected acquaintance with two very bold Frenchmen. Conversed with one of them. Drunkenness. Home. A drunken Englishman who knocked at my door by mistake.
[19 May] Near the *Café chantant*. The same strange and bold types . . . An American. Home. Strange dreams.
[2 June] Brandukov. To Golitsyn's with him. Still there was another handsome (flat-chested) youth, an elegant gentleman and a doctor. Injection of morphine.
[5 June] Got drunk all the same. Acquaintance with a strange Russian at the [*Café de la*] *Paix*. [6 June] At 6 o'clock went to Golitsyn's in the rain. Two sweet young men, particularly the darker one.[22]

There were infatuations within his own social circle too. In April 1889, the 21-year-old pianist Vasily Sapelnikov performed the Piano Concerto No. 1 in London, conducted by the composer. The next morning, Tchaikovsky crept into Sapelnikov's hotel room, where he gave the sleeping youth a kiss.[23] The return journey to Russia via Paris, Marseille and Tbilisi afforded yet more pleasures, this time in the form of Vladimir Sklifosovsky, the adolescent son of a Moscow surgeon, described in Tchaikovsky's diary as an 'agreeable youth'.[24] Writing to Modest from Istanbul, he penned a more detailed account of his travelling companions:

Two Russians were travelling with me: a fourteen-year-old boy *Sklifosovky* (son of the surgeon) and *Germanovich*, a student at Moscow University who accompanies him. Both are charming subjects with whom I have struck up a firm friendship. We shall part here; I am going on to *Batum*, and they to *Odessa*. We arrived here at 4 o'clock in the afternoon. We spent the entire evening strolling around the city; we spent the night on board the steamer. Today they are transferring to the Russian steamer. I shall miss them terribly. The steamship captain and his assistants, and indeed the entire staff, are very agreeable.[25]

Tchaikovsky's status as a moneyed gentleman meant that he could always either seek erotic satisfaction in the company of anonymous lower-class men in the major cities of Europe, and even in Russia itself, or meet his emotional needs through intense infatuations with young men and students from his own milieu.

In neither respect was Tchaikovsky very different from other homosexual men at that time, and in neither case was he the victim. Indeed, the frankness with which he wrote about his various sexual escapades to his brothers Modest and Anatoly suggested that he had little fear of exposure to blackmail, and in any case, when compared to other gay men in his social circle, his behaviour was decidedly restrained by the accepted conventions of the day. Those who suggest that Tchaikovsky's unlikely alleged involvement with the son of an influential member of the Russian court would inevitably have led to ignominy, ostracism and even death overlook the fact that the sexual morals of many other members of high society were far more brazen, and that despite this, they went unpublished or uncensored. Tchaikovsky's schoolmates Alexey Apukhtin and Prince Vladimir Meshchersky were far more public about their affairs, and the Imperial family itself knew more than its share of scandalous behaviour. Grand Duke Sergey Alexandrovich, for instance, was the brother of Alexander III and just one of a number of members of the Romanov dynasty who were rumoured to be homosexual.[26] On his appointment as Governor General of Moscow in 1891, one contemporary recorded the following witticism, which circulated in the city: 'Until now, Moscow has stood on seven hills, and now it is to stand on a single hillock' (the joke is based on the fact that the Russian word for hillock – *bugor* – is almost homonymous with the French slang for a gay man, *bougre*).[27]

All of these men survived and even flourished in the Russia of Alexander III and Nicholas II, despite their frequent and flagrant sexual transgressions (which, if they threatened propriety too much, were easily hushed up). Russian reaction to the Wilde trials of 1895 was incredulous and focused more on the hypocrisy of Victorian Britain than on the alleged immorality of the writer himself.[28] Indeed, late Imperial Russia did not use its anti-sodomy legislation with anything like the virulence of Britain or Germany at the time.[29] Russia was certainly no social paradise for a bashful gay man such as Tchaikovsky, but neither was it a repressive, tyrannical place – at least if one enjoyed the kind of Imperial patronage that he did. Attempts to reconstruct Tchaikovsky's last days on the basis of gossip and supposition overlook salient features of the historical context, as well as what is known of the composer's attitude to his own sexuality. They also neglect the simple fact that cholera was widespread in Russia at the time, especially in the rapidly growing urban environment of St Petersburg. Tchaikovsky may possibly have suffered a mild bout of the illness in the summer of 1892,[30] and in any case, his constitution was never particularly strong (something only exacerbated by his often immoderate consumption of alcohol).

When von Meck stopped his subsidy in September 1890, he described her actions to Jurgenson as 'some kind of banal, stupid joke, which makes me ashamed and sick'.[31] Is this not an apt description for the circumstances of his death too? Whatever his fame and eminence, the triviality of a death brought about by an easily preventable but all-too-prevalent illness represents the ultimate tragedy of his last days. For a composer who was painfully shy in society and guarded the often melancholy reality of his emotional life from all but the closest of friends, the public discussion of the circumstances of his death, both in the days immediately following it and in the years ever since, would have been a mortifying intrusion, as well as a distraction from what really constituted his greatest claim to fame – his creativity. Tchaikovsky's was certainly not a creativity nurtured and cultivated in romantic isolation from the society in which he lived, but a creativity that was fashioned in late Imperial Russia's new musical institutions – its conservatories, publishing houses, concert halls, opera houses and salons – and which both addressed and shaped the musical tastes of his nation. If we argue that Tchaikovsky's music speaks, then we may wish to concentrate less on interpreting what we think it might say and more on the means by which it achieves such a striking sense of expressiveness. And it achieves this not so much by translating psychology or even psychopathology into acts of seemingly sincere and truthful confession, but by employing all of Tchaikovsky's well-practised skills of artifice and artistry to create an abiding impression of absolute, yet always carefully projected, authenticity.

References

Introduction: 'The Intimate World of My Feelings and Thoughts'

1 I. D. Glikman, ed., *Pis'ma k drugu: Pis'ma D. D. Shostakovicha k I. D. Glikmanu* (Moscow and St Petersburg, 1993), p. 225.

2 Richard Taruskin, 'Pathetic Symphonist: Chaikovsky, Russia, Sexuality and the Study of Music', in Taruskin, *On Russian Music* (Berkeley, Los Angeles and London, 2009), pp. 76–104.

3 Modest Chaikovskii, *Zhizn' Petra Il'icha Chaikovskogo: po dokumentam, khranyashchimsya v arkhive imeni pokoinogo kompizitora v Klinu* (Moscow, 1901–2), trans. Paul Juon as *Das Leben Peter Iljitsch Tschaikowskys* (Moscow and Leipzig, 1901–3), and Rosa Newmarch as *The Life and Letters of Peter Ilich Tchaikovsky* (London, 1906).

4 Piotr Ilyich Tchaikovsky, *Letters to his Family: An Autobiography*, trans. Galina von Meck, ed. Percy M. Young (London, 1981).

5 Alexandra Orlova, *Tchaikovsky: A Self-portrait*, trans. R. M. Davidson (Oxford, 1990), and Alexander Poznansky, *Tchaikovsky: The Quest for the Inner Man* (New York, 1991).

6 Letter of 9 February 1878, in *P. I. Chaikovskii–N. F. fon Mekk: perepiska*, ed. P. E. Vaidman (Chelyabinsk, 2007–), vol. II, p. 71.

7 Letter of 7 November 1877, ibid., vol. I, p. 83.

8 P. E. Vaidman, ed., *P. I. Chaikovskii–P. I. Yurgenson: perepiska* (Moscow, 2011–13).

9 Ip. I. Chaikovskii, ed., *Dnevniki P. I. Chaikovskogo, 1873–1891* (Moscow and Petrograd, 1923), pp. 213–14.

10 Ibid., p. 257.

11 Letter of 9–18 August 1880, in *P. I. Chaikovskii–N. F. fon Mekk: perepiska*, vol. III, p. 427.

12 Letter of 9 February 1878, ibid., vol. I, pp. 73–4.

13　Letter of 24 June 1878, ibid., vol. II, p. 222.

14　Letter of 12 February 1878, ibid., vol. II, p. 80.

15　Modest Chaikovskii, *Zhizn' Petra Il'icha Chaikovskogo* (Moscow, 1997), vol. III, p. 151.

16　Letter of 1 August 1880, in Petr Il'ich Chaikovskii, *Polnoe sobranie sochinenii: literaturnye proizvedeniya i perepiska* (Moscow, 1953–81), vol. IX, p. 222.

1 'I Will Make *Something* of Myself'

1　Letter of 4 December 1861, in Petr Il'ich Chaikovskii, *Polnoe sobranie sochinenii: literaturnye proizvedeniya i perepiska* (Moscow, 1953–81), vol. V, pp. 71–2. Italics in original.

2　Letter of 14 January 1886, ibid., vol. XIII, pp. 241–2.

3　Modest Chaikovskii, *Zhizn' Petra Il'icha Chaikovskogo* (Moscow, 1997), vol. I, p. 40.

4　Letter of early January 1852, in Chaikovskii, *Polnoe sobranie sochinenii*, vol. V, p. 47.

5　Richard Taruskin, *Defining Russia Musically: Historical and Hermeneutical Essays* (Princeton, NJ, 1997), p. xiv.

6　Philip Ross Bullock, 'Women and Music', in *Women in Nineteenth-century Russia: Lives and Culture*, ed. Wendy Rosslyn and Alessandra Tosi (Cambridge, 2012), pp. 119–36.

7　Chaikovskii, *Zhizn' Petra Il'icha Chaikovskogo*, vol. I, p. 42.

8　Cited in Alexander Poznansky, ed., *Tchaikovsky through Others' Eyes*, trans. Ralph C. Burr, Jr and Robert Bird (Bloomington and Indianapolis, IN, 1999), p. 13.

9　Cited ibid., p. 16.

10　Ibid., p. 21.

11　Ibid., p. 24.

12　Chaikovskii, *Zhizn' Petra Il'icha Chaikovskogo*, vol. I, p. 447.

13　Letter of 10 March 1861, in Chaikovskii, *Polnoe sobranie sochinenii*, vol. V, pp. 60–61.

14　Cited in Poznansky, ed., *Tchaikovsky through Others' Eyes*, p. 17.

15　Cited ibid., p. 23.

16　Gustave Flaubert, *Correspondance*, ed. Jean Bruneau (Paris, 1973–2007), vol. V, p. 155.

2 'The Only Hope for Our Musical Future'

1 Letter of 11 January 1866, cited in Modest Chaikovskii, *Zhizn' Petra Il'icha Chaikovskogo* (Moscow, 1997), vol. I, pp. 188–9.

2 Letter of 30 December 1865, cited in P. I. Chaikovskii, *Pis'ma k blizkim*, ed. V. A. Zhdanov (Moscow, 1955), pp. 553–4.

3 Chaikovskii, *Zhizn' Petra Il'icha Chaikovskogo*, vol. I, p. 184.

4 Lynn M. Sargeant, *Harmony and Discord: Music and the Transformation of Russian Cultural Life* (Oxford and New York, 2011).

5 Letter of 15 January 1866, in Petr Il'ich Chaikovskii, *Polnoe sobranie sochinenii: literaturnye proizvedeniya i perepiska* (Moscow, 1953–81), vol. V, p. 94.

6 Letter of 23 January 1866, ibid., p. 96.

7 Letter of 10 January 1866, ibid., p. 91.

8 Letter of 24 December 1877, in *P. I. Chaikovskii–N. F. fon Mekk: perepiska*, ed. P. E. Vaidman (Chelyabinsk, 2007–), vol. I, p. 143.

9 David Brown, *Tchaikovsky: A Biographical and Critical Study* (London, 1978–91), vol. I, p. 185.

10 Cited in Alexander Poznansky, ed., *Tchaikovsky through Others' Eyes*, trans. Ralph C. Burr, Jr and Robert Bird (Bloomington and Indianapolis, IN, 1999), p. 66.

11 Letters of 18 and 31 March 1869, in M. A. Balakirev, *Vospominaniya i pis'ma*, ed. Yu. A. Kremlev, A. S. Lyapunova and E. L. Frid (Leningrad, 1962), pp. 127–32.

12 Letter of 2 October 1869, in Chaikovskii, *Polnoe sobranie sochinenii*, vol. V, p. 174.

13 Ibid. The second half of the sentence is censored in the complete Soviet-era edition of the composer's letters and is here cited from P. E. Vaidman, 'Neizvestnyi Chaikovskii – chelovek i khudozhnik', in *Neizvestnyi Chaikovskii*, ed. P. E. Vaidman (Moscow, 2009), pp. 9–31 (p. 18).

14 Balakirev, *Vospominaniya i pis'ma*, p. 146.

15 Letter of 9 January 1875, in Chaikovskii, *Polnoe sobranie sochinenii*, vol. V, p. 390.

16 Letter of 13 February 1873, ibid., p. 302.

17 Ip. I. Chaikovskii, ed., *Dnevniki P. I. Chaikovskogo, 1873–1891* (Moscow and Petrograd, 1923), p. 215.

18 'Pervyi kontsert russkogo muzykal'nogo obshchestva. – G-zha

Laura Karer. – 8-ia simfoniya Betkhovena. - Ital'yanskaya opera. –
G-zha Patti', *Sovremennaya letopis'*, XVM (November 1871), pp. 5–6,
reproduced in P. I. Chaikovskii, *Muzykal'no-kriticheskie stat'i*, 4th edn
(Leningrad, 1986), pp. 30–33 (p. 33).

19 Chaikovskii, *Zhizn' Petra Il'icha Chaikovskogo*, vol. V, p. 291.

20 Cited in Brown, *Tchaikovsky*, vol. I, p. 138.

21 Letter of 30 October 1878, in *P. I. Chaikovskii–N. F. fon Mekk: perepiska*,
vol. II, p. 317. The French can be translated as 'it is a menu overloaded
with spicy dishes.'

22 Caryl Emerson and Robert William Oldani, *Modest Musorgsky and Boris
Godunov: Myths, Realities, Reconsiderations* (Cambridge, 1994).

23 Gerald Abraham, 'Operas and Incidental Music', in *Tchaikovsky: A
Symposium*, ed. Gerald Abraham (London, 1945), pp. 124–83 (p. 136).

24 Chaikovskii, *Zhizn' Petra Il'icha Chaikovskogo*, vol. I, p. 406.

25 Letter of 21 November 1874, in Chaikovskii, *Polnoe sobranie sochinenii*,
vol. V, p. 379.

26 Brown, *Tchaikovsky*, vol. I, p. 226.

27 Chaikovskii, *Zhizn' Petra Il'icha Chaikovskogo*, vol. I, pp. 345 and 366.

28 Ibid., vol. I, p. 402.

29 Ts. A. Kyui, *Russkii romans: ocherk ego razvitiya* (St Petersburg, 1896).

30 Philip Ross Bullock, 'Ambiguous Speech and Eloquent Silence: The
Queerness of Tchaikovsky's Songs', *19th-century Music*, XXXII/1 (2008),
pp. 94–128.

31 Richard D. Sylvester, *Tchaikovsky's Complete Songs: A Companion with
Texts and Translations* (Bloomington, IN, 2004).

32 Terence Cave, *Mignon's Afterlives: Crossing Cultures from Goethe to the
Twenty-first Century* (Oxford, 2011).

33 Cited in Roland John Wiley, *Tchaikovsky* (Oxford and New York, 2009),
p. 75.

34 Letter of 2 December 1876, in Chaikovskii, *Polnoe sobranie sochinenii*,
vol. VI, p. 88.

35 Chaikovskii, *Zhizn' Petra Il'icha Chaikovskogo*, vol. I, pp. 481–2.

36 Letter of 29 October 1874, in Chaikovskii, *Polnoe sobranie sochinenii*,
vol. V, p. 372.

37 Letter of 29 October 1874, ibid., pp. 371–2.

38 Letter of 21–22 January 1878, in *P. I. Chaikovskii–N. F. fon Mekk:
perepiska*, vol. II, pp. 42–3.

39 Ibid., vol. II, p. 43.

40 Wiley, *Tchaikovsky*, p. 133.

41 Letter of 7 December 1877, in Chaikovskii, *Polnoe sobranie sochinenii*, vol. VI, p. 294.

42 Roland John Wiley, *Tchaikovsky's Ballets: 'Swan Lake', 'Sleeping Beauty', 'Nutcracker'* (Oxford, 1985), p. 61.

43 Ibid., pp. 242–74.

44 Letter of 8 August 1876, in Chaikovskii, *Polnoe sobranie sochinenii*, vol. VI, p. 65.

45 Letter of 26 November 1877, in *P. I. Chaikovskii–N. F. fon Mekk: perepiska*, vol, I, pp. 108–9.

46 Letter of 5 May 1879, ibid., vol. III, p. 119.

47 Alexander Poznansky and Brett Langston, eds, *The Tchaikovsky Handbook: A Guide to the Man and His Music* (Bloomington and Indianapolis, IN, 2002), vol. I, pp. 185–6.

48 Letter of 14 October 1876, in Chaikovskii, *Polnoe sobranie sochinenii*, vol. VI, pp. 80–81.

3 'For the Sake of *Qu'en-dira-t-on*'

1 Letter of 10 September 1876, cited in Aleksandr Poznanskii, *Chaikovskii* (Moscow, 2010), p. 224.

2 Letter of 28 September 1876, cited ibid., p. 227.

3 Letter of 16 April 1868, in Petr Il'ich Chaikovskii, *Polnoe sobranie sochinenii: literaturnye proizvedeniya i perepiska* (Moscow, 1953–81), vol. V, p. 136.

4 Letter of 1 February 1869, ibid., p. 155.

5 Letter of 26 December 1868, ibid., p. 149.

6 Letter of 22 November 1872, ibid., p. 290.

7 Cited in David Brown, *Tchaikovsky Remembered* (London and Boston, MA, 1993), p. 50.

8 Ip. I. Chaikovskii, ed., *Dnevniki P. I. Chaikovskogo, 1873–1891* (Moscow and Petrograd, 1923), p. 177.

9 Letter of 19 January 1877, cited in Poznanskii, *Chaikovskii*, p. 238.

10 Alexander Poznansky and Brett Langston, eds, *The Tchaikovsky Handbook: A Guide to the Man and His Music* (Bloomington and Indianapolis, IN, 2002), vol. I, p. 205.

11 Letter of 10 December 1872, in Chaikovskii, *Polnoe sobranie sochinenii*, vol. v, p. 293.

12 Letter of 9 January 1875, cited in Poznanskii, *Chaikovskii*, p. 204.

13 Kay Redfield Jamison, *Touched with Fire: Manic Depressive Illness and the Artistic Temperament* (New York, 1993).

14 Letter of 23 June 1877, in Chaikovskii, *Polnoe sobranie sochinenii*, vol. vi, p. 144.

15 Letter of 8 July 1877, ibid., p. 151.

16 Letter of 8 July 1877, ibid., p. 153.

17 Letter of 13 July 1877, cited in Poznanskii, *Chaikovskii*, p. 279.

18 Letter of 31 October 1877, cited in V. Solokov, *Antonina Chaikovskaya: istoriya zabytoi zhenshchiny* (Moscow, 1994), p. 54.

19 'Iz vospominanii vdovy P. I. Chaikovskogo', *Peterburgskaya gazeta*, 3 April 1893, cited ibid., p. 266.

20 Letter of 15 February 1877, in *P. I. Chaikovskii–N. F. fon Mekk: perepiska*, ed. P. E. Vaidman (Chelyabinsk, 2007–), vol. i, p. 22.

21 Letter of 7 March 1877, ibid., p. 25.

22 Letter of 16 March 1877, ibid., p. 27.

23 Galina fon Mekk, *Kak ya ikh pomnyu* (Moscow, 1999), pp. 32–3, cited in P. E. Vaidman, 'P. I. Chaikovskii i N. F. fon Mekk: Istoriya neobychnoi perepiski. Mify i realii cherez stoletie', in *P. I. Chaikovskii–N. F. fon Mekk: perepiska*, vol. i, pp. 181–280 (pp. 194–5).

24 Letter of 7 November 1877, in *P. I. Chaikovskii–N. F. fon Mekk: perepiska*, vol. i, p. 83, and letter of 6 January 1878, ibid., vol. ii, p. 21.

25 Letter of 22 January 1878, ibid., vol. ii, p. 45.

26 Letters of 1 May and 15 July 1877, ibid., vol. i, pp. 34 and 47–8.

27 Letters of 11 and 17 October 1877, ibid., pp. 66 and 69.

28 Letter of 14 September 1879, ibid., vol. iii, p. 232.

29 Letter of 13 March 1879, ibid., vol. iii, p. 93.

30 Letter of 16 February 1880, ibid., vol. iii, p. 339.

31 Letter of 8 March 1880, ibid., vol. iii, p. 347.

32 Letter of 17 October 1877, in Chaikovskii, *Polnoe sobranie sochinenii*, vol. vi, p. 190.

33 Letter of 12 November 1877, ibid., p. 236.

34 David Brown, *Tchaikovsky: A Biographical and Critical Study* (London, 1978–91), vol. ii, pp. 169–73.

35 Letter of 18 March 1878, in *P. I. Chaikovskii–S. I. Taneev: pis'ma*, ed. V. A. Zhdanov (Moscow, 1951), p. 32.

36 Letter of 27 March 1878, in Chaikovskii, *Polnoe sobranie sochinenii*, vol. VII, p. 200.

37 Letter of 18 March 1878, in *P. I. Chaikovskii–S. I. Taneev: pis'ma*, p. 32.

38 Letter of 27 March 1878, in Chaikovskii, *Polnoe sobranie sochinenii*, vol. VII, p. 201.

39 Letter of 1 May 1877, in *P. I. Chaikovskii–N. F. fon Mekk: perepiska*, vol. I, p. 31.

40 Letter of 1 May 1877, ibid., p. 34.

41 Roland John Wiley, *Tchaikovsky* (Oxford and New York, 2009), p. 165.

42 Letter of 17 February 1878, in *P. I. Chaikovskii–N. F. fon Mekk: perepiska*, vol. II, pp. 85–6.

43 Ibid., p. 83.

44 Letter of 18 May 1877, in Chaikovskii, *Polnoe sobranie sochinenii*, vol. VI, p. 136.

45 Letter of 24 December 1877, in *P. I. Chaikovskii–N. F. fon Mekk: perepiska*, vol. I, p. 143.

46 Richard Taruskin, *Defining Russia Musically: Historical and Hermeneutical Essays* (Princeton, NJ, 1997), pp. 53–60.

47 Cited in Wiley, *Tchaikovsky*, p. 173.

48 Letter of 24 September 1868, in Chaikovskii, *Polnoe sobranie sochinenii*, vol. V, p. 142.

49 Boris Gasparov, '*Eugene Onegin* in the Age of Realism', in *Five Operas and a Symphony: Word and Music in Russian Culture* (New Haven, CT, and London, 2005), pp. 58–94, and Emily Frey, 'Nowhere Man: *Evgeny Onegin* and the Politics of Reflection in Nineteenth-century Russia', *19th-century Music*, XXXVI/3 (2013), pp. 209–30.

50 Kadja Grönke, 'On the Role of Gremin: Tchaikovsky's *Eugene Onegin*', in *Tchaikovsky and His World*, ed. Leslie Kearney (Princeton, NJ, 1998), pp. 220–33.

51 In the initial version of the opera, Onegin's final words were in fact, 'O death, o death! I come to seek you out', but in correspondence with Albrecht, Tchaikovsky soon confessed his dissatisfaction with this version (letter of 3 February 1878, in Chaikovskii, *Polnoe sobranie sochinenii*, vol. VII, p. 93).

52 Letter of 30 August 1877, in *P. I. Chaikovskii–N. F. fon Mekk: perepiska*, vol. I, p. 62.

53 Letter of 9 June 1877, in Chaikovskii, *Polnoe sobranie sochinenii*, vol. VI, p. 141.

54 Letter of 3 December 1877, ibid., p. 275.

55 Letter of 4 February 1878, in *P. I. Chaikovskii–P. I. Yurgenson: perepiska* (Moscow, 2011–13), vol. I, p. 39.

56 Poznansky and Langston, eds, *The Tchaikovsky Handbook*, vol. I, pp. 38–9.

57 Letter of 4–8 February 1878, in Chaikovskii, *Polnoe sobranie sochinenii*, vol. VII, p. 98.

58 Letter of 1–4 January 1878, ibid., p. 19.

59 See for instance his letter to Jurgenson of 15 December 1881, in *P. I. Chaikovskii–P. I. Yurgenson: perepiska*, vol. I, pp. 315–16.

4 'I am a Free Man'

1 Letter of 13 February 1878, in P. I. Chaikovsii, *Pis'ma k rodnym*, ed. V. A. Zhdanov (Moscow, 1940), p. 374.

2 Letter of 18 February 1878, in *Neizvestnyi Chaikovskii*, ed. P. E. Vaidman (Moscow, 2009), p. 243.

3 Letter of 16 September 1878, cited in Aleksandr Poznanskii, *Chaikovskii* (Moscow, 2010), p. 182.

4 Letter of 26 February 1879, cited ibid., p. 413.

5 Letter of 13 February 1878, in Petr Il'ich Chaikovskii, *Polnoe sobranie sochinenii: literaturnye proizvedeniya i perepiska* (Moscow, 1953–81), vol. III, p. 115. The French phrase *péter plus haut que son cul* literally means 'to fart higher than one's own arse', and figuratively means something like 'to think very highly of oneself'.

6 Letter of 1 January 1878, in Chaikovskii, *Polnoe sobranie sochinenii*, vol. VII, p. 15.

7 Letter of 29 August 1878, in Chaikovskii, *Pis'ma k rodnym*, p. 442.

8 Letter of 16 September 1878, in Chaikovskii, *Polnoe sobranie sochinenii*, vol. VII, pp. 399–400.

9 Letter of 23 September 1878, ibid., vol. VII, pp. 405–6.

10 Letter of 7 October 1878, in *P. I. Chaikovskii–N. F. fon Mekk: perepiska*, ed. P. E. Vaidman (Chelyabinsk, 2007–), vol. II, p. 304.

11 Alexander Poznansky, *Tchaikovsky: The Quest for the Inner Man* (New York, 1991), pp. 132–3.

12 Letters of 21 August and 21 December 1881, in *P. I. Chaikovskii–N. F. fon Mekk: perepiska*, vol. III, pp. 579 and 626.

13 Modest Chaikovskii, *Zhizn' Petra Il'icha Chaikovskogo* (Moscow, 1997), vol. II, p. 465.

14 Letter of 22 July 1878, in Chaikovskii, *Polnoe sobranie sochinenii*, vol. VII, p. 343.

15 Letter of 29 July 1878, in *P. I. Chaikovskii–P. I. Yurgenson: perepiska*, ed. P. E. Vaidman (Moscow, 2011–13), vol. I, p. 59.

16 Letter of 5 December 1877, ibid., vol. I, p. 32.

17 David Brown, *Tchaikovsky: A Biographical and Critical Study* (London, 1978–91), vol. II, p. 274.

18 Letter of 23 November 1877, in *P. I. Chaikovskii–N. F. fon Mekk: perepiska*, vol. I, pp. 101–2.

19 Letter of 24 May 1881, in Chaikovskii, *Polnoe sobranie sochinenii*, vol. X, p. 120.

20 Letter of 4 August 1881, in *P. I. Chaikovskii–N. F. fon Mekk: perepiska*, vol. III, p. 574.

21 Letter of 17 January 1879, in Chaikovskii, *Polnoe sobranie sochinenii*, vol. VIII, p. 48.

22 Letter of 28 September 1883, ibid., vol. XII, p. 246.

23 Letter of 27 November 1879, in *P. I. Chaikovskii–N. F. fon Mekk: perepiska*, vol. III, p. 292.

24 Letter of 11 December 1883, in Chaikovskii, *Polnoe sobranie sochinenii*, vol. XII, p. 285.

25 Letter of 21 November 1878, in *P. I. Chaikovskii–N. F. fon Mekk: perepiska*, vol. II, p. 331.

26 Letter of 17 January 1891, in *P. I. Chaikovskii–P. I. Yurgenson: perepiska*, vol. II, p. 345.

27 Roland John Wiley, *Tchaikovsky* (Oxford and New York, 2009), p. 268.

28 Letter of 28 July 1883, in *P. I. Chaikovskii–P. I. Yurgenson: perepiska*, vol. I, p. 452.

29 Letter of 29 July 1883, ibid., vol. I, p. 454.

30 Chaikovskii, *Zhizn' Petra Il'icha Chaikovskogo*, vol. II, p. 530.

31 Leslie Kearney, 'Tchaikovsky Androgyne: *The Maid of Orleans*', in *Tchaikovsky and His World*, ed. Leslie Kearney (Princeton, NJ, 1998), pp. 239–76.

32 Alexander Poznansky, 'The Petrolina Letters', in *Tchaikovsky: The Quest for the Inner Man*, pp. 131–50.

33 Letter of 5 October 1879, in *P. I. Chaikovskii–N. F. fon Mekk: perepiska*, vol. III, p. 245.

34 Letter of 21 August 1878, in Chaikovskii, *Polnoe sobranie sochinenii*, vol. VII, p. 374.

35 Richard Taruskin, *Defining Russia Musically: Historical and Hermeneutical Essays* (Princeton, NJ, 1997), pp. 266–76.

36 Letter of 24 June 1878, in *P. I. Chaikovskii–N. F. fon Mekk: perepiska*, vol. II, p. 222.

37 Letter of 9 September 1880, ibid., vol. III, p. 438.

38 Letter of 24 August 1881, ibid., vol. III, p. 580.

39 Letters of 22 November 1882, in Chaikovskii, *Polnoe sobranie sochinenii*, vol. XI, p. 287, and 1 April 1884, ibid., vol. XII, p. 341.

40 Letter of 1 August 1880, ibid., vol. IX, p. 223.

41 Letter of 24 April 1884, ibid., vol. XII, p. 360.

42 Letter of 30 June 1884, ibid., vol. XII, p. 397.

43 Letter of 19 April 1884, ibid., vol. XII, p. 353.

44 Ip. I. Chaikovskii, ed., *Dnevniki P. I. Chaikovskogo, 1873–1891* (Moscow and Petrograd, 1923), pp. 15 and 24.

45 Poznansky, 'X and Z at Kamenka', in *Tchaikovsky: The Search for the Inner Man*, pp. 425–46.

46 Letter of 18 January 1885, in Chaikovskii, *Polnoe sobranie sochinenii*, vol. XII, p. 25.

47 Letter of 20 March 1891, in *P. I. Chaikovskii–P. I. Yurgenson: perepiska*, vol. II, p. 371.

5 'Where is My Home to Be?'

1 Letter of 3 December 1884, in Petr Il'ich Chaikovskii, *Polnoe sobranie sochinenii: literaturnye proizvedeniya i perepiska* (Moscow, 1953–81), vol. XII, p. 509.

2 Cited ibid., vol. XIII, p. 15.

3 Letter of 19 July 1886, in *P. I. Chaikovskii–P. I. Yurgenson: perepiska*, ed. P. E. Vaidman (Moscow, 2011–13), vol. II, pp. 45–6. The letter was published in Jurgenson's own German translation in *Musikerbriefe aus fünf Jahrhunderten*, ed. La Mara (Leipzig, 1886), vol. II, pp. 380–82.

4 Alexander Poznansky and Brett Langston, eds, *The Tchaikovsky Handbook: A Guide to the Man and His Music* (Bloomington and Indianapolis, IN, 2002), vol. I, p. 151.

5 Letter of 21 September 1888, in Chaikovskii, *Polnoe sobranie sochinenii*, vol. XIV, pp. 542–3.

6 Letter of 13 June 1885, ibid., vol. XIII, p. 101.

7 Letter of 22 December 1885, ibid., vol. XIII, p. 229.

8 Poznansky and Langston, eds, *The Tchaikovsky Handbook*, vol. I, p. 154.

9 Marina Riztarev, *Tchaikovsky's 'Pathétique' and Russian Culture* (Farnham and Burlington, IN, 2014), pp. 17–46.

10 Letter of 5 May 1886, in Chaikovskii, *Polnoe sobranie sochinenii*, vol. XIII, p. 351.

11 Letter of 19 May 1886, ibid., vol. XIII, p. 349.

12 César Cui, *La Musique en Russie* (Paris, 1880).

13 Modest Chaikovskii, *Zhizn' Petra Il'icha Chaikovskogo* (Moscow, 1997), vol. III, p. 59.

14 'Avtobiografichekoe opisanie puteshestviya za granitsu v 1888 gody', in P. I. Chaikovskii, *Muzykal'no–kriticheskie stat'i*, 4th edn (Leningrad, 1986), pp. 286–316 (p. 312).

15 Letters of 20 October 1888, in Chaikovskii, *Polnoe sobranie sochinenii*, vol. XIV, pp. 553–4.

16 'Avtobiografichekoe opisanie puteshestviya za granitsu v 1888 gody', p. 298.

17 Letter of 28 October 1887, in Chaikovskii, *Polnoe sobranie sochinenii*, vol. XIV, p. 250.

18 Letter of 27 September 1885, ibid., vol. XIII, p. 159.

19 Letter of 5 March 1885, ibid., vol. XIII, p. 45.

20 Richard Wortman, *Scenarios of Power: Myth and Ceremony in Russian Monarchy* (Princeton, NJ, 1995–2000).

21 Cited in David Brown, *Tchaikovsky: A Biographical and Critical Study* (London, 1978–1991), vol. IV, p. 185.

22 Roland John Wiley, *Tchaikovsky* (Oxford and New York, 2009), p. 346.

23 Letter of 7 July 1886, in Chaikovskii, *Polnoe sobranie sochinenii*, vol. XIII, p. 391.

24 Aleksandr Pushkin, 'Pikovaya dama', in *Polnoe sobranie sochinenii*, vol. VIII, book 1, p. 241.

25 Ibid., p. 247.

26 Claire Whitehead, *The Fantastic in France and Russia in the Nineteenth Century: In Pursuit of Hesitation* (London, 2006), pp. 13–39.

27 Boris Gasparov, 'Lost in a Symbolist City: Multiple Chronotopes in

Chaikovsky's *The Queen of Spades*', in *Five Operas and a Symphony: Word and Music in Russian Culture* (New Haven, CT, and London, 2005), pp. 132–60.

28 Simon Morrison, 'Chaikovsky and Decadence', in *Russian Opera and the Symbolist Movement* (Berkeley, Los Angeles and London, 2002), pp. 45–114.

29 Puskin, 'Pikovaya dama', p. 244.

30 Wiley, *Tchaikovsky*, pp. 398–9.

31 Tim Scholl, *Sleeping Beauty: A Legend in Progress* (New Haven, CT, and London, 2004), p. 167.

32 Luba Golburt, *The First Epoch: The Eighteenth Century and the Russian Cultural Imagination* (Madison, WI, 2014), pp. 12–15.

33 Letter of 2 October 1886, in Chaikovskii, *Polnoe sobranie sochinenii*, vol. XIV, p. 554.

34 Letter of 21 January 1883, in *P. I. Chaikovskii–P. I. Yurgenson: perepiska*, vol. I, p. 413.

35 Letter of 2 September 1889, in Chaikovskii, *Polnoe sobranie sochinenii*, vol. XVa, p. 175.

36 Brown, *Tchaikovsky: A Biographical and Critical Study*, vol. IV, p. 309.

37 Letter of 22 September 1890, in Chaikovskii, *Polnoe sobranie sochinenii*, vol. XVb, pp. 263–4.

38 Ip. I. Chaikovskii, ed., *Dnevniki P. I. Chaikovskogo, 1873–1891* (Moscow and Petrograd, 1923), p. 273 (slightly modified).

39 Letter of 25 June 1891, in Chaikovskii, *Polnoe sobranie sochinenii*, vol. XVIa, p. 156.

40 Cited in David Brown, *Tchaikovsky Remembered* (London and Boston, MA, 1993), p. 179.

41 Brown, *Tchaikovsky: A Biographical and Critical Study*, vol. IV, p. 388.

42 Letter of 11 February 1893, in Chaikovskii, *Polnoe sobranie sochinenii*, vol. XVII, p. 42.

43 Gerald Norris, *Stanford, the Cambridge Jubilee and Tchaikovsky* (Newton Abbot and North Pomfret, VT, 1980).

44 Letter of 21 September 1893, in Chaikovskii, *Polnoe sobranie sochinenii*, vol. XVII, p. 186.

45 Letter of 24 December 1892, ibid., vol. XVIb, p. 215.

46 Letter of 20 August 1893, in *P. I. Chaikovskii–P. I. Yurgenson: perepiska*, vol. II, p. 489.

47 Letter of 18 October 1893, ibid., vol. II, p. 495.

48 Letter of 15 April 1893, in Chaikovskii, *Polnoe sobranie sochinenii*, vol. XVII, p. 81.

49 Letter of 1 August 1893, ibid., vol. XVII, pp. 153–4.

50 Wiley, *Tchaikovsky*, pp. 437–9.

51 Letter of 11 February 1893, in Chaikovskii, *Polnoe sobranie sochinenii*, vol. XVII, p. 43.

52 Pauline Fairclough, *A Soviet Credo: Shostakovich's Fourth Symphony* (Aldershot and Burlington, IN, 2006), and David Fanning, *The Breadth of the Symphonist: Shostakovich's Tenth* (London, 1989).

Conclusion: 'Some Kind of Banal, Stupid Joke'

1 The best and most detailed account of the circumstances surrounding Tchaikovsky's death is Alexander Poznansky, *Tchaikovsky's Last Days: A Documentary Study* (Oxford, 1996).

2 William Nickell, *The Death of Tolstoy: Russia on the Eve, Astapovo Station, 1910* (Ithaca, NY, and London, 2010).

3 Richard Buckle, *Diaghilev* (New York, 1979), p. 23, cited in Poznansky, *Tchaikovsky's Last Days*, p. 134.

4 Ip. I. Chaikovskii, ed., *Dnevniki P. I. Chaikovskogo, 1873–1891* (Moscow and Petrograd, 1923).

5 V. A. Zhdanov and N. T. Zhegin, eds, *P.I. Chaikovskii: Perepiska s N.F. fon Mekk* (Moscow and Leningrad, 1934–6), and *P. I. Chaikovskii: Perepiska s P. I. Yurgensonom* (Moscow and Leningrad, 1938–52).

6 V. A. Zhdanov, ed., *P. I. Chaikovskii: Pis'ma k rodnym* (Moscow, 1940).

7 Marina Raku, *Muzykal'naya klassika v mifotvorchestve sovetskoi epokhi* (Moscow, 2014), pp. 564–659.

8 C. Hubert H. Parry, *Summary of the History and Development of Mediaeval and Modern European Music* (London, 1905), p. 119.

9 Ibid., p. 120.

10 C. Hubert H. Parry, *Style in Musical Art* (London, 1911), p. 206.

11 Malcolm Hamrick Brown, 'Tchaikovsky and His Music in Anglo-American Criticism, 1890s–1950s', in *Tchaikovsky and his Contemporaries: A Centennial Symposium*, ed. Alexandar Mihailovic (Westport, CT, and London, 1999), pp. 61–73, republished in *Queer*

Episodes in Music and Modern Identity, ed. Sophie Fuller and Lloyd Whitesell (Urbana and Chicago, IL, 2002), pp. 134–49.

12 Byron Adams, '"Thor's Hammer": Sibelius and British Music Critics, 1905–1957', in *Jean Sibelius and His World*, ed. Daniel M. Grimley (Princeton, NJ, and Oxford, 2011), pp. 125–57.

13 Edward Carpenter, *The Intermediate Sex: A Study of Some Transitional Types of Men and Women* (London and Manchester, 1908), pp. 37–8.

14 Havelock Ellis, *Studies in the Psychology of Sex* (Philadelphia, PA, 1900–1928), vol. II, p. 295.

15 Michelle Fillion, *Difficult Rhythm: Music and the Word in E. M. Forster* (Urbana, IL, 2010), pp. 93–107.

16 Klaus Mann, *Symphonie pathétique* (Amsterdam, 1935).

17 Nina Berberova, *Chaikovskii: istoriya odinokoi zhizni* (Berlin, 1936).

18 Catherine Drinker Bowen and Barbara von Meck, *Beloved Friend: The Story of Tchaikowsky and Nadejda von Meck* (London, 1937).

19 Alexandra Orlova, 'Tchaikovsky: The Last Chapter', *Music and Letters*, LXII (1981), pp. 125–45.

20 Richard Taruskin, 'Pathetic Symphonist: Chaikovsky, Russia, Sexuality and the Study of Music', in *On Russian Music* (Berkeley, Los Angeles and London, 2009), pp. 82–5.

21 Alexander Poznansky, *Tchaikovsky: The Quest for the Inner Man* (New York, 1991), pp. 455–9.

22 Chaikovskii, ed., *Dnevniki P. I. Chaikovskogo*, pp. 60, 61, 65 and 67.

23 Cited in David Brown, *Tchaikovsky: A Biographical and Critical Study* (London, 1978–1991), vol. IV, p. 182.

24 Chaikovskii, ed., *Dnevniki P. I. Chaikovskogo*, p. 233.

25 Letter of 8 April 1889, in Petr Il'ich Chaikovskii, *Polnoe sobranie sochinenii: literaturnye proizvedeniya i perepiska* (Moscow, 1953–81), vol. XVa, p. 93.

26 Dan Healey, *Homosexual Desire in Revolutionary Russia: The Regulation of Sexual and Gender Dissent* (Chicago, IL, and London, 2001), p. 93.

27 V. N. Lamzdorf, *Dnevnik, 1891–1892*, ed. F. A. Rotstein (Moscow and Leningrad, 1934), p. 106.

28 Evgenii Bershtein, 'The Russian Myth of Oscar Wilde', in *Self and Story in Russian History*, ed. Laura Engelstein and Stephanie Sandler (Ithaca, NY, and London, 2000), pp. 168–88, and '"Next to Christ": Oscar Wilde in Russian Modernism', in *The Reception of Oscar Wilde in Europe*, ed.

Stefano Evangelista (London and New York, 2010), pp. 285–300.

29 Laura Engelstein, *The Keys to Happiness: Sex and the Search for Modernity in Fin-de-Siècle Russia* (Ithaca, NY, and London, 1992).

30 Roland John Wiley, *Tchaikovsky* (Oxford and New York, 2009), p. 446.

31 Letter of 28 September 1890, in *P. I. Chaikovskii–P. I. Yurgenson: perepiska*, ed. P. E. Vaidman (Moscow, 2011–13), vol. II, p. 318.

Select Bibliography

In addition to the published titles listed below, the Tchaikovsky Research website, www.tchaikovsky-research.net, constitutes an indispensable source of information about Tchaikovsky's life and works.

Abraham, Gerald, ed., *Tchaikovsky: A Symposium* (London, 1945)

Adams, Byron, '"Thor's Hammer": Sibelius and British Music Critics, 1905–1957', in *Jean Sibelius and His World*, ed. Daniel M. Grimley (Princeton, NJ, and Oxford, 2011), pp. 125–57

Balakirev, M. A., *Vospominaniya i pis'ma*, ed. Yu. A. Kremlev, A. S. Lyapunova and E. L. Frid (Leningrad, 1962)

Berberova, Nina, *Chaikovskii: istoriya odinokoi zhizni* (Berlin, 1936)

Bershtein, Evgenii, '"Next to Christ": Oscar Wilde in Russian Modernism', in *The Reception of Oscar Wilde in Europe*, ed. Stefano Evangelista (London and New York, 2010), pp. 285–300

—, 'The Russian Myth of Oscar Wilde', in *Self and Story in Russian History*, ed. Laura Engelstein and Stephanie Sandler (Ithaca, NY, and London, 2000), pp. 168–88

Bowen, Catherine Drinker, and Barbara von Meck, *Beloved Friend: The Story of Tchaikowsky and Nadejda von Meck* (London, 1937)

Brown, David, *Tchaikovsky: A Biographical and Critical Study* (London, 1978–1991)

—, *Tchaikovsky: The Man and His Music* (London, 2006)

—, ed., *Tchaikovsky Remembered* (London and Boston, MA, 1993)

Brown, Malcolm Hamrick, 'Tchaikovsky and His Music in Anglo-American Criticism, 1890s–1950s', in *Tchaikovsky and his Contemporaries: A Centennial Symposium*, ed. Alexandar Mihailovic (Westport, CT, and London, 1999), pp. 61–73; republished in *Queer Episodes in Music and Modern Identity*, ed. Sophie Fuller and Lloyd

Whitesell (Urbana and Chicago, IL, 2002), pp. 134–49

Bullock, Philip Ross, 'Ambiguous Speech and Eloquent Silence: The Queerness of Tchaikovsky's Songs', *19th-century Music*, XXXII/1 (2008), pp. 94–128

—, 'Women and Music', in *Women in Nineteenth-century Russia: Lives and Culture*, ed. Wendy Rosslyn and Alessandra Tosi (Cambridge, 2012), pp. 119–36

Carpenter, Edward, *The Intermediate Sex: A Study of Some Transitional Types of Men and Women* (London and Manchester, 1908)

Cave, Terence, *Mignon's Afterlives: Crossing Cultures from Goethe to the Twenty-first Century* (Oxford, 2011)

Chaikovskii, Ippolit Il'ich, ed., *Dnevniki P. I. Chaikovskogo, 1873–1891* (Moscow and Petrograd, 1923)

Chaikovskii, Modest Il'ich, *Das Leben Peter Iljitsch Tschaikowskys*, trans. Paul Juon (Moscow and Leipzig, 1901–3)

—, *The Life and Letters of Peter Ilich Tchaikovsky*, trans. Rosa Newmarch (London, 1906)

—, *Zhizn' Petra Il'icha Chaikovskogo* (Moscow, 1997)

—, *Zhizn' Petra Il'icha Chaikovskogo: po dokumentam, khranyashchimsya v arkhive imeni pokoinogo kompizitora v Klinu* (Moscow, 1901–2)

Chaikovskii, Petr Il'ich, *Letters to his Family: An Autobiography*, trans. Galina von Meck, ed. Percy M. Young (London, 1981)

—, *Muzykal'no-kriticheskie stat'i*, 4th edn (Leningrad, 1986)

—, *Polnoe sobranie sochinenii: literaturnye proizvedeniya i perepiska* (Moscow, 1953–81)

Cui, César, *see* Kyui, Ts. A.

Ellis, Havelock, *Studies in the Psychology of Sex* (Philadelphia, PA, 1900–1928)

Emerson, Caryl, and Robert William Oldani, *Modest Musorgsky and Boris Godunov: Myths, Realities, Reconsiderations* (Cambridge, 1994)

Engelstein, Laura, *The Keys to Happiness: Sex and the Search for Modernity in Fin-de-siècle Russia* (Ithaca, NY, and London, 1992)

Fairclough, Pauline, *A Soviet Credo: Shostakovich's Fourth Symphony* (Aldershot and Burlington, IN, 2006)

Fanning, David, *The Breadth of the Symphonist: Shostakovich's Tenth* (London, 1989)

Fillion, Michelle, *Difficult Rhythm: Music and the Word in E. M. Forster* (Urbana, IL, 2010)

Frey, Emily, 'Nowhere Man: *Evgeny Onegin* and the Politics of Reflection in Nineteenth-century Russia', *19th-century Music*, XXXVI/3 (2013), pp. 209–30

Garden, Edward, *Tchaikovsky* (Oxford, 1993)

—, and Nigel Gotteri, eds, *'To My Best Friend': Correspondence between Tchaikovsky and Nadezhda von Meck, 1876–1878*, trans. Galina von Meck (Oxford, 1993)

Gasparov, Boris, *Five Operas and a Symphony: Word and Music in Russian Culture* (New Haven, CT, and London, 2005)

Glikman, I. D., ed., *Pis'ma k drugu: Pis'ma D. D. Shostakovicha k I. D. Glikmanu* (Moscow and St Petersburg, 1993)

Golburt, Luba, *The First Epoch: The Eighteenth Century and the Russian Cultural Imagination* (Madison, WI, 2014)

Grönke, Kadja, 'On the Role of Gremin: Tchaikovsky's *Eugene Onegin*', in *Tchaikovsky and His World*, ed. Leslie Kearney (Princeton, NJ, 1998), pp. 220–33

Healey, Dan, *Homosexual Desire in Revolutionary Russia: The Regulation of Sexual and Gender Dissent* (Chicago, IL, and London, 2001)

Jamison, Kay Redfield, *Touched with Fire: Manic Depressive Illness and the Artistic Temperament* (New York, 1993)

Kearney, Leslie, ed., *Tchaikovsky and His World* (Princeton, NJ, 1998)

Kyui, Ts. A., *La Musique en Russie* (Paris, 1880)

—, *Russkii romans: ocherk ego razvitiya* (St Petersburg, 1896)

Mann, Klaus, *Symphonie pathétique* (Amsterdam, 1935)

Mihailovich, Alexandar, ed., *Tchaikovsky and his Contemporaries: A Centennial Symposium* (Westport, CT, and London, 1999)

Morrison, Simon, *Russian Opera and the Symbolist Movement* (Berkeley, Los Angeles and London, 2002)

Nickell, William, *The Death of Tolstoy: Russia on the Eve, Astapovo Station 1910* (Ithaca, NY, and London, 2010)

Norris, Gerald, *Stanford, the Cambridge Jubilee and Tchaikovsky* (Newton Abbot and North Pomfret, VT, 1980)

Orlova, Alexandra, *Tchaikovsky: A Self-portrait*, trans. R. M. Davidson (Oxford, 1990)

—, 'Tchaikovsky: The Last Chapter', *Music and Letters*, LXII (1981), pp. 125–45

Parry, C. Hubert H., *Summary of the History and Development of Mediaeval and Modern European Music* (London, 1905)

—, *Style in Musical Art* (London, 1911)

Poznanskii, Aleksandr, *Chaikovskii* (Moscow, 2010)

—, *Petr Chaikovskii: biografiya* (St Petersburg, 2009)

—, *Tchaikovsky: The Quest for the Inner Man* (New York, 1991)

—, *Tchaikovsky's Last Days: A Documentary Study* (Oxford, 1996)

—, ed., *Tchaikovsky through Others' Eyes*, trans. Ralph C. Burr Jr and Robert Bird (Bloomington and Indianapolis, IN, 1999)

—, and Brett Langston, eds, *The Tchaikovsky Handbook: A Guide to the Man and His Music* (Bloomington and Indianapolis, IN, 2002)

Pushkin, Aleksandr, *Polnoe sobranie sochinenii* (Moscow, 1937–59)

Raku, Marina, *Muzykal'naya klassika v mifotvorchestve sovetskoi epokhi* (Moscow, 2014)

Riztarev, Marina, *Tchaikovsky's 'Pathétique' and Russian Culture* (Farnham and Burlington, IN, 2014)

Sargeant, Lynn M., *Harmony and Discord: Music and the Transformation of Russian Cultural Life* (Oxford and New York, 2011)

Scholl, Tim, *Sleeping Beauty: A Legend in Progress* (New Haven, CT, and London, 2004)

Solokov, V., *Antonina Chaikovskaya: istoriya zabytoi zhenshchiny* (Moscow, 1994)

Sylvester, Richard D., *Tchaikovsky's Complete Songs: A Companion with Texts and Translations* (Bloomington, IN, 2004)

Taruskin, Richard, *Defining Russia Musically: Historical and Hermeneutical Essays* (Princeton, NJ, 1997)

—, *On Russian Music* (Berkeley, Los Angeles and London, 2009)

Tchaikovsky, *see* Chaikovskii

Vaidman, P. E., ed., *Neizvestnyi Chaikovskii* (Moscow, 2009)

—. ed., *P. I. Chaikovskii–N. F. fon Mekk: perepiska* (Chelyabinsk, 2007–)

—, ed., *P. I. Chaikovskii–P. I. Yurgenson: perepiska* (Moscow, 2011–13)

Vaidman, Polina, Ljudmila Korabel'nikova and Valentina Rubcova, eds, *Thematic and Bibliographical Catalogue of P. I. Tchaikovsky's Works*, 2nd edn (Moscow, 2006)

Warrack, John, *Tchaikovsky* (London, 1973)

Whitehead, Claire, *The Fantastic in France and Russia in the Nineteenth Century: In Pursuit of Hesitation* (London, 2006)

Wiley, Roland John, *Tchaikovsky* (Oxford and New York, 2009)

—, *Tchaikovsky's Ballets: 'Swan Lake', 'Sleeping Beauty', 'Nutcracker'* (Oxford, 1985)

Wortman, Richard, *Scenarios of Power: Myth and Ceremony in Russian Monarchy* (Princeton, NJ, 1995–2000)

Zhdanov, V. A., ed., *P. I. Chaikovskii: Pis'ma k rodnym* (Moscow, 1940)

—, *P. I. Chaikovskii–S. I. Taneev: pisma* (Moscow, 1951)

—, and Zhegin, N. T., eds, *P. I. Chaikovskii: Perepiska s N. F. fon Mekk* (Moscow and Leningrad, 1934–6)

—, and Zhegin, N. T., eds, *P. I. Chaikovskii: Perepiska s P. I. Yurgensonom* (Moscow and Leningrad, 1938–52)

Select Discography

The *Tchaikovsky Edition* is a comprehensive survey of almost all of the composer's works, many of them in historic performances (Brilliant Classics: 94650, 60 CDs).

Operas

Cherevichki (aka *The Tsarina's Slippers*): Olga Guryakova, Vsevolod Grivnov, Larisa Dyadkova, Maxim Mikhailov, Sergey Leiferkus; Orchestra of the Royal Opera House, conducted by Alexander Polyanichko, directed by Francesca Zambello (Opus Arte: OA1037D, DVD, recorded 2009)

Eugene Onegin: Evgeny Belos, Galina Vishnevskaya, Sergey Lemeshev; Bolshoi Theatre Orchestra and Chorus, conducted by Boris Khaikin (Melodiya: MELCD1001945, 2 CDs, recorded 1955)
—: Dmitry Hvorostovsky, Nuccia Focile, Neil Shicoff, Olga Borodina; Orchestre de Paris and St Petersburg Chamber Choir, conducted by Semyon Bychkov (Philips: 4757017, recorded 1992)
—: Wojciech Drabowicz, Elena Prokina, Martin Thompson; London Philharmonic and Glyndebourne Festival Chorus, conducted by Andrew Davis, directed by Graham Vick (NVC Arts: 0630140142, DVD, recorded 1994)
—: Mariusz Kwiecień, Tatyana Monogarova, Andrey Dunaev; Bolshoi Theatre Orchestra and Chorus, conducted by Alexander Vedernikov, directed by Dmitri Chernyakov (Bel Air Classiques: BAC046, 2 DVDs, recorded at the Palais Garnier, Paris, 2008)

Iolanta: Anna Netrebko, Sergey Skorokhodov, Alexey Markov, Vitaly
    Kovalyov; Slovenian Philharmonic Orchestra and Slovenian
    Chamber Choir, conducted by Emmanuel Villaume (Deutsche
    Grammophon: 4793969, 2 CDs, recorded 2012)

The Maid of Orleans: Irina Arkhipova, Sergey Yakovenko, Vladimir
    Valaitis; All-Union Big Symphony Orchestra and Choir, conducted
    by Gennady Rozhdestvensky (Melodiya: MELCD1002053, 3 CDs,
    recorded 1969)

Mazepa: Sergey Leiferkus, Anatoly Kocherga, Larisa Dyadkova, Galina
    Gorchakova, Sergey Larin; Gothenburg Symphony Orchestra and the
    Chorus of the Royal Opera, Stockholm, conducted by Neeme Järvi
    (Deutsche Grammophon: 775637, 3 CDs, recorded 1993)

The Queen of Spades (*Pique Dame*): Peter Gougaloff, Regina Reznik,
    Galina Vishnevskaya; Orchestre National de France and Maîtrise
    de Radio France, conducted by Mstislav Rostropovich (Deutsche
    Grammophon: 4636792, 3 CDs, recorded 1977)
—: Gegam Grigoryan, Mariya Gulegina, Lyudmila Filatova, Sergey
    Leiferkus, Olga Borodina; Orchestra and Chorus of the Kirov
    Opera, St Petersburg, conducted by Valery Gergiev, directed by Yuri
    Temirkanov (Philips: 0704349, DVD, recorded 1992)

Ballets

The Nutcracker: Alina Cojocaru, Anthony Dowell, Ivan Putrov, Miyako
    Yoshida, Jonathan Cope; Royal Ballet and Orchestra of the Royal
    Opera House, conducted by Evgeny Svetlanov (BBC Opus Arte:
    OA0828D, DVD, recorded 2000)
—: Kirov Orchestra, conducted by Valery Gergiev (Philips: 462114, CD,
    recorded 1998)

The Sleeping Beauty: Alina Cojocaru, Federico Bonelli, Genesia Rosato,
    Marianela Nuñez; Royal Ballet and Orchestra of the Royal Opera

House, conducted by Valery Ovsyanikov (BBC Opus Arte: OA0995D, DVD, recorded 2006)

—: Russian National Orchestra, conducted by Mikhail Pletnev (Deutsche Grammophon: 4779788, 2 CDs, recorded 1997)

Swan Lake: Ulyana Lopatkina, Danila Korsuntsev; Ballet and Orchestra of the Mariinsky Theatre, St Petersburg, conducted by Valery Gergiev (Decca: 0743216, DVD, recorded 2006)

—: Bergen Philharmonic Orchestra, conducted by Neeme Järvi (Chandos: CHSA51242, 2 CDs, recorded 2012)

Symphonies, concertos and orchestral works

The six symphonies, with *Manfred* and selected symphonic poems and overtures. Russian National Orchestra, conducted by Mikhail Pletnev (Deutsche Grammophon: 4778699, 7 CDs, reissued 2010)

Symphonies 4, 5 and 6. Leningrad Philharmonic Orchestra, conducted by Evgeny Mravinsky (Deutsche Grammophon: 4775911, 2 CDs, recorded 1960)

Orchestral Suites Nos 1–4. New Philharmonia Orchestra, conducted by Antal Doráti (Deutsche Grammophon: 4781708, 2 CDs, recorded 1966)

Piano Concertos Nos 1–3, Concert Fantasia. Stephen Hough and the Minnesota Orchestra, conducted by Osmo Vänskä (Hyperion: CDA67711-2, 2 CDs, recorded 2009)

Piano Concerto No. 1. Martha Argerich and the Bavarian Radio Symphony Orchestra, conducted by Kirill Kondrashin (Philips: 4466732, CD, recorded 1980; coupled with Rachmaninoff, Piano Concerto No. 3)

Piano Concerto No. 1 (1879 version). Kirill Gerstein and the Deutsches Symphonie-Orchester Berlin, conducted by James Gaffigan (Myrios:

Kmyr016, CD, recorded 2014; coupled with Prokofiev, Piano
Concerto No. 2)

Variations on a Rococo Theme. Mstislav Rostropovich and the Berliner
Philharmoniker, conducted by Herbert von Karajan (Deutsche
Grammophon: 4474132, CD, recorded 1968; coupled with Dvořák,
Cello Concerto)

Violin Concerto. Kyung-wha Chung and the London Symphony
Orchestra, conducted by Andre Previn (Decca: 4757734, CD, recorded
1970; coupled with Sibelius, Violin Concerto)

Songs

Joan Rogers and Roger Vignoles (Hyperion: CDH55331, CD, recorded 1992)
Olga Borodina and Larisa Gergieva (Philips: 442013, CD, recorded 1993)
Christianne Stotijn and Julius Drake (Onyx: 4034, CD, recorded 2008)
Dmitry Hvorostovsky and Ivari Ilja (Delos: DE3393, 2 CDs, recorded 2009)

Chamber and instrumental music

Eighteen Pieces for Piano, Op. 72. Mikhail Pletnev (Deutsche
Grammophon: 4775378, CD, recorded 2004)

Piano Trio. Martha Argerich, Gidon Kremer and Mischa Maisky
(Deutsche Grammophon: 4593262, CD, recorded 1998; coupled with
Shostakovich, Piano Trio No. 2)

The Seasons. Pavel Kolesnikov (Hyperion: CDA68028, CD, recorded 2013)

String Quartets Nos 1–3 and *Souvenir de Florence*. Borodin Quartet
(Chandos: CHAN9871, 2 CDs, recorded 1964)

Acknowledgements

The research for and writing of this biography would not have been possible without the generous help, expert advice and wise suggestions of the following individuals: Lucinde Braun, Ada Bronowski, Caryl Emerson, Lizzy Emerson, Narve Fulsås, Diana Greenwald, Daniel M. Grimley, Kadja Grönke, Saija Isomaa, Emma Kingsley, Mauro Mattia, Sandra Mayer, Robin Feuer Miller, Jonathan Paine, Dick Passingham, Mika Perala, Alexander Poznansky, Jane Shuttleworth, Emma Sutton, Anastasia Tolstoy and Catherine Tolstoy. In particular, it has been a particular pleasure to write in parallel with Julie Curtis, whose own distinction as a biographer has been a constant source of inspiration. I am indebted to the A. Bakhrushin State Central Theatre Museum, Moscow; the Tchaikovsky State House-Museum, Klin; and the State Tretyakov Gallery, Moscow, for help in providing the images. I am grateful to Michael Leaman for suggesting that I should undertake this project in the first place, as well as to the whole team at Reaktion for seeing the book so carefully into print. Inevitably, Stefano Evangelista's unquantifiable involvement went far beyond reading a number of draft chapters and listening to more Tchaikovsky in a few years than most people manage in a lifetime. The dedication of this book to my sister, brother-in-law, nephew and niece doesn't mean they have to read it, but I hope they might.

Photo Acknowledgements

The author and publishers wish to express their thanks to the following sources of illustrative material and/or permission to reproduce it:

A. A. Bakhrushin State Central Theatre Museum: p. 83; P. I. Tchaikovsky State House-Museum, Klin: pp. 8, 24, 25, 27, 29, 32, 38, 42, 53, 61, 65, 73, 79, 87, 105, 131, 138, 139, 144, 147, 167, 168, 170, 172, 175, 177, 183, 189; State Tretyakov Gallery, Moscow: p. 173.